DEAD-HANDED

DEAD-HANDED

A Nut Cracker Investigation

Katherine Ramsland

First published by Level Best Books 2024

This novel is entirely a work of fiction. The names, characters and incidents portrayed in it are the work of the author's imagination. Any resemblance to actual persons, living or dead, events or localities is entirely coincidental.

Author Photo Credit: Noelle Means

First edition

ISBN: 978-1-68512-700-8

Cover art by Level Best Designs

This book was professionally typeset on Reedsy.
Find out more at reedsy.com

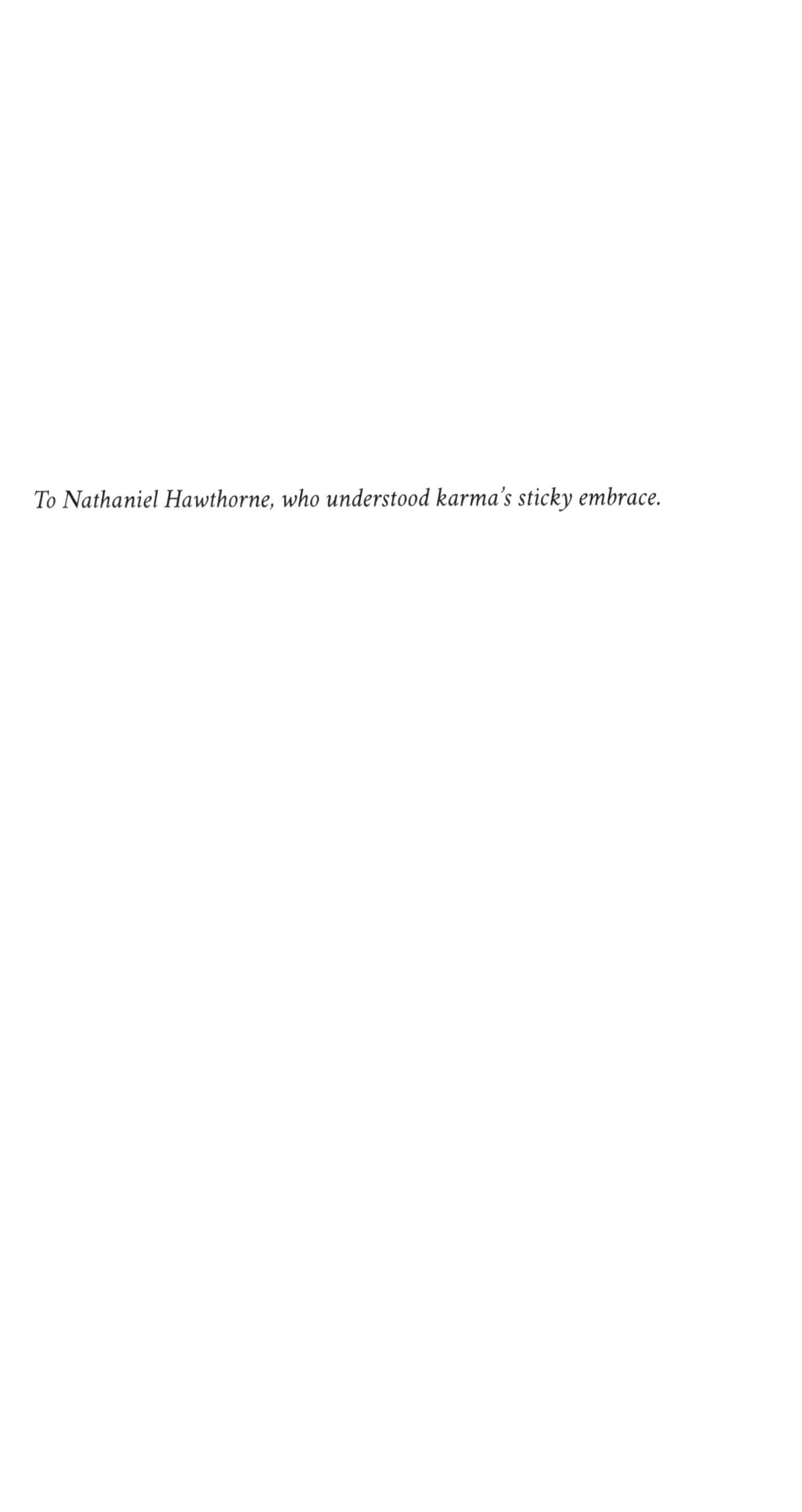

To Nathaniel Hawthorne, who understood karma's sticky embrace.

Praise for Dead-Handed

"Set in the heady environs of the New England transcendental movement, this taut forensic thriller unites an ancient Scots legend, a biological disaster and a cursed family worthy of Nathaniel Hawthorne himself. Prepare for an all-night read: in *Dead-Handed,* Katherine Ramsland is at her spooky storytelling best."—Juilene Osborne-McKnight, author *The Story We Carry in Our Bones: Irish History for Americans*

"A creepy old mansion, a wealthy dying man, a mysterious enclave, and a tenacious investigator all add up to form an intriguing mystery. Katherine Ramsland's *Dead-Handed* is a well-plotted, devilishly twisted tale of murder and mayhem."—Bruce Robert Coffin, international bestselling coauthor of The Turner and Mosley Files

Prologue

The teenage girl they pulled from the pond had been the envy of her peers. The "Most Likely to Succeed" track star and honor student, Marti Fielding, had just won a scholarship to Yale. Everyone thought nothing could stop the blonde dynamo.

Then she went missing.

Half of Dunbury had turned out for the search. It was three days before a hiker discovered Marti's partially submerged body in Gilly Pond. By then, her skin was mottled, her green eyes glazed, and her pert nose disfigured by worms. The determination was suicide.

A week later, I stood at the edge of this pond amid odors of wet pine and clumped leaves. Besides some bird squawks, the place was silent. On a map, I noted how close I was to a decrepit settlement called Dacretown. This creepy spot had a reputation for being cursed. It even had a western boundary called the Dead Line. Such places can trigger desperate acts, especially in kids.

But I don't just accept a medical examiner's call. Sometimes they see only the surface. Once officials decide on suicide, they rarely take more steps. I sought a bigger picture.

Marti's autopsy report showed pond water in the lungs and no external injuries. There was no tox analysis yet to say if drugs were involved. Still, this seemed a poor spot for ending a life, and the girl had left no note. No one knew where she'd been during the hours leading up to her death. I needed to find out.

"Why here?" I wondered out loud. I looked back toward the parking area. "Where was your car? No one mentioned one in the report. You couldn't have walked here. Did someone bring you?"

I made a mental note to ask about her mode of transportation. She'd attended an elite boarding school, so I guessed she'd had a car.

To add to the tragedy, this death was the latest of three recent incidents involving teens. A boy had jumped from a cliff, and another had run at a train. The second boy survived but was in a coma. Although Marti's demise was distinct, I saw links to the others. Same age. Some friends in common. A recent party two had attended. And all three had selected a spot near Dacretown.

Parents had begged town officials to do something to stop these incidents. Those officials had decided they needed an expert. That's how I got involved. Not many psychologists are suicidologists. I was one of four on the East Coast, and by chance, I'd been in the area.

Or maybe it wasn't chance. Looking back, it seems like we were meant to cross paths. Marti was caught in a web spun by people aware of me before I knew about any of them.

I thought about the brief notes in the girl's file. She was in a training program to improve her college potential. She'd been doing well. Her parents had no clue why she'd done this. Yet, a study buddy said Marti thought someone was stalking her. A girl on Marti's pole vault team said she'd hung out with a college guy who ran a secret club.

I'd identified the club, thanks to a resourceful reporter, Rob Galloway. He'd called it the Skeleton Crew. There were membership levels, with the Bone Heads in charge. They'd built a clubhouse, the Crypt, near Dacretown.

So, there was a club, a possible stalker, three seemingly related incidents, and a wooded property with dark repute.

I donned my gloves against the chill and stepped around snow that lingered from a surprise October storm. It was mostly gone from where the rescuers had rushed to pull Marti from the water. I moved away to look elsewhere.

"Was anyone here with you?" I asked. "A friend? Perhaps an enemy?" I've had cases in which kids in distress invited a witness. This was an age of selfies and influencers and reckless online challenges, including for suicide. Some kids want to make a mark or simply have a social presence, even in death.

I hadn't ventured far when I spotted an imposing chain-link fence that bore a sign: *Private Property: Keep Out.* I approached it. On the other side, behind a long thatch of weeds, I saw a moss-covered crumbling stone wall, two feet high. This fence, I thought, had to mark the Dead Line. I was closer to Dacretown than I realized.

I felt a prickle and turned. "Hello?"

A glob of snow fell off a branch.

I walked to my left, then stopped. Something glinted in the grass. I crouched down. The item was small, easy to miss. I inched closer. A gold hoop, perhaps an earring. I pulled out my phone and took a photo. Then I looked for a rock to use as a marker. I wasn't losing this potential piece of evidence. I spotted a rock nearby. Replacing my right glove with a rubber one, I grabbed it and set it close to the item, then took a picture.

Turning toward my SUV, I counted my steps to the parking lot. There, I opened the police report to read the inventory of items found with the body. "Okay, you were wearing jeans, a black bra, black panties, a pair of socks and ankle boots, a navy shirt, a ring on your right ring finger, a round gold earring in your right ear. No mention of its mate." I hesitated. It had been as cold that day as it was today. "Where was your jacket? Your gloves?" This didn't add up.

I grabbed a six-inch ruler and returned to my marker. Recalling the police chief's quick dismissal of my professional credentials, I took a photo to text to her. *Send someone to Gilly Pond to collect this.*

I stepped back and looked around. Four feet north of the earring, I saw a distinct boot print in a patch of mud. It was too large to be Marti's. Other footprints were present but obscured. I estimated at least two people here, maybe a third. Could be lookie-loos. Could also be witnesses with important information. Could be the person who'd ripped an earring from the ear of the girl in the pond. Placing the ruler next to the clear print, I photographed it from different angles. Then I returned to my car to wait for the cops. This place had to be sealed off and fully processed.

Yesterday, I was begging for cases. Today, I had three. I also had the mystery of my grandfather's dying plea.

Chapter One

A terse voicemail gave little hint of the trouble ahead. "My father is quite ill. He won't last long. Are you able to come?"

That was my Aunt Bree, a.k.a. Briana Duncan. We hadn't spoken in years. My grandfather, Judson Hunter, had to be in bad shape for Bree to urge me there. *Really* bad. Considering the stress I'd caused the last time I was there, I knew Bree wanted me as far from the Hunter estate in Concord, Massachusetts, as possible. When I returned the call, she said, "He can hardly breathe. And he's hallucinating…he's…talking…to *dead* people. No one's there."

She sounded unnerved. Yet I thought it could just be a case of terminal lucidity, an end-of-life phenomenon many people experience. I didn't say it, though. I offered a softer response. "That must be difficult. I'll come as soon as I can."

In truth, I didn't want to be anywhere near the man. When I'd visited Judson five years ago, my father—his son—had recently vanished. Judson had the resources from his real estate business to help me search. But he'd refused. I'd stormed out. We hadn't spoken again. Bree had sided with him, so it made little sense now that she wanted me there. Unless…maybe Judson had "seen" Dad among his "visitors." Maybe Bree hoped to prove to me I was chasing a ghost. That would leave her, my dad's half-sister and Judson's only other child, his unchallenged heir.

I strode to my office, down the hall from my living area in my Outer Banks house in North Carolina. I run a PI agency. I call it Nut Cracker Investigations because we accept baffling cases, i.e., hard nuts to crack.

I also use my clinical training to advise on sleuthing tactics and death investigations.

The smell of fresh hazelnut coffee signaled company. I needed it. I found Natra Gawoni, my case manager and confidante, sitting on the leather couch. Her Doberdor sniffer dog, Mika, rose from the floor to greet me. She wagged her tail as she licked my hand and searched for a treat. Natra's long dark hair was wound into a single braid, and she wore gray sweats, which told me she'd been on the beach training Mika. She lives here, too, in a second-floor apartment on the other side. We share a kitchen, but she's usually the only one cooking.

Natra held up a clinical report I'd asked her to proofread. "Almost done. Three typos, all fixed. Ready to go."

"Good. You can send it. I don't need to read it again. I'm heading to Concord. My grandfather appears to be dying."

Her brown eyes widened. She knows the story. "They called you?"

"Yes, big surprise."

"Change of heart?"

"I doubt it. My Aunt Bree called, and she certainly doesn't want me shouting at Judson that Dad's still alive. She says Judson's seeing people, as in end-stage hallucinations. Maybe she wants to tell me he's seen Dad."

I hugged myself against a sudden chill. When Dad disappeared five years ago, we'd found no body. There was just a note about ending his life. Via legal work, he'd assigned his oceanfront house to me, his only child. He'd divorced my mother two decades ago when I was fifteen. I knew Dad had been depressed over something that had happened to a colleague, and he seemed to have put his affairs in order. The verdict for Lang Hunter was suicide. It was hard to contest.

Yet I believed it was pseudocide: he'd faked his death to disappear. With the trail still warm, I'd gone to see Judson. I'd brought what I thought was proof of life, but he'd rebuffed me.

"Why won't you help me?!" I'd shouted. "You have plenty of money. We can hire people to look. How can you turn your back on your only son?"

He'd just stared at me with his icy blue eyes. "Leave it. He's gone. It's better for everyone to accept it."

It hadn't been better for me. I still conducted searches, tracking Dad here and there, including in other countries. He'd done a good job of seeming to be dead, but I'd found some breadcrumbs in two renewed subscriptions.

Natra looked skeptical. "Couldn't your aunt just tell you over the phone what he's seeing?"

"She seems disturbed by it, like she'd picked up someone's trash. I don't know if she'll tell me at all. But if he's dying, I guess I should be there."

Natra nodded. She knows when I'm trying to talk myself into something. She wants no part of that monologue.

I poured myself a cup of coffee before I took a seat. Mika sat in front of me, full of eager anticipation. "Maybe Judson's decision to cut off my dad is haunting him. He made that move long before Dad disappeared. By the time I was twelve, they were pretty much estranged. I may be Judson's granddaughter, but he's treated me like a bothersome appendage. My dad's from his first wife, and Judson favors his second wife, though she divorced him too."

Mika touched her warm tongue to my hand. I gave her a quick pat on the head.

Natra unfolded her legs and set down the report she'd been reading. "What about JoLynn's cases?"

I shrugged. "I won't be gone long, and we're just providing support. I can check in by video."

JoLynn Wilde's a forensic meteorologist and anthropologist with experience at several fieldwork facilities, also known as "body farms." She'd been invaluable in a recent case in which we were searching for buried victims via enigmatic codes. JoLynn had set up a drone with a special sensor that helped to identify trees that had absorbed "unusual" nutrients from the soil. Pairing her work with sniffer dogs, we'd found a body. JoLynn wasn't a Nut Cracker, not officially, but I'd accept her assistance any time. Ayden Scott, my PI, was learning a lot from her about the impact of weather on corpses.

And she'd just drawn me into an investigation. She'd recently discovered that a death in Tennessee believed the result of a tornado was a homicide staged as an accident. A week later, she'd noticed something similar in another case. Natra, with her talent for charts and organization, was developing a victimology. I cocked my head. "Have you heard anything more?"

"Nothing links these victims personally, not that I've found. Two different states, Tennessee and Oklahoma. One female, Carmen Ashford, thirty-four, and one male, Craig Warren, thirty. But both died in severe weather, and the events were six months apart."

"Same cause of death?"

"No. One was hit in the head, the other buried under debris where she suffocated, but it looks intentional, like the items were carefully placed over her. They trapped her but didn't crush her. Sadistic."

I considered this. "So, a killer might be traveling to storm systems in order to use weather to cover his crimes?"

Natra shrugged. "Anything's possible."

"Not probable, though. Yes, we've seen a few random killers who just wanted to kill, with no victim target, no predictable MO, but still…"

"The county sheriff's checking it out."

"Are you researching deaths in other weather events?"

She raised her chin.

"Right. Sorry. You've probably already set up your database."

"Me and JoLynn. We got this. I'll work with her until we have something solid. We're even watching future potential storm systems. I'll loop you in when it's time."

I sipped my coffee. "I'm finished with my case evals. I can afford to be away for two or three days."

"Isn't Kamryn coming tonight for the weekend?"

That's my daughter, just turned ten. I share custody with my ex-husband, Wayne Worth. I nodded. "I can tell Wayne to keep her until I'm back. Maybe I shouldn't go at all. What would I really gain for my trouble? Not to mention, they just had snow in Concord." I grimaced. "Five inches." I gestured around me. "Nothing makes me embrace this place more than my childhood memory of eye-level drifts."

Natra snorted. "It's October." She got up to fetch more coffee.

"And they've had some fierce early-season storms up there."

"You're talking yourself out of it."

"Trying. But I should go."

"Kam will love it. Take her. You'll have company."

Natra was right. Kamryn had been in Concord once before. She'd been too young to remember much, but the snow had delighted her. When I asked her, she said she wanted to go. Wayne approved, so I packed us both a bag for three days.

I should've known better.

Chapter Two

On the flight to Boston, Kamryn asked me to pose with her in the plane seats for a selfie. Or is that a we-fie? She studied it, then showed me. The contrast between us, with my medium-length blond curls and her straight brunette hair, my blue eyes and her brown, seemed a physical manifestation of our less visible disconnects. I'm focused and organized; Kamryn is anything but. I probe deeply into mental processes; she dismisses my queries into why she likes things with "I just like it."

I'd explained that she'd gotten her father's physical traits, including his dark hair and height. I didn't add that she also had his restlessness. Wayne and I had split when Kamryn was six, and we'd agreed that she'd live with him in South Carolina during the school year, spending alternate weekends and most vacations with me.

I was glad to have her along. Sometimes, I thought I'd become like my own mother, distant and detached. Until Dad vanished, I'd looked to him as the parent who'd be there for me. I wasn't a great mother, I feared, but I did try to attend to what engaged Kam's interest. I wished I could tell her my grandfather would appreciate our visit, but I doubted he would. He was a successful real estate developer, but not big on family connection. Dad had told me very little about him.

Kamryn looked at me. "Do you have a picture of Grampa?"

She meant my dad. He'd vanished when she was five. I had a framed photo in my bedroom, but Kam hardly paid attention. I looked through the photos on my phone and located one of him posing with her on the beach when she was four.

"He looks like you," Kam commented. "But his hair is white."

"It's light, yes, but not white." Not then, anyway. Now fifty-seven if he were still alive, he might have more gray than blond. For me, he hadn't aged beyond the last day I'd seen him.

"Can you text this to me?" Kamryn asked.

"Of course." I forwarded the photo to her phone. I liked that she was curious. I wasn't sure she'd see any images of Dad in Judson's house. I suspected he'd thoroughly ejected his son.

We took a bus and a commuter train for the quick trip to Concord. Kamryn loved watching the snow-laden countryside roll by, with many trees still in leaf. The colors had mostly changed to red and gold, but a few were still green.

Bree had sent a car to meet us at the station. My chest felt tight at the thought of returning to Judson's imposing 8,000-square-foot colonial mansion. He'd inherited it from his own grandfather, Merrick Hunter. The historic house, worth millions, held bad memories for me from arguments I'd overheard between father and son.

The car took us to one of Judson's guesthouses, half a block from his mansion. I'd lived here when I was eight, as Dad had tried working for Judson. He'd failed, eliciting scorn from both Judson and my mother. She'd thought Dad was wrecking his chance to inherit everything. That was the beginning of the end for them. It had been a difficult year.

Judson's house manager, Shona Teagan, met us at the door. Shona's thick mahogany hair framed a round face. She looked to be in her late thirties. She wore a dark green uniform-type dress that showed a plump figure. Crinkles around her brown eyes suggested she liked to laugh.

"I'm Judson's granddaughter," I explained. Shona nodded as if she knew, then looked at Kamryn. "Is this your daughter?"

"Yes, Kamryn. She's just turned ten."

With a shy grin, Kam reached out her hand. Shona smiled and took it. "I have two daughters a little older than you. One's at school in Boston, but Elyse lives here. She's twelve."

Kamryn brightened. "Can I meet her?"

Shona looked at me. I nodded. To Kam, she said, "I'll arrange it. She'd love some company."

I noticed Shona's faint accent and asked, "Are you from Scotland?"

"My family's from the western coast," she said, "going a long way back. I grew up in Glasgow." She added that "Ms. Duncan" was still at work and would be home soon.

Shona showed us around the three-story Colonial-style wood-frame house. Judson used it for business associates and short-term guests. He owned several properties in the historic area, but this was my favorite. To my relief, the furnace was on, and the place was warm. Built two hundred years ago, the house had been updated with private baths for each bedroom and a kitchen a master chef would envy. The house also had a library with a large fireplace and restored woodwork. I hoped the hidden staircase was still intact. I'd taken refuge in it many times when my parents were fighting. My mother had hated the drawbacks of historic homes—the musty odors and drafts in the winter—but I'd enjoyed how close we were to a large rural cemetery where I could spend time alone.

Shona led us to the kitchen to show us that she'd stocked the place with basic items. "I can get anything else you might need."

I looked around, impressed. "Thank you. I know where the grocery store is. I used to live here."

"Of course. Mr. Hunter has cars he offers to guests. Ms. Duncan said you can use one. I'll show you where they're parked and give you a key. Please let me know when you're ready to visit Mr. Hunter." She gave me a number to text her before she left us to explore.

The house had been freshly painted. Kam loved the gray-trimmed white grand entrance and central staircase. I smiled at the original dark wood floors that showed ruts and scratches from two centuries of use. The artwork on the walls from local painters remained the same as from my time here.

"This looks like a good place for finding me!" Kamryn exclaimed. That's a game we play that benefits us both. I learned it in a SWAT class. I've taught her how to "meter" a room from various angles at the doorway before she enters so she's aware of what to expect. When she hides, it gives me a chance to sharpen my own instincts for surprises, and Kamryn can be quite innovative.

"We don't have the squirt guns," I reminded her. The one who sees the other first squirts them.

Kam shrugged. "We can buy some."

"We can't use water in here. These floors would stain. Let's go look at the bedrooms. You can pick one."

The place smelled stuffy but clean. I showed Kamryn the room I'd had when I was here. With light gray walls and white trim, it now included a massive inset TV screen. Books filled two shelves, and a vase held fresh daisies.

"I like this one!" Kam exclaimed.

"Go ahead and unpack."

I took the room my parents had shared, at least at first. It smelled like wood cleaner and laundered sheets. Roomy, with a lovely view of a wooded back yard, it made me feel close to Dad. A layer of snow coated the ground outside. Deciding against fully unpacking, I placed my suitcase on the dressing table. I wasn't ready to settle in. I wanted to believe I could leave at once. I'd made sure our return tickets were flexible.

Kamryn strode in with a thick paperback. She held it up. *Ghost Story*, by Peter Straub. All about a vengeful shapeshifter that terrorized four men bound by a terrible secret during an interminable snowstorm. "It was in my room."

I raised an eyebrow. "That might be a hard one." Not to mention too explicit for her age.

She smirked. "It's about snow, right?"

"Yes, but the weather won't get that bad. The forecast is for warmer temps. And we won't be here long. Don't you have a better book on your tablet? If not, there's a library downstairs. I can pick one for you. Maybe by an author who once lived here in the area? My favorite is Nathaniel Hawthorne."

Kamryn shook her head. "I wanna read this one." When she got stubborn, there was no point trying to change her mind. *This* we had in common.

I smoothed her long hair into place. Despite her quirky smile, she was growing into quite a pretty girl, which made me proud but nervous. She was nearly as tall as me and would soon surpass my five-foot-five height. "Leave it here for now. Take the guidebook I bought you so you can learn about the area. Several prominent authors lived here, including Louisa May Alcott."

Kamryn's face lit up. I'd read *Little Women* to her, and she'd loved it. She went to fetch the guidebook. That's one thing I can count on: she's eager to learn about new places.

I picked up *Ghost Story*. The plot was dark. Not only did snow pile up many feet, trapping an entire town in upstate New York, but the storm was more aggressive than spooky. And it had occurred in October.

I opened it. The first page bore a quote from a Nathaniel Hawthorne story: "The chasm was merely one of the orifices of the pit of blackness that lies beneath us, everywhere." Charming. I recalled characters in this tale named Hawthorne and Maule, which referred to Hawthorne's tale about the price of family secrets, *The House of the Seven Gables*.

I needed no such reminder. Just down the street, I had my own grim family to face.

Chapter Three

We walked over to Judson's mansion, which I'd always called the Big House. I told Kamryn this is where her great-grandfather lived, then rang the bell.

Shona led us through a long hallway full of expensive paintings and up the tall staircase to Judson's oversized master bedroom. On the way, she chatted easily with Kamryn about school and where she lived.

"If you need assistance, I'm in the cottage in back," she told me. "I have things for girls there." I realized she was telling me she was available if I wanted to shield Kamryn from what lay ahead with Judson.

"I appreciate that."

Shona opened the door. Judson was asleep. The smell of disinfectant hit me.

I took a seat on a cushioned chair near his carved mahogany king-size bed. Kamryn went over to a cushioned window seat and plopped down with her book. The sun would set soon, but a small lamp nearby gave her light for reading.

Judson snored softly through rumbles of suffocating emphysema. Pink Stargazer lilies burst from bronze vases on matching bed tables. Their spicy perfume didn't quite cover the odor of incontinence. Barely visible behind one vase, a heart monitor beeped its quiet rhythm. An antique quilt that matched the color of brooding clouds outside registered Judson's shallow breaths. It was startling to see a man who'd wielded power in this town with his "financial rewards" reduced to this helpless state.

I barely thought of him as a grandfather. He'd never been kind or affectionate, never told jokes or stories with a twinkle in his eye. Distinguished and proud, he'd wanted us all—including kids—to treat him with deference. I'd been told to call him "sir" rather than Grandpa or Grandad.

I glanced at Kamryn. Engaged with the guidebook, she twisted a lock of her hair.

"Doing okay?" I asked. She nodded.

Kamryn was independent, but we'd grown close recently after an ordeal in which she'd been abducted by an associate of my ex-husband's. She'd proven herself resourceful, but in the end, she'd been a little girl who'd needed her mom. And her mom had needed that from her.

Judson's house suffocated me. I despised the dark wood that dominated the tone and the heavy floral curtains that blocked sunlight. It reminded me of the constant tension between him and Dad. To evict this memory, I looked for a text from Natra. Nothing yet. Ayden was at a seminar in Texas on drawing from decomposed faces for John Doe identifications. Jackson Raines, my legal partner and more, was in Europe. Even Joe Lochren, my part-time cyber guy, was at an AI conference.

I felt left out. My Nut Crackers were my family. We'd been through a lot. We've taken on cases so hard to crack we've sometimes risked our lives. But we love the work.

I grabbed a newspaper from a pile on Judson's dresser. I wanted to scan the local events to find something for Kam. On page three, an article caught my eye: a rundown of three incidents that signaled a possible suicide cluster.

A high school senior in Dunbury named Owen Kringle had thrown himself at an oncoming train. He'd survived but was in a coma, with significant injuries. He'd broken a leg, an arm, and several ribs, and had a head injury. The reporter had linked this incident to two recent completed suicides by teens from the same town: Ralph Steiner had gone off a cliff, and Marti Fielding had drowned in a pond. I leaned over the article.

This was my thing. I taught workshops on such phenomena to coroners and cops. Many suicide clusters happened in affluent areas, mostly involving teens. No one knows what causes a suicide contagion, but media coverage plays a role. So does a location's reputation. The reporter wrote about a grim legend associated with the area. That's how I first heard of Dacretown. The former community had seen an over-the-top number of calamities. This had all happened during the eighteenth century, but the lore persisted. I was about to look it up on my phone when I heard the assertive *tap, tap* from high-heeled shoes on the wood floor in the hall that announced Briana Duncan.

Chapter Four

A navy wool skirt and sweater accented Bree's slender figure. She saw me, stopped, and lifted her chin. She had my father's intense eyes, blond hair, and chiseled cheekbones, but her sour expression diluted her beauty.

"Hello, Ann."

She knew I hated to be called Ann. You'd never know from her frosty tone that she'd once taken me for walks and read me stories. I'd played with her daughter, Maisie, a year younger than me.

I stood and nodded.

Bree squinted at Kamryn. I suspect she'd forgotten I have a daughter too. Bree was reportedly estranged from Maisie, but I hadn't heard why. I knew only that Maisie had been a gifted child but also rebellious and difficult. When I was around her, she'd repeatedly set me up for pranks, then say in a snarky way, "Idiots always respond." Eventually, I'd just avoided her.

"May I speak with you privately, please?" Bree gestured with her head toward the hallway.

To Kam I said, "I'll be right back." There was no need to bring her into the Hunter family spats. I was sure she sensed the tension.

Bree closed the heavy door to Judson's bedroom before she clasped her hands and gave me a fierce look. "What did you say to him?"

I blinked. "To whom?"

"My father."

I tried to assess the situation. *Something* had happened. I watched Bree's body language for some hint. Her stiff posture oozed anger. I shook my head. "He's been asleep since we arrived."

"I mean before."

"I haven't talked to him since we fought over my dad. You were there."

Her eyes narrowed. "That can't be true."

"It is. When he wouldn't help me find Dad, I stopped calling."

She flinched but recovered. "Then he must have called you."

I shook my head. "Never once checked on me or Kamryn. As far as I knew, we were dead to him."

"Ann, you're exasperating!"

I crossed my arms.

Bree put her hands on her hips. "Then how do you explain him changing his will? Why would he name *you* as his executor?"

I was stunned. This was news to me. I shook my head. "No idea."

Bree glowered. "He summoned Peter Hillman, his attorney, to make the change. That's how I know. But it's always been *me*. I manage his business and take care of him. I was the executor. I earned it!"

I raised a finger to my lips. Judson might be unconscious, but her shrill voice could penetrate. "It's got to be a mistake," I said. "Maybe—"

"There's been a mistake, all right, and I plan to fight this! He's been forgetful, anxious, unable to make decisions. I'll challenge his testamentary capacity. I have witnesses."

I raised my hands in defense. "Okay, okay. We'll figure it out. I didn't ask for this, and I don't know why he'd do it. Let's hope he… Hey, you said he's had visions recently. Who did he describe? End-of-life visions can affect people."

Bree drew herself up and touched her coiffed hair. "He saw…my mother."

I narrowed my eyes. She'd hesitated. I thought she was lying. But at least she hadn't said the name I dreaded to hear. Her mother was Judson's second ex-wife. She'd died a few years after she left him. "Look, Aunt Bree, I can't afford to be up here sorting through all his affairs. What a pain! But I'd like to hear it from his lawyer first. And, anyway, Judson's still alive. He could still change his mind."

But I knew these visions signaled his decline. A high percentage of dying people reported them, especially when very close to the end.

"Mom?"

Kamryn's shout startled us. Bree opened the door, and I rushed in. Kam leaned over Judson. Her wide eyes alarmed me. I hoped Judson hadn't died right in front of her.

Bree approached her father's other side. She checked the heart monitor and bent close to him. "He's breathing."

I moved Kam away. "What's wrong? What happened?"

She gave a wary look toward Bree and shook her head. "I just thought he was breathing weird."

"I'll call the hospice team," Bree said. "Please stay with him." She left the room.

Kamryn pulled me away from the bed. In a low voice, she said, "He wanted something. He looked at me. When I went to him, he whispered something."

My heart raced. "Whispered? He was awake?"

"It didn't make any sense."

"Kamryn, what did he say?" *Please don't say he saw—*

"I'm not sure. He looked scared."

"So, you couldn't make it out?"

She swallowed and nodded. Her eyes were wide when she delivered the message. "He said, 'Don't let her take it.'"

Chapter Five

That evening, a hospice team took over. From a window in the guesthouse, I watched several vehicles drive by. Then Bree came over. She told me a nurse believed the end was near but said it could still be several days. I thought Bree could've just texted this, but then she squinted and asked, "Did your daughter see or hear anything I should know?"

I decided to keep Judson's outcry between Kamryn and me. "She called us in as soon as she saw he'd woken up."

Bree lifted her chin. She didn't believe me. We were even. We were both holding back.

"Are you comfortable here?" she asked. It seemed like an odd question. I'd lived here for nearly a year, and up until five years ago, I'd been back several times, sometimes staying in this house.

I opted to be civil. "We're fine. Thank you for stocking the refrigerator."

"If you need something, tell Shona." She turned and strode toward the front door before she stopped and looked back at me. "Just…be careful. You don't understand the situation." Then she was gone.

She was right about that. I had to think about today's rush of startling information. I was Judson's executor. He was scared about someone—a female. I wondered if telling Bree the content of his plea might pry loose her secret. Who *had* he seen? What was *she* hiding? Why had she lied? For that matter, why had *I* been so cagey?

For dinner, I took Kamryn to Merchants Row. The aroma of maple-roasted vegetables, cooked meat, and squash soup welcomed us in. Kamryn admired the heavily wooded features of the historic hotel that housed this restaurant. We ordered fish and chips. As she bit into a vinegar-soaked fry, she asked, "What did Great-Grampa mean? Who was he talking about?"

"I don't know, Kam. I haven't spoken to him in a while."

"Maybe he meant, don't let her take *me*."

"That's possible. Or maybe he didn't say it right, or you didn't hear it right."

She cocked her head. "I heard it. He grabbed my hand, like it was really important. Did you tell Aunt Bree?"

I hesitated. Kamryn had just turned ten, but she understood death. She'd recently been part of a case that involved a murdered boy. She also knew we might be attending a funeral here. I ran a fork through my peas. "I'll tell her when the time is right. She's overwhelmed. He's probably not even aware of where he is or what he's saying. We'll have to wait, so let's focus on what else we can do here."

Kam's eyes opened with excitement. "I read some stuff about Concord."

"Great. What do you want to see?"

"I wanna see where Louisa May Alcott lived. She was in two different houses."

"Okay. I'll show you around. It's a good place for you to learn some history."

Aside from us, there was one other person in the restaurant, a dark-haired man in a navy suit at a corner table, tapping on a laptop. I wondered if he were listening to us. I turned my chair a little so I could see him from the corner of my eye while Kamryn recited what else she'd read about the town's former residents. Hawthorne, Thoreau, Emerson. She'd picked up a lot. When we left the restaurant, I looked back, but the man seemed intent on his work. Outside, a skiff of snow and some flurries made Kamryn squeal in delight. I let her run ahead while I called Bree. She told me there'd been no change.

When I tucked Kamryn into bed that evening, she asked me to read her a story. I picked Nathaniel Hawthorne's "Feathertop," in the hope of hooking her on this author like Dad had once hooked me. The story was about a scarecrow made human by a witch. "Hawthorne lived nearby in the Old Manse," I told her. "That's where he wrote short stories like this. I'll show you tomorrow."

Kam didn't last two pages before her eyes closed and her breathing deepened. Since the story ended with Feathertop's horrified discovery of his false life, this was probably for the best. Hawthorne wasn't bedtime fare for kids.

I went into the library to call Natra and tell her the recent events. "I can't imagine why I'd be the executor. It makes no sense."

"Maybe you're getting dead-handed."

"Dead-handed? What does *that* mean?"

"It's a real estate term. *Mortmain*. People keep control over their property after they die by gifting it with stipulations, typically to a church or corporation. It's kind of a legacy thing."

"So, he'd expect me to donate his fortune?"

"More like manage it, probably, according to his wishes."

"Wow. That's a Hawthorne theme if I ever heard one. These cloistered New England families and their secrets. Now I'm interested in what's in that will. Are you on the deck?"

"I am. It's lovely here tonight."

I could picture her listening to the rhythmic ocean waves, twisting her hair, and sipping a glass of wine. "I hope I won't be here long," I said. "Kam's learning things, but Wayne won't want her missing school. She'll miss at least Monday."

"Any ideas what Judson's outcry meant?"

"Wish I knew. I'd like to find out what he's recently said, but Bree hasn't opened up. We're heading for a showdown over the will, I think. But there's something else." I told her about the news article on the recent suicide incidents. "I'd like to follow this story. Suicide contagion, if that's what we have, is an interest of mine. I'll send you the info. See if there's more context. Anything else on JoLynn's cases?"

"She's getting the investigation reports, but there won't be much. Accidents like these aren't investigated unless an insurance company gets involved. Since both victims were outside in poor weather conditions, evidence probably washed away, but we'll keep on it. How's Kam?"

"Eager for snow."

Natra laughed. "Sounds like her—oh, hey, JoLynn's calling."

"Go! I'll call you tomorrow."

I checked on the weather. The row of daily icons that showed a stable pattern reassured me. But I knew that sudden shifts can occur.

I thumbed through Hawthorne's *Mosses from an Old Manse* collection. It looked like the same book I'd found on my father's bedstand when we lived here. Touching it helped me feel close to him. Bree had read some of this collection to me and her daughter. I remembered the dark-haired Maisie fidgeting. She'd always try to guess the endings and ruin the magic. I'd heard that she'd run away a lot as a teen, breaking up Bree's marriage. Dad had said she'd gotten involved with a guy who'd been trouble, but he wouldn't elaborate. I wondered what had happened to her. By now, she was in her mid-thirties, but Bree hadn't mentioned her.

From the story collection, I picked "The Birthmark," one of my favorites. A scientist has a beautiful wife with only one thing marring her perfection: a small red birthmark on her face shaped like a hand. The scientist believes he can surgically erase this blemish. It doesn't bother the wife, but the man is so obsessed with making her perfect she submits. It ends badly. The red hand is so deeply rooted the extraction kills her. The scientist's pursuit of an ideal leaves him with nothing but loss.

I thought about this. My father was that red hand—the birthmark Judson wanted to obliterate from his esteemed family. At some point, Judson might have loved his son, but he'd come to view Lang as a defect, a disappointment. Yet shutting him out—extracting him—had likely ensured the family's demise. Hawthornean karma.

I closed the book. The story made me sad, like all pointless loss from dysfunctional greed. I saw it too often in the crimes I investigated.

Before retiring, I checked on Kamryn. She looked peaceful. I loved that she was in my former room, at nearly the same age I'd been when I lived here. I locked up the house and got ready for bed, then looked at my phone.

Ayden had texted his assessment of the drawing seminar: *Useful. Challenging. Glad I came. Hi to Kam.* Natra had also texted. *We might have another one.*

It was too late to call her. I hated to wish for Judson's death, but I wanted to go home.

Chapter Six

In the morning, Bree knocked at the door. She was dressed to go to her office. Her eyes were rimmed in red. Her Chanel perfume brought back memories of the hugs she once gave me. She held up a bag. "Fresh cranberry scones. Shona made them for the hospice team. I thought your daughter might like some."

I accepted the bag. "Thank you. I'm sure she will."

"My father had a difficult night. The medical staff will be tending to him 24-7, so they'll be in and out." I sensed she was trying to sound calm, but she twisted a ring on her left hand. "They want to limit the number of people in his room. It's probably not good for your daughter to see, anyway."

"I understand." In other words, I was more a visitor than family. "I'll be in town, nearby, if anything happens. I'd like to show Kamryn around."

She stared as if she wanted to say something, but then abruptly thanked me and walked away.

Kamryn was still asleep, so I called Natra by video. "What did your text mean? Another what?"

"JoLynn said the pattern in the first two murder-by-weather cases shows up again. This time, it was a flood. About two years ago. Michael Levy's the victim. He was thirty-two. It's like some weather freak's studying disturbances so he can put himself in places where deaths can be blamed on them."

I snorted. "That's a new one. Controlled but still random, like Israel Keyes. He'd pick a spot, purchase items for a kill kit, bury them in a plastic bucket, and wait for a year or so before he'd go back and kill someone who crossed his path. He wouldn't target a specific person. He'd kill just to do it. Then he screwed up and got caught."

"This seems methodical, too," Natra agreed.

"It doesn't make much sense, though. It can't be easy figuring out where a storm will be that's so severe it will cover up a murder. How would he know he'd find someone outside?"

"Maybe it's hit-n-miss. It works in some places, not others. Who knows how much time he puts into it? Maybe he has money, so he can travel on short notice."

I considered this. "He'd be like a storm chaser. We can probably locate people like that online. Maybe see if someone's talking about those three events."

"We're looking into it, but he, or they, seem too smart for that kind of error."

"Smart killers are caught all the time on stupid mistakes. But I suspect any discussion would be on the deep web. Or it will be coded."

"We need more details. The police reports are basic. It took JoLynn's expertise in Chattanooga to figure that one out. There aren't many forensic meteorologists. She's working on it. If we need a meeting, we'll loop you in."

"Hope it doesn't rev up. I need to be here for now. Any storms tracking?"

"A couple. A tropical storm and a cold front."

"Ah! Sounds like you'll be cold, too, eh?"

"Not as cold as you."

"Keep me posted." I decided to refocus. "What about my case up here in Dunbury?"

"I found some articles. It's intriguing, especially the local lore. The area has a reputation for negative energy."

"Meaning?"

"Curses, bad luck, psychotic breaks. Goes back in history, *deep* history. I'll gather it into a document and email it, with a map that shows the incident locations. They're all close to that Dacretown property."

"Call an official in Dunbury. Offer my services as a consultant. Parents are already demanding some action."

Natra cocked her head. "You'll consult with Kam there?"

"Just wanna get my foot in the door. Could be a good case for my research, not to mention a fee. If they hire me, I might need Ayden up here to help with PI work, so he should be ready."

"I'll make some calls."

Everywhere I turned so far that morning, I ended up with more questions than answers. I buffered my frustration by giving Kamryn a walking tour of Concord. It was a sunny day, cold but still.

Kamryn seemed delighted by each place we stopped. Questions bubbled out of her. I showed her the site at North Bridge of the battle in April 1775 that had ignited the Revolutionary War. Close by, I pointed out the single gabled window on The Old Manse, an imposing three-story beige mansion where Hawthorne had penned his first story collection.

"I read you one from a later edition," I told her.

We cut over to Lexington Street to see the former homes of Louisa May Alcott and Ralph Waldo Emerson. During the mid-1800s, Concord had been a hub of intellectual and literary creativity. Further along this street, Hawthorne had lived in a unique yellow house, the Wayside, once owned by the Alcotts. Kam wanted to linger at both, but the dark gray, two-story Orchard House where Louisa had lived especially delighted her. Snow prevented a walk through the woods to Henry David Thoreau's renowned wilderness retreat, but I promised to drive her there if we had a chance.

"It's hard to make plans when we don't know how long we'll be here," I told her.

Kamryn looked up with a smile. "I hope we stay till it snows again."

A text came from Shona inviting us to lunch. I accepted. If her daughter got along with Kamryn, it could afford me time to consult. And if Shona warmed up to me, I might get information about Judson or Bree. *Don't let her take it!* I'd watch for an opportunity.

Chapter Seven

We had just enough time to see my favorite spot, Sleepy Hollow Cemetery. On the lane inside that parallels Bedford Street, we skirted piles of melting snow mixed with brown leaves. The sodden boneyard felt dark today, even with trees stripped nearly bare. The 31-acre burial ground was founded in 1855, with rows of rounded headstones, some so eroded they couldn't be read. It's one of the original rural cemeteries, designed by the architects for New York's Central Park. Oak, maple, and pine trees made the place feel like we were in the woods.

Kamryn wandered from one gravestone to another to shout out the dates. She looked at me. "Will we see the headless horseman?"

I shook my head. "That's a different cemetery. It's in New York. Same name, different place. I believe this one was named first."

Kamryn pouted. She always wants to see a ghost. We arrived at a sculpted figure at the center of the dominating Melvin monument, an oversized angel emerging from a cavern. "This was commissioned by James Melvin to honor his brothers, who died during the Civil War."

Kamryn glanced at it before she went to see another vault. I'd learned to appreciate her ability to leap from one thing to another. Like the scientist in "The Birthmark," I'd once viewed this trait as a flaw and had tried to erase it with behavioral controls. But then I'd understood its advantages. For one thing, she didn't anchor for long in a bad mood.

I steered Kam along a winding paved road toward a hill called Authors Ridge. I'd spent a lot of time there during my reluctant residence in this town. I'd found it comforting to sit among the gravestones that marked the remains of great minds. Sometimes, my father had accompanied me.

Kamryn took my hand. "What was your dad like?"

The question startled me, as if she'd read my mind. "He was like you, in a lot of ways, always thinking about many different things at once."

She smiled. "Did he like puzzles?"

"He did. He spent his life trying to solve really tough puzzles about people who went missing."

Kam went silent, as if absorbing this. "Did he find anyone?"

"Sometimes. But he took on mysterious cases, the ones that were hard to explain. They weren't people who'd just run off. They often had lives they liked, but one day they just weren't there. They'd leave meals half-eaten, or cars abandoned, or even leave their kids." *Like me.* "He thought there might be some common thread."

Kamryn's eyes widened. "Like aliens?"

I shrugged. "I don't know if he ever figured it out."

"Maybe that's what he's doing. Maybe he's where *they* are. So, he can't tell you."

"That's possible."

Kamryn leaned into me. "Did you figure out what Great-Grampa meant? Are we s'posed to do something?"

"I don't know, Kam. Sometimes, when people are very ill, they have visions and get notions that don't make sense."

"Why did he say it to me?"

"He's seen you only twice. He doesn't know you, not really."

"He looked right at me. He made me come over to him, and he grabbed my hand! He seemed scared."

This was new information. "He *made* you come over?"

"Yes. He waved me over to the bed."

Judson likely had secrets that haunted him as he faced his own death. Perhaps bad ones. "Maybe he'll wake up later and explain it." I doubted this but didn't know what else to say. Judson didn't like kids. I'd never seen him show affection even to Maisie, Bree's daughter. Why would he have beckoned to Kamryn?

I'd seen how easily her neurodiverse mind connected with people who dabbled in alter realities. It was like my father's attunement to people's auras and moods. There could be more to Judson's focus on Kamryn than her being by chance the only one in the room. Unless Maisie had kids somewhere, Kamryn might be the final Hunter heir.

Across the cemetery, I noticed a couple of people. One was a lone male figure in a long, black coat and dark knit cap. He had a thinner build than the man from the restaurant. The other was a female. She placed something at a headstone. I steered Kamryn in the other direction.

We ascended the rocky path on Authors Ridge. To our left, I pointed out the impressive rough-hewn monument for the Transcendental thinker, Ralph Waldo Emerson, and his relatives. Kamryn counted the names. "How did they get so many people in there?"

"Bone coffins."

She turned her brown eyes on me. "What's that?"

"Small containers. After someone's been buried for several years, their survivors acquired more space by putting the bones in a smaller box."

Kam made a face. "That's weird."

"Not really. People were in closer touch with death. These old cemeteries in the middle of towns had limited space. It was a way to keep large families together, close enough for visits. I think there might be more than twenty people buried in this grave."

We moved on, but I flashed on an Emerson sentiment I'd always liked: *Do not go where the path may lead; go instead where there is no path and leave a trail.*

Higher up on the rocky path, we stepped over tree roots and stopped at a simple rounded gravestone. Across the front was just a name: *Hawthorne.* A scattering of pennies, some folded notes, and a dozen pens lay on the ground between the headstone and a smaller footstone. A few pens stood straight up in the dirt. I pointed at them.

"See? That's for authors. Bring a pen, take a pen, and carry on the muse." I dug into my purse and handed Kamryn a pen. "Put this with the others and pick one to take with us. Grab whichever pen you like."

She looked at me. "Won't they come back to get it?"

"No. The point is to leave it for someone who might get inspiration from it, just from it being on this grave."

"How?"

I shrugged. "It's magic. The transference of the spirit of creativity."

Kam bent down and grabbed a thick purple pen, smiled, and showed me.

I nodded. "Nice one." I placed a pen down, too, and selected a black one. "I used to come up here on summer evenings when I was your age. I'd sit and read *The House of the Seven Gables* or *Mosses from an Old Manse* and spook myself. Hawthorne could be scary."

Kam nodded. "Was that story last night scary? I didn't hear the end."

"No. It's sad, though. Hawthorne wrote about human flaws that caused others harm." I wondered what the great literary writer might have thought of Judson. No doubt he'd be made into a character like the heartless Colonel Pyncheon.

I guided Kam over to the clump of ordinary headstones for Henry David Thoreau and Louisa May Alcott, pointing out the cluster of coins, pens, tiny dolls, stuffed animals, and fading flowers at each of these graves.

Kamryn looked at them, then asked, "Why doesn't Aunt Bree like me?"

Surprised, I cocked my head. "Why do you think that?"

"She looks at me like I'm in the way."

"She's just worried, maybe tired."

Kamryn shrugged. She stepped over to the Alcott's plot and crouched near the inauspicious white headstone for Louisa. She brushed a chunk of ice off it. Flat rather than raised, it served as a rectangular platter for coins and pens. Kam held up the purple pen from Hawthorne's grave. "Can I put this here and take a different one?"

"Of course."

With some reverence, she placed it on Alcott's headstone and selected a red pen to carry away. I looked around for that lone man, didn't see him, and took Kamryn down the other side of the ridge. These stones reminded me of the call I'd made that morning to Judson's attorney. Peter Hillman had assured me that a witness had confirmed that Judson's mental state was sound.

"Why me for the executor?" I'd asked.

"He didn't say. I have an accountant ready to assist you. Judson left more than enough to cover the fees, including for your time. It's generous, and everything's organized."

The overcast sky seemed darker as we took the path to the exit. Kamryn read several epitaphs out loud. I felt a chill and glanced toward a cluster of gravestones as if I might see Judson's ghost. To my surprise, the man in black was closer, some thirty yards away, focused on a square monument. Just past him, the woman still lingered too. I touched Kamryn's shoulder to urge her to move.

"But I want to read the stones!" she protested.

"It's time for lunch. You can meet Elyse."

I wanted to get away from this isolated spot. Just before we exited, I looked back at the two sightseers. Both were gazing in our direction.

Chapter Eight

Shona's home behind Judson's house was a cozy modern Scottish cottage. Against soft green walls sat simple oak furniture with knitted wool throws over a tweed couch. There was even a wooden rocking chair. The paintings featured breathtaking Highlands landscapes. I wondered if this was Shona's taste or Judson's decorator's. Regardless, it felt warm and relaxed. Piles of books bore titles that showed a love of history.

"I apologize for a tight squeeze," said Shona, "but I have just forty-five minutes for my break today, and I'm on call for emergencies. At least the girls can meet."

I held up a hand. "I completely understand. There's probably a lot of activity with healthcare workers in and out. How's my grandfather?"

"The same. I have a list of people to call. It'll be a busy day. But, please, join us."

She'd set a lovely table with hot chowder, fresh crusty bread, hunks of cheese, and several treats common to New England. The blue pottery plates and bowls, set with pewter cutlery, reinforced the informal atmosphere. Shona offered me a glass of wine, but I declined. Elyse entered the room, and Shona introduced her.

Elyse Teagan had large greenish-brown eyes and auburn hair that hung in waves past her shoulders. She sat straight in her chair during lunch, acting polite, but from her sidelong looks at Kamryn, I sensed she had a lively side. Once she was free to show Kam her room, I heard plenty of reassuring giggles. While the girls explored each other's worlds, I asked Shona about her background. "You mentioned you're from the western side of Scotland.

In the Highlands?"

"Morvern. Or some say Morven. It's a peninsula among the islands, but it's easiest to take a ferry to see it. Most people go from Mull to Iona or the Inner Hebrides, but Morvern has its charm and an impressive natural shoreline. It's just as dramatic as the others but undamaged by tourists. There's a lovely nature reserve, a castle, a medieval church, and a distillery."

I smiled. "Every place in Scotland has a distillery."

"That they do. But Morvern has other things to distinguish it, like a wishing stone with a large hole, where you fill your mouth with water, pass through the hole, turn three times, and receive your heart's desire." She laughed. "And, of course, there's a distinctive coffin road."

I sat up. "Coffin road?"

"Ah, yes. In ancient times, they'd carry the dead in coffins to the west along specially marked roads to remote burial grounds. The Highlands and western islands have many such tracks. It was the way of the sun as it sets, and the soil was less rocky. If the road was especially long or the person had high social status, they'd have wakes along the way. They'd sing and lament and build cairns on which to place the coffins during resting periods. You dare not let it touch the ground, or the spirit might haunt you. The custom was to carry the dead with their feet pointing away from home so they couldn't find their way back." Shona smiled.

"I'm surprised I don't know about this," I said. "My father took me to Scotland several times. Never said anything about coffin roads."

I noticed a slight change in Shona's expression. I'm trained in micro-expressions. They're quick, and they reveal feelings a person might wish to hide. Her eyes had widened, and her mouth tightened when I'd mentioned Dad. I guessed she'd heard negative things about him from Judson or Bree.

"I suppose these roads aren't well known," Shona continued. "Maybe a bit morbid, especially the stories about processions that were attacked or robbed during the night."

"Wouldn't robbers be nervous about interrupting a journey like that?"

"You would think. But some consider only their own gain. Of course, a curse might make them regret their error." She poured me another cup of coffee. "Did you ever see any of your grandfather's collection?"

"Collection? Of what?"

"Oh, artifacts, coins, crafts."

"He wasn't a grandfatherly type. If he had stuff like that, he wasn't about to let a child handle it. He had locked rooms, that much I remember. Plenty of hands-off warnings. Dad didn't mention a collection."

"It's quite precious to him. He showed me a few items, but I know he has more."

This seemed an odd remark. "How would you know that?"

She hesitated, as if she knew she'd said too much. "He's bought things from other collectors. Some items are Scottish relics."

"Like stolen things? Stuff he shouldn't have?"

"Well, I wouldn't know. The things he showed me are mostly old pottery, jewelry, and pieces of art."

"Is there something specific you think he has?"

"No, no, of course not." She waved a hand dismissively and collected the lunch dishes. But she'd made me curious. I glanced at the mantel and noticed a distinct hand-painted gray jar with a cap. Shona followed my gaze. "That's mine. From Morvern."

"It looks like an urn. From a coffin road, perhaps?"

She smiled. "That's grim."

This was getting awkward. I wanted to lighten the mood. "When were you there last?"

"Oh…" she seemed to consider. "It's been some time. I've traveled back and forth, but I've been in Concord a year. I was hired to manage the household."

"Knowing Judson's moods, you must have a lot of patience."

Shona smiled. "I understand you lived here for a year."

A deflection. "I did. I was eight. My father was just out of graduate school and needed support. He tried working for Judson, but they didn't get along. Real estate wasn't Dad's passion."

"And what was?"

I took a sip of coffee. "He was more of an investigative researcher. He made some investments, which paid the bills, and acquired some properties, but he traveled a lot. He looked for missing people."

Shona leaned closer. "Did he find anyone?"

"I think he found good leads, but his cases were complicated. I guess I'm like him in that way. I seem to always take on the twisty ones."

"Did you help him on any?"

"I did. That's how I learned how to investigate. But he kind of got lost in ideas about portals and thin places. I'm sure you know what those are."

"Oh, yes." She nodded. "Morvern is considered one."

"He's probably been there, then. He thought he could crack the mystical codes and show the portals to be natural phenomena. Then *he* disappeared. If he had any secrets about locating the missing, he didn't leave them behind."

Shona moved her fingers over her lips before she said, "I heard. I'm sorry for your loss."

I felt the familiar tightening in my chest when I thought I should insist that Dad was alive. Instead, I thanked her and changed the subject. "Since you've been here a while, have you heard about this place called Dacretown? It's near Dunbury, half an hour or so from here. Seems to be some recent trouble there related to its legends."

I thought I saw annoyance in Shona's expression before she said, "It's an old settlement that's rotted away. Such places have ghost stories. Kids try to get in, and they quickly find out it's private property."

"Who owns it?"

"I'm not sure."

The fingers of her right hand clenched, and one side of her mouth tightened. I recognized these signals and sensed a wall. She knew more than she'd say. This lunch had not gone as well as I'd hoped. I thought of a way to keep things light. "I'm taking Kamryn over to Thoreau's cabin this afternoon. Shall I take Elyse with us?"

Shona's face brightened. "She'd enjoy that. She's read his work."

"That's great. Kamryn's missing school, so I'm trying to supplement with some history lessons."

"She could come when our tutor's here. During weekdays, I have a grad student, Jeannette Criner, come in for Elyse. She's a local. I don't think she'd mind including your daughter. She teaches American history, geography, composition, and literature."

This seemed ideal. I agreed to try it. An arrangement like this might produce more information. Shona had practically told me that Judson was hiding something. I believed she also knew things about my father. I had to strengthen our connection.

Chapter Nine

Bree had alerted relatives and associates who might have to travel. She expected her father to die soon. "There's nothing for you to do," she told me by phone. "Feel free to use one of the cars. We'll talk this evening."

In the six-bay garage, I walked past a Lexus, a Cadillac, and two Mercedes. I decided to use Judson's white Range Rover SV. Both girls approved. As I drove, I watched for vehicles on my tail. The couple in the cemetery had spooked me.

Taking Elyse proved to be a benefit. She kept Kamryn busy, and she also knew quite a bit about the literary enclave that Concord had once been. For a twelve-year-old, she was well-versed in obscure writers. Kam was getting the education I'd hoped for. And she listened to her new friend better than if I were telling her the same things.

Our first stop was the cabin where Thoreau had spent a couple of years writing and communing with nature.

"The original cabin's gone," Elyse said. "There's a sign if you want to see where it was."

I shook my head. "Snow's blocking the path. Let's look at the reconstructed one."

We parked near the tourist area and walked to the cabin. A male guide told us about the conditions under which Thoreau had lived. He hadn't exactly been a survivalist, since he could easily walk to town, and his mother brought him lunch. Kam thought this was funny, but Elyse warned her not to underestimate him. She pointed out how he'd connected with nature in a poetical sense. "He wanted us to take care of it."

By the time she was done, Kamryn wanted to read more about him. Goal accomplished.

I checked the sky. Still clear. A storm was brewing in the northern Plains, I knew, but it could dissipate before it reached us. I hoped for that.

I drove toward Dunbury, the town associated with the suicide cluster. I wanted to know the route should I get the gig. Soon, we entered a small New England village with historic charm: well-kept frame houses, a town square, several tall church steeples, and some sweet little coffee shops. It seemed ordinary, but it did have both commuter and freight rail tracks. Strangely enough, suicide clusters often happened near tracks.

I stopped in a drugstore to pick up a local paper. When I got in line to pay, I heard a woman near a display rack say, "I just don't believe these kids are doing this. Especially not that girl."

I tuned in. The woman's female companion had a response. "I heard she'd been bullied."

"I know her mother. She said Marti'd been acting odd. Something about this doesn't feel right. Probably that strange boyfriend."

I wanted to hear more. I thought about looking for another item, but Kamryn tugged on my sleeve. She hated to wait. I bought my paper and walked out. I'd heard enough to see a lead.

In the middle of the town square, I spotted a monument that looked familiar. I pulled out my phone.

Kamryn looked at me. "What?"

I opened a map app. "Just curious about something. Give me a sec."

We were near an area I'd explored several times with my father. I had a faint memory of a place nearby with multiple boarded-up buildings. An abandoned asylum. The place had given my eight-year-old self the creeps. Later, I'd learned that the layout had been the "campus model" for late-nineteenth-century psychiatric facilities. Many had closed, leaving buildings empty. I recalled broken windows and green window frames with peeling paint.

I decided to drive by. Elyse and Kamryn chatted in the back seat. Elyse seemed to enjoy being a tour guide. When we arrived at the entrance to the place I remembered, I pulled in. A locked iron gate and a *No Trespassing* sign barred the way, but several reddish-brown brick buildings were within view. My memories returned in a flood. I was in the right place. I'd walked these grounds with Dad.

Kamryn sat up. "What's this?"

"An old hospital," I told her. "Abandoned places like this exist all over the East Coast."

"Why're we here?"

"It's a place I used to visit."

"I've been here," Elyse said. "It's just old buildings. No one lives here."

I looked at the girls. "I thought maybe we could go in, but it's restricted now."

Kam shook her head. "I don't want to."

"It'll be dark soon," Elyse added.

"Okay, you're right. We should be getting back." I put the Range Rover in reverse to back out when a large black Suburban pulled up behind me and blocked my way. My heart beat faster. Kamryn looked behind us.

I held up a hand. "Don't worry." I got out to watch the hefty man in a security uniform approach.

He looked annoyed. "Are you aware you can't be on this property?" The bulge under his jacket told me he was armed.

I held out my hands to look vulnerable. "I apologize. I thought this place was open to the public. I used to come here."

"That's been a while."

"I didn't trespass. Just drove up to the sign. Did something happen to close it?"

He put his hands on his hips. "These kids won't stay out. It poses a liability."

I wondered if this was the area where the Dunbury kids had come to end their lives. A track ran nearby. "Well, I can see that it's being developed. If you'll let me back up, we'll go ahead and leave."

His eyes narrowed. "You a reporter? Sniffing around?"

I wondered why he'd jump to that conclusion. There must be something here. "No, I'm not. I don't even live here. I'm visiting family. Just out for a drive."

The man scrutinized the Range Rover with the girls inside. Then he nodded. "You can leave. But I have that plate number. I'll know if you come back."

"Thank you. I won't be back." *At least, not in this vehicle.*

When I got back on the road, Kamryn asked, "What did he want?"

"He's a security guard. I guess they're concerned about people going through there."

"Maybe 'cuz of the ghosts," Elyse stated.

I looked at her in the rearview mirror. "Ghosts?"

"That's what my sister said. People come here looking for ghosts. Some lady went crazy here."

"Well, it was a psychiatric facility once."

"No, on the other side." She pointed. "All the way across. Past the Dead Line."

"Dead Line?"

"That's what they call it. There's a bad place back there."

I flashed on my father walking with purpose into the woods.

"What happened?" Kamryn asked.

"Oh, it was a long time ago. A man killed his whole family, an' there was other bad stuff. I heard when they were digging there, they found things, like bones, maybe. They had to stop. That's when they made the Dead Line."

Kam's eyes were big. "Did they see ghosts?"

"One guy got something on camera a few months ago. You can watch it online. It's a recording. A dark shape. He said it was creepy in there. He was gonna camp out and run the camera all night, but then someone made him leave. He said there were markers on the ground and deep holes and blood on the trees."

I made a mental note. Creepy tales about a long-abandoned town were one thing; fresh digging at a place associated with suicides was another, especially since I remembered my dad in that area…digging.

Chapter Ten

As we left the garage, I saw lights in Judson's windows. I called Bree but got her voicemail. I left a message asking her to please let me know Judson's status. I couldn't figure out why she'd invite me here only to avoid me.

On the front porch, I paused. Stuffed into a crack in the door was a business card. I pulled it out and urged Kamryn into the house. I didn't like knowing that someone had been on the porch. There was an alarm here but no video security.

In better light, I looked at the card. The embossed name, dark blue lettering on light blue stock, was *Richard Lehr*, with a phone number. A line beneath the name listed one item: *Privacy Consultant*. There was no address. I turned the card over. On the back was a note, "Please call: Urgent."

I texted the number to Natra to trace, sent a photo of the card, and let her know I'd call her once Kam was occupied. *If the number's blocked, send it to Joe.* That's my moonlighting digital guy. He helps in exchange for using my high-end digital equipment. I appreciate his creativity in maneuvering around tricky cyber laws without quite breaking them.

"I'm gonna read, Mom," Kamryn said. "Do we have anything by Thoreau?"

Elyse was having some impact. I'd been influenced myself at Kam's age by seeing where authors lived and wrote. "I'm sure there's a book in here somewhere, but it might be a little advanced for you. How about a book that describes the local writers? You can learn about his life."

Kamryn gave me an odd look. "I thought you want me to read more."

"I do, but I don't want you to get discouraged. He writes grown-up stuff."

I couldn't think of a way to describe Concord's esoteric transcendental movement. "If you read *about* him first, that could help you understand his essays."

"But we heard all that stuff about him today."

I sensed she wanted to impress her new friend. It gave me an opening. "Kamryn, how would you like to take some lessons with Elyse from her tutor?"

She frowned.

"Her tutor's a local historian. Your teachers will be pleased."

Kam shrugged. "Okay. I have some writing assignments. Maybe she can help me."

We looked through the library for an appropriate book. Kamryn tried the door to the hidden staircase, but it was locked. "Can we get a key?"

"I'll ask, but it's probably locked to keep guests out."

"Did you use it?"

"Yes, but we were living here. And as I recall, the steps are steep. Maybe Aunt Bree didn't want anyone to fall and get hurt."

Being in the library brought back a time when Dad and I were playing Hide 'n' Seek, much like the Find Me game I now played with Kam. One day, I couldn't find him and panicked. I'd cried, which brought Dad out of the hidden staircase—my introduction to it. I didn't forgive him. In retrospect, I must have sensed his intent to leave one day. First, he divorced my mother, dividing our family and leaving me with her bitterness and blame. Then he erased himself from my life altogether, aside from the house he'd left to me. I'd give up the house to have him back.

I found a book for Kamryn that offered a history of Concord. "There should be quotes in here from Thoreau's work." By then, she'd discovered another book, *Famous Storms of New England*. She took both to her room.

I ordered a pizza, then opened my laptop and looked up information about the abandoned property. The psychiatric complex took up one square mile, and the wooded area northwest of those buildings featured a large plot that comprised the former Dacretown settlement. It had an irregular shape, with roads that entered from five different spots. I estimated it at several hundred acres. The village had probably been a farming homestead. That's where Dad had taken photos and dug his holes.

I found an article that described a scandal with the asylum over patient abuse and misuse of public funds. The facility was forced to close after losing several lawsuits over inhumane conditions. Patients had been bound to their beds or radiators, left in their excrement, force-fed, and used for experiments. To make feeding easier, teeth were removed. A small unlicensed cemetery had turned up some mass graves holding unidentified patients. Some were missing body parts. What a nightmare for those who'd had to endure it. That was the kind of thing that inspired spooky stories. I noted the usual collection of rumors about creatures in the woods and lingering ghosts. Phantom screams, white figures, weird howls, crazy ladies—the expected stuff. But for some reason, the place was getting renewed notice. That reporter, Galloway, had mentioned it in the context of the suicides.

A news article from a few years earlier caught my attention. An educational organization, the Institute for Mentalistics, had purchased the psychiatric property to develop a research and training facility. There'd been some resistance, as the bid had included Dacretown.

This article described Dacretown as an area with historical significance. A couple of brothers had settled there during the early eighteenth century. With their growing families, they'd founded a thriving village, but an illness had swept through and killed many of the residents. All that remained were a few crumbling building foundations and overgrown cellar holes. An organization called the Gray Hollow Group protected the place, and the business of selling it seemed murky. Soon after the Institute made its bid, one of the GHG members, a man named Gregory Hawkins, had died in an accident. An investigation had turned up some questions, but the police closed the case. Still, the sale went south. The developers settled for just the asylum grounds. Dacretown remained in someone else's hands.

I started a search on this mysterious conservancy group when a video call from Natra interrupted me.

"Got some info," she said. "Your privacy consultant might be a former skip tracer. He learned the ways people disappear and now he makes money helping others do the same. Like…"—she gestured—"someone you know."

I blinked. She meant Dad. That had gone right over my head. I was here in the town where Dad grew up, he'd vanished, and a privacy consultant had noticed my presence and contacted me. "God, I'm an idiot. I need to call this guy."

"Hold up. I ran the number. It doesn't track to an address, so I sent it to Joe. Probably goes to a burner and it's likely sophisticated. Privacy consultants have more tricks than most. Don't meet him without backup, especially not with Kamryn there."

"I know someone who can watch her. But I'll at least call him."

Natra raised a finger. "I also have more on your suicide cluster and that property. Apparently, a local legend was tied to some suicides there in the past, which possibly attracted these kids."

"Happens all too often. Like the suicide forest in Japan that lures depressed people to join others who hanged themselves."

"There was once a village on that property that some people think was cursed."

I nodded. "Right, right, Dacretown. I've just been reading about it."

"You'll like this since it's got Scottish roots. It seems that during the eighteenth century, someone in Scotland stole a relic or artifact from a powerful clan. When this clan caught and tortured the thief, his two sons fled to America. Actually, three sons did, but one was lost at sea. They brought the item with them. Apparently, the clan leader had attached a curse to the relic, so whoever had it would suffer great harm. Pestilence and death, et cetera, et cetera. The brothers either didn't know or didn't care. They settled together at Dacretown with their wives and started families. Others joined them, and they developed a farming community. Then, the string of bad luck started. Or maybe it started with the brother lost at sea."

I made a face. "I was near that place today. I hope it didn't infect me."

"I don't think the town's still there."

"Some remnants are. The property appears to be fenced off and protected by some private group. It borders a large psychiatric complex."

"I saw that. Just a bunch of old buildings now."

"Yes, it's shuttered, but my father and I used to walk there when I was a kid. He never said anything about a curse. So, what was the bad luck? I saw something about a contagion, but what else?"

Natra pulled a pad of paper in front of her. "There's a lot of nasty stuff for a small community. First, a massive storm damaged most of the buildings and killed off crops and the animals they needed for farming. They tried rebuilding, but then some kids were struck with a mysterious fatal illness. One of the mothers went insane. But get this: by the end of that year, one of the founding brothers had murdered his entire family before turning the gun on himself."

"Yikes! The curse was real."

"An Indian attack finished off a couple more families. Another town leader moved away after his wife wandered into the woods and vanished, but he ended up in an asylum. The last of the settlers decided the ground was cursed, so they abandoned it."

Elyse had mentioned some of this. "No one ever found the stolen item?"

"Not that I've seen. Apparently, the records don't say what it is. Lots of things have been suggested, from a sacred symbol stone to a document to a weapon, even a skull, but the only people who might know are descendants of the clan."

"Or of the thieves. Maybe we should consult a historian or an archaeologist." I thought of Jeannette Criner, the tutor.

"Here's a little more. There was an attempt to resettle the place at the end of that century, but bad luck came to them as well. Let me read you what one article says." Natra put on some dark-framed reading glasses. "Over the years, the Dacretown buildings deteriorated. Kids playing in them accidentally burnt down the main structure, a community hall. When a kid died in an accident there, the area was fenced off. Next to it, the state cleared several acres and built a psychiatric hospital."

I nodded. "And now some business has purchased that property for development. The Institute for Mentalistics. I wanted to go on the property today, but a security guard warned me off. How's this related to the suicide cluster?"

"The curse, apparently. That's the draw. A decade ago, a kid wrote a journal about the bad luck he'd experienced after digging around in the old foundations to locate the item. Claimed he'd discovered a map to its location. After he ran in front of a train, his parents found his journal."

"With the map?"

"No mention of that. He'd persuaded himself that he was doomed because he'd gotten close to the cursed object. Then another kid claimed he'd found it but buried it again after someone threatened him. Later, he hanged himself in the Dacretown woods. Not quite a cluster, but a month ago on the tenth anniversary of the first death, the local paper ran an article about it. So, then this recent series happened."

"Media coverage has an impact."

"Now the place is patrolled." Natra sorted through her pile of papers. "I found this on social media. Some kids who know Owen Kringle, the train kid in the hospital, said a club had formed dedicated to finding the object to neutralize the curse."

I remembered the report. "Was this group called the Skeleton Crew?"

"Doesn't say."

"Hmm. Too many questions. I need to find the reporter who wrote the article I read. I can see how a place like that could seem all dark and creepy to teens. Still, nothing suggests a strong suicide attraction, not like we see in other places."

Natra held up a finger. "That's the romantic part. The rumor is that the relic had the power to make people successful. Like a magic lamp with a genie. Finding the relic would guarantee their success and free them from stress. Or so the story goes." She looked over her shoulder. "Sounds like Ayden's here. That truck's unmistakable. Wanna talk to him?"

"You fill him in. But I'd like him to be ready to catch a plane. If I get this gig, I'll need him here. No weapons. There won't be time to get a gun registered. I just need some sleuthing. Nothing dangerous."

Or so I thought.

Chapter Eleven

I left Kamryn with Shona and Elyse while I made a run to the grocery store. "I won't be long."

"Okay, Mom. Will you get us some M&Ms?"

"It's on my list."

I looked around before I entered Judson's garage. A puddle at my feet had frozen over. Cars were parked along the street, but they looked empty. Judson had security cameras on his properties, so I wasn't concerned. Once I was in the Range Rover, I watched for cars that might start up and pull out behind me. Nothing. I relaxed.

At the grocery store, I noticed a darker shade to the clouds. They looked heavy, but I'd seen no weather alert. I soon had what I needed for a couple more days. I loaded the bag on the passenger side and closed the car door.

"Dr. Hunter."

I looked to my left. A man approached. I recognized him as the guy from the Merchants Row restaurant. So, he *had* been listening to me. I stood still. He strode with purpose, as if he'd been waiting for me to come out. I felt like I'd stumbled across a snake and had to see how it would act before I could make my move. When he stopped, I felt him bristling with energy.

He held out a hand. "I'm Richard Lehr." Even in this cold air, a sheen of perspiration hugged his nose. A parking lot light caught the intensity of his dark eyes. From the gray strands that ran through his clipped dark hair, I placed him in his mid-fifties. "I left my card for you. I expected you to call."

I hesitated, then shook his hand. His grip felt as if he were trying to pull me with him over a cliff. I cleared my throat and let go. "I have your card,

Mr. Lehr, but I'm in town for family business."

"I know. I'm acquainted with Judson Hunter and Briana Duncan. She said you were coming. I must speak with you."

This surprised me. "She didn't mention—"

"There's a reason. In fact, if you ask her, she'll deny it, I promise you. She doesn't want me to talk with you. I can explain."

I took a step back. "Have you been following me? I saw you in the restaurant."

"I hoped to speak to you there but saw your daughter, so I waited."

"You've been watching me."

"Guilty. What I have to say concerns you, something you want."

Lehr seemed quite sure of himself. I didn't like this, not out here where I had no protection. "I'll call you when I can, Mr. Lehr. Maybe tomorrow. Right now, I don't—"

"Make time." He cocked his head and fumbled with a button on his coat. "You should hear this before Judson dies. He'll be gone soon."

His imperious manner annoyed me. "This really isn't the—"

Lehr stepped closer. I recoiled from the sweet smell of his cologne. He leaned slightly toward me. I drew myself up. "I know what a privacy consultant is, Mr. Lehr. You help people disappear. What's so pressing?"

"Your father has something of mine. I need it."

I felt punched in the gut. I narrowed my eyes. Lehr moved his coat to show he was armed. "Just so you know, you're safe with me."

My heart sped up. *Safe?* Why did he think he should show me his weapon? A snow flurry melted on his cheek. Several more fell around us. I looked toward the store. I wanted to go back inside, get away from this man. "I really need to get back. Judson's ill—"

"Here's the gist, Dr. Hunter. I was in business with Judson for years. He's been my partner, even my mentor. He promised me something your father took. So, either Lang has it, or you do. If it's you, I have an offer. A good one. We'll both get something we want."

I had my out. "Didn't Briana tell you? My father killed himself."

Lehr crossed his arms. "Nice try. You don't know me, so I won't hold that against you, but I have plenty of informants. You think he's still alive. You've been searching for him. You had a falling out with Judson over it." Another punch. I opened my mouth, but he continued. "You need me. We can help each other. We can find him. But then I want you to turn over the item to me. It belongs to me. So, we pool our resources. It's that simple. A *quid pro quo*. Think it over. Then call me. There's a time limit." He looked at his watch. "I want your answer by this time tomorrow."

"And if I don't call?"

"You're better off with me as a friend. Don't bother looking me up. Whatever you and your assistant, even your ex-husband, the detective, might find won't be what it seems. I'm a ghost." He snapped his fingers. "You can't lose. You'll find your father, and you'll pay for my help with something you won't even want."

"I don't care to be pressured by someone I—"

Lehr's expression turned nasty, and he looked down his nose. "I just want what's already mine."

He obviously knew where I was staying and knew my daughter was here. I had to get back.

"Call me tomorrow," he said. "Better yet, meet me at the bar where you saw me before. I'll show you proof of life."

"Proof?"

"That's right. I know who helped Lang Hunter disappear. Ours is a small society."

"Then why not just go to that person?"

"Tomorrow, Dr. Hunter. It's a simple proposition. If you need more incentive, look up Gregory Hawkins. See what happened to him."

Lehr bowed slightly and strode to his car, a maroon Mercedes G-Wagon. He *was* good at this. That was an expensive vehicle.

I sensed he'd made a veiled threat. I recalled a Hawkins associated with the Dacretown sale. He'd died in an accident. I had to find out more. I texted Natra to send Ayden ASAP. No matter what happened with Dunbury, I needed my best investigative resource here. I was sliding down a hill I didn't know I'd been on.

Chapter Twelve

L ehr had rattled me. He knew too many details about my life. Some were easily found because I had a podcast and website, but what I thought about my father's status was limited to a few close associates. And Lehr supposedly knew things about how Dad had vanished. If he really had proof of life, I had to hear it.

Once Kamryn was tucked in with her book, I called Bree. She sounded frazzled.

"Is there anything I can do to help?" I asked.

"Ann, I appreciate the offer, but the professionals will take care of everything." She paused, then added, "And just so you know, I have my own attorneys looking at undoing that will."

"Fine with me. I don't want the extra work." I didn't tell her what Peter Hillman had said. "I'll arrange to stay a couple more days, but I'm having my investigator come to assist me."

Her silence made me realize she thought it was about her or Judson, so I added, "I have cases pending. I'll put him up in a hotel. But I want to ask you something. I just had an encounter with a man named Richard Lehr. He claims he was Judson's partner."

I heard Bree draw a breath. "That was years ago, and they weren't partners. Just associates. What does he want?"

"He said you told him I was coming."

"I haven't spoken to anyone about you aside from telling Shona to prepare the guesthouse. He's probably trying to find out about Judson's condition. Maybe he thinks he's getting something. You should avoid him. I expect there will be more like him."

"Thanks for the tip." We ended the call. One of them was lying. I wasn't sure which.

I called Natra on the video line. It was always a comfort to see her face. She kept my life organized. Before I could tell her what happened, she said, "Ayden's booked for tomorrow morning. Couldn't find a Jeep, so I rented him a Tahoe. He wasn't keen about it, but he'll live with it. Figured he'd need an SUV up there. And you have an appointment with a member of the Dunbury town council and the police chief."

"Wow. That's great! When?"

"Tomorrow morning, 9:30 am. Hope you can get away."

"I've got someone to watch Kam. In fact, she'll be with a tutor. She's connecting with the history here."

"She told me. She loves the old houses, with all their gables and grand staircases. She showed me her room. Nice."

"So, tell me about the meeting."

"They're interested in your advice. I convinced them you're busy but will make the time. I gave your credentials, including your cop trainings on suicide, and offered a discounted fee, since they won't have to pay for travel. Apparently, desperate parents are harassing them to do something. I told them to bring police files, autopsy reports, anything that will help."

"Perfect. You're a wiz, my friend. And Ayden's support up here will expand my services if the need arises. Plus, he can fill in if I have to focus on Judson."

"FYI, there's some pressure in Dunbury to resolve this, because one of the deaths happened near where that development's about to start, and it's been delayed. I expect that's holding up benefits for interested parties."

"The complexities of small-town politics. Noted. Just tell me when and where."

Natra gave me the address. "There's one more thing, Annie."

"What's that?"

"Remember that skip tracer you used to track down your father?"

"Yeah."

"I called her. Wanted to know what she'd heard about this Lehr character.

She warned me to stay away from him, said he's a fraud and a pest."

"So, he's not a privacy consultant?"

"Nope. Like *he* said, it's a small community. Some know of him, and not in a good way. He probably used that credential to hook you. So, be careful."

"Well, he just approached me. He's an oddball and I can see how he'd be a pest. Talks in clipped sentences, constantly interrupting. He's rude and abrupt and seems to expect I'll just do what he wants."

"Where'd you see him?"

"He's been watching me, apparently. Knows a lot about me. Too much. He approached me in a parking lot this evening. Claims to have proof that Dad's alive, but he wants something for it. He didn't say what, but he gave the impression that Dad or Judson owes him something. He says he was Judson's business partner, but Bree dismisses it. Says it was years ago and told me to avoid him."

"Family secrets, sounds like."

"Which I hope won't entangle me. He wants an answer tomorrow. Not sure yet what I'll do, but Ayden will be here by then. Oh, and Lehr alluded to a man formerly associated with this Dacretown place who died in an accident a few years ago. Lehr said it like I should take it seriously."

"Like a threat?"

"I don't know. Can you try to get the story? I assume there will be articles, maybe an obit. Gregory Hawkins, as I recall. And while you're at it, see if you can track down this Gray Hollow Group. Apparently, they're the guardians of that Dacretown property. Maybe he was part of it."

"Will do, Annie. And lock up tonight."

"I've checked every door, every window. Nothing about this trip so far has felt right."

Chapter Thirteen

lyse's tutor arrived at 8:30 a.m. to meet Kamryn and take her to Shona's. Ordinarily, Kam would've complained about the early hour, but she was excited to see Elyse again.

I appreciated that Jeannette introduced herself before taking charge of my daughter. The brown-skinned young woman explained that she'd grown up in nearby Lexington but preferred the rich literary history of Concord. In her late twenties, she worked as a tutor while she finished her dissertation. She rented an apartment in a historic home up the street.

Kamryn ran upstairs to get the things she wanted to take over. I used the opportunity to ask Jeannette if she knew about Dacretown.

She pushed her glasses up. "Oh, that's such a strange place. I went over with friends once, but we couldn't get in. Whoever owns it threatens trespassers, and the cops take that seriously. I wish I could explore it. I'm not as bold as those kids who ignore the signs. Some of them have gotten hurt there."

"I've heard. Did you ever meet a man named Gregory Hawkins?"

She shook her head. "I've heard the Hawkins name, though. They restore historic properties. Try the guy who runs Gardiner Preservation. It's in town. I think he knows them." She gestured around us. "They worked on this property. I remember the van outside. Maybe their card is in a drawer."

Kamryn came clomping down the steps. She extended her hand with some shyness, but I could tell she was eager to see what Jeannette could teach her. I thanked Jeanette for the information and urged Kam to have a good time. "I'll be back by mid-afternoon, but I'll check in before that. And, by the way, Ayden's coming today."

Kam couldn't have been more excited. After they left, I called Shona about Judson. There'd been no change. I also texted Wayne about the tutor to reassure him that Kamryn was getting some lessons. He gave that a thumbs up.

I hoped to accomplish a lot that morning. I'd meet with the officials, perhaps find some people to interview, and look at one or two of the death scenes. I had Natra's map, a list of names with their contact info, and a good sense of my goals. Better yet, I felt no guilt over leaving Kamryn with a tutor. I liked the woman and Kam had seemed eager for an adventure.

As I drove, I considered how much to tell the Dunbury officials about the development of suicide clusters. They'd be most interested in tips for thwarting more such acts, but they should also learn the facts.

A cluster involves multiple suicides in a tight area during a limited period that exceeds the typical suicide rate—usually about three months. The victims are close in age. Sometimes, kids make a pact to act together or use the same method.

There'd been a few clusters in Massachusetts in recent times. Three high school kids on Nantucket had killed themselves in 2009. Four had done it in Needham between 2004 and 2006, and three in Wellesley in 2007. About five percent of suicides are part of a cluster, mostly involving high school and college students. They tend to occur in affluent Caucasian communities. The original or "instigating" suicide usually serves as a model. If one kid jumps in front of a train or parks a running car in a garage, the others follow the leader.

For the potential Dunbury cluster, we had three incidents within five weeks, two of them a week apart: Owen Kringle chose a train, Ralph Steiner picked a long drop, and Marti went into a frigid pond. Marti had lived here just over two years, while both boys were locals. That raised the possibility of a suicide *contagion*, the impact of a publicized suicide on vulnerable people. These incidents can happen as a widespread cultural response, like to a celebrity's suicide, or as a local cluster or even an echo cluster that occurs on the first cluster's anniversary.

Despite Dacretown's disturbing lore, it didn't qualify as a "suicide shrine." People travel specifically to kill themselves at special places like the Eiffel Tower, the London Underground, the Golden Gate Bridge, and the Empire State Building. In 1933, a heartbroken woman jumped into a volcano to achieve spiritual transformation. This act had inspired more than a hundred others to follow her example.

At a community building in Dunbury, a plump, balding Bradley Cresswell welcomed me. He tugged at his blue striped bowtie as he said, "I'm part of the public safety council. I speak on the mayor's behalf, as a liaison with the parents." He seemed flustered as he introduced me to Chief Emily Blackburn, as if he either didn't know her well or didn't get along with her. I figured the latter once I experienced her squinty eyes and painful grip as she shook my hand.

Taller than me, and bulky, Blackburn styled her hair in a slicked-back bob. When she spoke, she held her face at an angle, as if she didn't want to look directly at me. I sensed she wasn't keen about hiring a consultant.

"We're pleased to have your assistance," Cresswell said. "But no one on the council thinks there's an actual cluster. There's nothing wrong with our community. We're sure these incidents are unrelated, but as you advised, we're limiting media coverage. Don't glorify the victims. No memorial tribute pages online."

Cresswell was trying to lead me. I listened patiently. He had his reasons, largely invested in the town's image.

"I'd like to see the reports," I said. "I've done a lot of research on these types of incidents. Clusters are hard to understand, but they don't mean there's something wrong with the community or the families. If I can learn more about the connections among the three kids, I can better judge if there's a contagion effect. Victims of suicide might not even realize they—"

"It's not a copycat situation." Blackburn's tone was sharp. "We've got three completely different incidents. It's just a coincidence they happened so close together. And Owen's still alive. We expect him to revive. When he does, we'll know if the first one influenced him."

"We'd just like to expedite this," Cresswell added. In other words, they were doing this to reassure parents, but they wanted me finished ASAP.

"Well, teens are susceptible to what other kids do," I said. "If they know someone who's completed a suicide, they're three times more likely to make an attempt themselves, even if they don't seem depressed. There were earlier suicides in the area, so this could be what we call an echo cluster. Kids get to talking about past incidents, and some start thinking more seriously about problems in their own lives. If there's a suicide spot, they might think they're infected."

Blackburn snorted her dismissal of such an idea. But training in suicide analysis for law enforcement tends to be superficial. Dunbury needed someone like me, whether they knew it or not.

The tone of the meeting continued like this for ten more minutes, with both officials defending their town and minimizing my work. Blackburn finally hinted at the stakes. "We've got a business development going in over there. We don't need any more delays before winter. We've had attorneys blocking it, and now we've got you."

"I promise to be as efficient as I can," I assured her. "But you yourself should know that when death investigations are rushed, things get over-looked." I'd already told them the reports I'd need. I now gave them a list of people I'd like to speak to. Blackburn looked it over with a sour expression. "Some of these people are grieving. We've just had the Fielding girl's funeral."

"I'm aware of that, and I'm trained in speaking with grieving people. But first, I'd like to see the reports and look at the pond. If I think you have a genuine cluster here, I'll make a list of tips for the community. If not, I'll give you reasons why not, and you can use that to reassure parents."

With a frown, Blackburn picked up a handful of files and gave them to me. "You'll find the police reports and autopsy reports here. A few interviews. We've been thorough."

"I'm sure you have been." I wasn't, given what I'd just heard, but I thanked her and took my leave.

This work wasn't going to be easy. I'd expected that. No cop wants to be second-guessed, but I'd hoped for more support from Cresswell. He'd let Blackburn take the lead, as if she had more clout, and she'd made it clear she wanted me gone. With the files in my arms, I strode from the building.

Outside, I noticed a slender young man with a mop of curly dark hair sitting on a metal bench across the street. Maybe twenty or so, he stared in my direction. It felt too cold to be just sitting outside, so I thought he had some purpose. I waited, hoping he'd approach and add a piece to this puzzle. Instead, he cocked his head, stood, and strode away.

I went around the side of the building to the parking lot. As I approached the spot where I'd left the Range Rover, a man got out of his car. He made it clear his business was with me. He held out his hand. "Rob Galloway. I'm a reporter."

He couldn't have had better timing.

Chapter Fourteen

Galloway was nearly a foot taller than me, slender, and carried an air of Ivy League privilege. He wore a sky-blue shirt and a navy blazer under a black cashmere peacoat. Thin blond streaks ran through his wavy chestnut hair.

"I heard you've been hired to consult on our situation," he said. "I report for several local papers." His nasal accent placed him squarely in New England, but it wasn't distinctly Boston. Maybe New Hampshire. The s's sounded closer to sh, and 'ar' was 'ah,' so 'dark' was 'dahk.' He dropped ts, ds, and gs from the ends of many words, but not like Southerners did, yet he'd clearly been trained to minimize these quirks.

"I've seen your stories," I said. "You know how to dig."

He offered a broad smile with straight, white teeth. "I do. I enjoy weaving a gripping narrative. So, you won't be surprised that I'd like to interview you about what you just said to our esteemed officials."

"I'm not sure it qualifies as gripping. But how do you even know?"

"I have my ways. How about it? I've never met a suicide expert before." He held out his hands in the same way I often did when trying to reassure a resistant client.

From what I'd read of his work, I suspected he'd side with me. I'd need someone local to connect me with the right people and reinforce my message. He seemed connected. I held out a hand. "Give me your card. I'll consider it."

Galloway handed me a white card embossed with elegant black print. "When I heard last night they were inviting you to discuss this, I listened to your podcast, two episodes so far. Rather witty. I have a YouTube channel devoted to small-town politics. Maybe you can check it out. Whatever you need. I'm keen to hear more."

"Who told you I'd be here today?"

"Cresswell. He wants me to let the community know they're actually doing something. Tit for tat, as they say."

I narrowed my eyes. "What's your take on this town council?"

Galloway folded his arms. "One word: fractured. You just saw representatives from opposing sides. They're divided on almost everything. Some have vested interests. You'll want to watch out for them. They might be guided by, let's just say, outside influences."

"Money? As in development money?"

"Allegedly. I suspect you'll be frustrated, like you look right now. But they did hire you to do an evaluation, correct? So, you'll get some to listen, especially the ones with teenagers. But any of them will resist a threat to delay or reduce local revenues."

"I noticed. I have some time right now. Shall we get coffee?"

He smiled. "I know just the place."

We ended up nearby in a cozy coffee house with dark wood paneling. Galloway seemed familiar with the waitress, who flirted with him and gestured toward a booth. "Your spot's available."

After we ordered, Galloway leaned toward me. "So, Dr. Hunter…"

"Annie."

"Great. I'm Rob. So, Cresswell thinks you're up to speed about the history of our tragic events, or, as you say, our cluster."

"Partly thanks to you. I read your article two days ago. It's the kind of thing I research, so it grabbed me. You seem to think these incidents are related to that old ghost town."

"Dacretown, yes. According to my source, there's a definite link."

"Has anything about Marti Fielding caught your attention? Maybe something not generally known?"

His brown eyes lit up. "Who's the investigator now?"

"That's what I do. I don't just accept police or ME reports. On behalf of families, I dig deeper. Suicide's a fraught subject, with parents defending themselves and cops just wanting to move on. But suicide clusters involving kids is a community concern. It's about prevention because it's hard to predict who might decide to add their name."

"Can I quote you on that?"

"Sure, fine. Just be careful about raising the anxiety levels."

Rob gestured for the waitress to refill his mug. "I get it. Our public safety committee's been slow to act. What do you want to know about Marti?"

"What's this club she supposedly belonged to?"

He nodded. "Ah, yes. Her boyfriend's club."

"What's his name?"

"John Hawkins, but he goes by Kip. He started the club after his father died."

Now I was getting somewhere. Kip Hawkins could be related to the Gray Hollow Group member Lehr had mentioned. I put that aside for the moment. "So, Kip's in the Skeleton Crew. What's the story there?"

"Works for his cousin in Concord restoring properties. Does stone work, tiles, stuff like that. He's talented. Has a real feel for wood and stone. The club's just half a dozen kids, I believe, including his two brothers. Kip's sharp. He used to talk to me, but then he pulled away. He knows things about these deaths, I'm sure of that. Somehow, Marti got involved, but I don't know the details. Just some rumors."

"Intriguing."

"Secrets always are. I tried a backdoor to him through another kid, Owen Kringle, but *he* ran at the train. He's alive but not talking, not yet. Now the others are spooked about saying anything to me."

"They think you're to blame?"

He shrugged. "They just don't want to be outed. Kip's especially wary."

"Is he related to Gregory Hawkins, who died in a fatal accident?"

Rob raised an eyebrow.

"I looked up the Dacretown lore and came across an article about a pending sale, a conflict, and an untimely death."

"Well, okay, yes, Gregory's Kip's father, but as for an accident, Kip thinks he was murdered."

"Ah. Any evidence?"

"No. And I agree with the ME, so Kip's not happy with me."

I tilted my head. "So, the members of this Skeleton Crew decide to investigate a man's death, and now two have come to harm? What about the other teen who died? Ralph."

"Not in the club, as far as I can tell." Rob cocked his head. "Maybe you can suss it out. You're the expert. There's no real mystery about the facts. Gregory Hawkins was on his way to meet someone who supposedly had important information for him about an illegal enterprise. He'd set up the meeting at a hotel in Boston. When no one heard from him, they sent police to his room. They found him dead in the bathtub, like he'd slipped and hit his head, then drowned. There was no forced entry."

"What about the person he was meeting? No notes in the room about that?"

"None that led to a source. That person was supposed to connect with him, but there were no calls on his phone, no texts, and no notes."

I tapped my mug. "Still, the death does seem suspicious, especially if someone had reason to stop the meeting. They could've removed the notes, used burner phones, things like that."

"Well, that's what Kip says. He thinks someone didn't want that information getting out. Kip said his dad had received some threatening calls before the meeting. If those were to a burner, that's gone. Greg told Kip that if anything happened to him, it wouldn't be an accident. Still, Greg did suffer from depression."

"Are you suggesting suicide rather than accident?"

Rob shrugged. "Just stating some facts."

I took a sip of coffee. "I sense you knew him."

"I did. I thought his claims were wild, but he insisted he had proof, so I listened. He said he just needed one more confirmation from a person deeply involved, and he could blow the whole thing wide open."

"That could feel threatening. Any problems in his family?"

"A divorce, eight years ago. Gregory got custody of Kip and his brothers."

"And now Kip's girlfriend's dead from suicide. That's rough. Sounds like I should talk to Kip."

Rob moved his spoon around. "He's tough. If you approach him as part of an investigation, he'll shut down. He hates the local cops. Thinks they failed his family. He ended up back with his mother, whom he dislikes. Now he's an adult, though. He's twenty-one."

"Dating a seventeen-year-old?"

"Apparently." Rob shook his head. "Wouldn't have lasted. She was college-bound, with sponsors and big plans. He's been to college, even finished early, but has no driving ambition."

"Maybe depressed, too, like his dad?"

"I don't know if he'll be much help. But you can try. I'm sure he already knows about you. One thing this Skeleton Crew does well is their spy games."

"Okay. Whom do you suggest I talk to?"

Rob sat back and gazed at me. "If Owen regains consciousness, that's a good start."

"On my list. Who else?"

He leaned forward. "Tell you what. Give me an interview, and I'll make you a list."

"Deal. But not today. I'm on a schedule. Maybe tomorrow."

We parted with tentative plans for Rob to meet me in Concord. I needed to check him out first. And I had to do something else while I still had time.

I drove away and found a secluded place to pull over. I made some notes on things I'd ask Rob when I saw him next. I wondered if this Skeleton Crew was watching me. I texted Kamryn to make sure she was okay. She responded, *We went through Louisa May's house!* I smiled. She was having fun.

I skimmed the reports I'd received on Marti Fielding and found GPS coordinates for Gilly Pond's location. Then I headed to the place where Marti had drowned. That's when I spotted the earring and tracks mentioned earlier and realized her death looked suspicious.

When Chief Blackburn arrived, I told her, "By the way, I saw no winter coat or gloves in your inventory. Maybe someone should find out if they're at, or missing from, Marti's house. You also didn't mention locating a car, so someone brought her here. I don't think she walked."

Blackburn frowned. "Could've been on drugs. Heated her up. We don't know that yet."

Unlikely. I gave my statement to one of her deputies and drove away.

The possibility of a suicide cluster here was weakening, but mystery remained. I was glad I'd decided to get Ayden here. I'd send him looking for Kip. That guy, I believed, had info I needed. Maybe he was also in danger. I'd get Natra to find a photo of him, so I'd know him when I saw him.

Before I arrived back in Concord, Rob Galloway texted me: *Good catch. Watch your back. You just made some enemies.*

Chapter Fifteen

On my way from the garage to pick up Kamryn, I noticed Bree at a window. She beckoned for me to come into the Big House. I dreaded to hear whatever news she might have or, worse, to endure another blast of her anger. Had I come to Concord alone and not gotten involved with a case, I'd have left by now.

I noted Bree's gray business suit and tailored pink blouse. She seemed out of breath. Her dark blue eyes lit up. "I have good news! My father's better today. He's recovering. He's been sitting up, and he even ate some soup. He's still coughing, but he's been talking."

Not the news I'd expected.

"You can probably go home," Bree continued. "I'm sorry to have gotten you here. I'll pay for your flight, for both of you. I'm about to let others know not to come."

"Wait, Aunt Bree." I wasn't sure how to break it to her that Judson's supposed recovery might just be the "surge." It's a brief period of vitality that some people experience just before death. It seems as if they've revived. It can last just moments or endure for a few hours. It gives false hope. Then I realized something. This pocket of clarity offered an opportunity to connect. Judson could say why he'd named me executor. I drew myself up. "I've seen this before. Don't call anyone. It might not be what it looks like."

Bree's expression darkened. "You don't know what you're talking about." She turned away.

I stepped around her to stop her. "I do know, and you're aware that this is my work because we've talked about this before. Now is our chance to find out what Judson wants. He can explain why he changed his will. Or he can say it's a mistake. He likely won't last more than a day or two. We have to ask him. Together. In front of a witness."

Bree hesitated. Her fight to regain control could be won or lost in the next few moments. She'd want to know his reason and even get a chance to change his mind, but she wouldn't want *me* to know, nor have any witness.

Then Judson yelled. He sounded angry. We sprinted up the steps, Bree ahead of me in her precarious heels. I wanted to find Shona, but there wasn't time. I followed Bree through the door and saw a young brunette nurse in a blue uniform trying to get Judson back into bed. He yelled at her, "Leave me be! Who are you? Why are you in my house?"

"Mr. Hunter, please—" She reached for him.

"Don't handle me!"

Then Judson saw me and stood up straight. "Ann. You're here." His eyes were red, and he coughed so harshly I thought he'd fall over. I saw spatters of blood on his beige pajama shirt. But he did recognize me, and he seemed to accept my presence. He pulled his green robe around his frail body and leaned back against the bed. He stared at me. "Have you seen him?"

I wasn't sure if he was talking to me or to someone he saw inside his own head. I moved toward him and touched his arm. His breath smelled sour, like a man with one foot in the grave. His sallow skin sagged. "Seen whom, Judson?"

"He was here, out there…" Judson gestured toward a window. "He shouldn't be here!"

Bree gestured for the nurse to help her. "Please, Father, get back in bed. You might fall and hurt yourself."

He glared at her. "What are you doing here?"

"You're ill. You need care."

He waved her away. To me, Judson said, "Find him. Tell him."

"I will," I said. The best course during terminal lucidity is just to listen. "What shall I tell him?"

"Ann, stop!" Bree insisted. "Please leave the room."

Judson pushed away from the bed and strode to the window that overlooked his backyard. His energy surprised me. He seemed to have shed years from his age. He unlocked and pulled the window up until he got it open about a foot, letting in a rush of cold air.

Bree looked at the nurse. "We need to get him back in bed. He doesn't know what he's doing." She stepped toward Judson and tried to move him away from the window. Judson pushed Bree so aggressively she fell back against a chair.

"Mr. Hunter, sir," the nurse implored him. "You need to—"

Judson returned to the window and forced it further open. He leaned out and yelled, "Don't stay! He's here! Get away! He'll see you!"

Bree rose and urged the nurse to grab his left arm. They got him into the chair. Bree closed the window and locked it. She pulled the curtains over it, as if to prevent her father from even looking outside. Judson stared at me, his mouth hanging open. Drool seeped out and stained his robe. He was fading. He'd exerted his last bit of gumption in an apparent attempt to warn someone.

I stepped over to stand in front of him. "Judson, I need to know why you made me your executor. Do you finally believe me about my father? Is that why?"

Bree stood still, her eyes wide, as if shocked at my bluntness. She gestured for the nurse to leave. I couldn't fight her on this, but I could do my best to get an answer from my grandfather.

Judson looked confused. He blinked and shook his head. I wondered now whether he'd been in his right mind as Hillman had assured me. The old man stared at me. His lips moved. He ran a hand through his thinning gray hair.

I felt Bree tug on my arm. "Let him rest."

"No!" I shrugged her off. He'd heard me. I wanted an answer.

"It's all in the—" He coughed hard. Bree put her hand on his shoulder. He kept coughing. I helped Bree get Judson to his feet. He shuffled with short steps toward the bed. Bree removed his robe, and he lay down. His eyes looked vacant now. He seemed shrunken, resigned to the end, as if he'd been climbing a mountain and finally realized he wouldn't reach the top. Bree flashed me a look to leave him alone. I shook my head. He had something to tell me. I had to know. We both had to know.

Bree pulled the quilt over Judson. I thought he looked as if he'd passed out. I leaned close and said, "Judson, tell me. Now."

His eyelid twitched. His hand formed into a fist. He looked at Bree. One finger came out, as if he were pointing at something or someone that only he could see. In a voice I could barely hear, he said, "Hawkins. Tell him no more. It stops with us."

Chapter Sixteen

I fetched Kamryn from Shona's house. To my dismay, it was snowing. Kam jumped up and down in the flurries and skipped all the way back to the guesthouse. I felt much less enthused, and not just from the snow.

Judson had said nothing more before he'd closed his eyes and begun to snore in raspy breaths. Bree had insisted that I leave, nearly pushing me out the door, but I'd warned her that she was misreading his behavior. "Don't tell anyone he's recovered. Just keep doing what you were doing. He won't get up like that again."

I'd seen the nurse in the hall and told her to go in. I had things to say to Bree, but not when strangers could overhear us. Hawkins, he'd said. Was that the same man I'd been hearing about? And what did Judson mean by "stops with us"? Whom did Judson think he was yelling at outside? I'd looked around before I went to Shona's, but I'd seen no one in the yard. I'd entered Judson's room with one burning question and come out with a dozen more. Bree had essentially shut me down. I'd finally left.

I vowed that the next time I got Bree alone, I'd confront her. She hadn't seemed at all surprised at Judson's outburst. One thing I'm good at: spotting behavior that *should* be present but isn't. I was sure Bree knew what he'd been talking about.

Judson hadn't answered my question about the will, but I guessed from what he did say that his attorney had some document that would make it all clear. *It's all in the...* Judson's choice for executor wasn't a mistake. When I'd asked about it, he hadn't looked at me as if I'd lost my mind. There was a reason for it. Apparently, he hadn't told Bree what it was. She wasn't pretending about that. Whatever was going on, Judson seemed to think it was urgent that we do something. If we didn't, dire things would happen.

In the house, Kamryn bubbled over with enthusiasm for what she'd learned that morning. I felt less guilty for leaving her here. Over an afternoon snack of fresh apple crisp I'd bought for her on my way back, Kam gave me the Cliff Notes version of the Battle of Lexington and Concord. Her brown eyes shown bright as she told me about how they'd watched an interactive exhibit from the Concord Museum of Paul Revere's ride, and now she wanted to see all those places in person. This was a good thing, an unexpected justification for bringing her here. I suppressed my agitation over Judson's behavior to focus on my daughter.

"Maybe we can see Paul Revere's house when we head back to Boston," I told her. "You'll be surprised at how many people lived in it."

"You've seen it?"

"Sure. I went to Boston a lot."

Kamryn took a bite of her snack. "I'm so glad I met Elyse. She's great. She knows so much and can play piano, and she knows sign language. She showed me some." Kam demonstrated several gestures.

"So, you're enjoying it."

She nodded. "It's fun. Better than school. Jeannette can play guitar and wants to show me how. She's teaching Elyse. You know why she has a tutor?"

"No."

"She got kicked out of school for two weeks."

I blinked. "For what?"

"They said she picked a lock and stole a book from a display."

I didn't like the sound of that. "Did she?"

"She wanted to read it. They said she couldn't touch it."

I sat down. My stomach fluttered. I had to handle this carefully. "And what do you think, Kam? Should she have done that?"

She shrugged. "Why shouldn't they just let her read it?"

"Well, it was probably a rare book and had to be protected. That's why books are under glass. Touching them can ruin the pages, and then no one else can read them."

Kamryn's eyes widened. "Really?"

"And if it's locked, there's probably a reason. They're trusting people to respect that."

Kam chewed a little before she said, "Like the staircase?"

"Like the staircase. This house doesn't belong to us, and we respect that."

"Okay. But Elyse gave me the key." Kamryn dug into her pocket, removed a dark metal skeleton-type key, and placed it on the table. "Should I give it back?"

I stared at it. "Elyse found this?"

"I told her about the staircase, and she said she knew where the keys were to all the houses. Her mom keeps them because she usually opens them for people and manages the cleaning crews. Elyse got it for me. She said she's been in there, and there's a little room."

I slid the key toward me. "I'll take it back."

"Okay. When will Ayden be here? I hope it keeps snowing so he can see it."

"It's just some flurries. And he'll be here in an hour or so. He's landed, but he has to pick up a car. He'll call from the inn."

"Why doesn't he just stay here?" she asked. "There's lots of room."

"Because we're guests here. Plus, he'll have a suite there. It'll be more private."

Kamryn shrugged as if I made no sense. "Can I go back to Elyse's tomorrow? We're gonna draw some things."

"We'll see. I need to talk to my Aunt Bree and to Shona first."

"We heard Great-Grampa yelling out the window today. Is he better?"

This startled me. "No, he's not. He's having trouble remembering where he is."

"Elyse said he's done that before. Her mom told her not to say anything, just ignore it."

I suddenly realized that Elyse could be a source of information. That kid was attentive if a bit slick-fingered. She seemed to like to do things she knew she shouldn't. What else had she gotten into?

Kamryn finished her snack and asked to go to her room. "I wanna read some stuff that we learned about today."

"Of course." Nothing could have pleased me more.

She took her dishes to the sink and went up the steps. I looked at the staircase key. I knew I should return it to Shona right away, but I was curious about why the staircase was locked. It's not like anyone would use it. As I recalled, the shaft was tight. It was more a novelty than a useful means to get upstairs, especially for an adult. I'd been in it, going up and down from the second floor to get books, but I'd been small.

I felt the key's shaft. Kamryn was upstairs. She wouldn't even know if I just peeked in for a second to see if the staircase was how I remembered it.

I went into the library and listened. I heard Kam close her bathroom door. With quiet steps, I moved toward the door for the staircase.

Maybe there was nothing inside. Maybe Bree had locked it to keep guests from using it.

Yet I burned to see it. I'd been inside before. It was all right to have a quick peek. I stepped over and slid the small metal key from my pocket. I was crossing a line. I didn't like myself right now. But that wasn't enough to make me stop. I had to see.

Chapter Seventeen

I stepped over to examine the nearly invisible crack along the raised wood paneling that revealed the opening. I noticed a fresh layer of white paint. The keyhole, I knew, was hidden behind a cover that blended with the paint. I'd found it myself when I was eight. My father had looked up the architectural plans. Next to the stairs, about halfway up, was a cubbyhole with a bare light bulb, a built-in set of shelves, and a hinged wooden seat over a hidden compartment. He'd found some old papers in it from a prior owner.

After we'd cleaned it out, Dad realized that I'd sometimes sneak back in, especially when he and Mom were fighting. He started to leave things in the cubbyhole for me to discover. Sometimes, they were notes from him, sometimes children's books, and even photos he'd taken of the area. It was our game. I'd left him notes as well and even a map to my favorite part of the cemetery. The cubbyhole was my special place. I'd look forward to seeing what he left me.

I slid the keyhole cover open. My heart raced, and my brain supplied conflicting assaults from my devils and angels. *Don't do this. There's no harm in just looking.*

I put the key in and applied pressure as I moved it to the right. The lock resisted. I went the other way, but it still didn't budge. I worked the key back and forth until I heard the telltale click. That was it. The lock had opened. I breathed out, removed the key, and put it back in my pocket. Around the keyhole was a thin metal ring, now tarnished, that helped to move the door outward, toward me. I pulled the ring out and tugged. The door didn't budge.

I stopped, afraid I might break the ring. I wondered how long this door had been locked. I knew the staircase was easier to enter at the top, on the second floor, because I could use my weight to push the door inward. But then Kamryn would hear me. I tugged again. Then pushed and pulled. Still stuck.

The impasse afforded a chance to reconsider. I could walk away and tell Kam to give the key back to Elyse, so no one got in trouble. But I'd already opened the lock. I took a deep breath. Out the window, I saw white flakes still falling.

Maybe I can just ask Bree for the key, I thought. *Do this the right way.* But then she'd ask Shona for it, and they'd discover it missing. That could put Shona in danger of losing her job and get Elyse in trouble.

Just do it. Then you can discreetly return the key.

I tugged the metal loop again. The door yielded a little. I saw enough of its edge to think I could pull it open with my fingertips.

I tried this move. No go.

I stepped back. It felt as if I needed a code word to break the magic seal. How had I managed this before? I used to go freely in and out. It's not as if it were summer, with swollen wood.

I had a thought. Maybe it was locked from the inside. Yes, that was it. I remembered now. You could lock it on both ends from inside. But someone would have to be inside to do it.

I needed a knife with a thin blade.

I went into the kitchen to look for one and listened again for movement from Kamryn. Then I noticed a text from Natra on my phone. I hadn't even heard the alert. *Call when you can.*

I returned to the library to shove the door back in place. I'd unlocked it. Good enough for now. No one would know. I could try again when Kam was asleep. I placed the key back on the table where Kam had shown it to me, then called Natra.

Chapter Eighteen

"Can you get on a video chat?" she asked. "JoLynn's here. I've sent you a packet of files and photos to look at. Is Ayden there yet?"

"He'll be here shortly. Boston traffic is challenging. He'll call once he's settled at the inn. Give me a few minutes to look at the files, and I'll call you back."

On my laptop, I downloaded the folder Natra had sent. There were several brief news reports, some police and autopsy reports, and JoLynn's analysis of each incident. These were the three weather deaths she'd been investigating. I scanned the details, aware that each death had been determined an accident. One was later proven to have been a murder. The autopsy reports commanded more attention. There were two, and both were cursory, as if the pathologists were just going through the motions.

I turned on the video. In moments, I saw Natra and JoLynn together at a table. JoLynn waved. This lissome woman, with her thick hair, pretty eyes, and pouty lips, should have been a model. Instead, she'd chosen a career that kept her close to the dead.

"There's not much here," I commented. "Like you said, accidental deaths don't generate much attention."

"Did you read my report?" JoLynn asked.

"Skimmed it. You think there are links."

"I do. Each looks like an accidental death during a weather event, but on closer inspection, the accident scenario fails to match the mechanism of death. Just small things, but no one caught the inconsistencies." She leaned forward. "And there's more. We have different weather events in different locations, but it looks like two of the victims were lured out. Despite the weather, they went. They didn't just get caught in the rain, so to speak. I'm still working on the third one. No one yet suspects anything about it, and I don't want to ask the family for his phone."

I thought she had barely enough evidence to be this confident. "What do you mean, 'lured'?"

"Two were informed through a text that someone they cared about needed urgent assistance. The messages were nearly identical."

I nodded. "Interesting. So, you're saying we've got a killer who watches for nasty weather patterns, travels to the area, hijacks someone's phone number to send a message as bait, and then kills them. That's a new one. Lots of planning. Thrill? Mission?"

"That's what we're stuck on," Natra offered. "You're the shrink. But the similar content in the texts is striking. Each seems to be from an acquaintance, which we've determined were actual people. Each says their car is broken down, and they need a ride. Each says they're two miles away."

"Both say two miles?" I asked.

"Yes. That's part of what flags them. That's an unlikely coincidence."

"A phone hack, then?"

"Unclear, but it could be a spoof. We have just the two, as JoLynn mentioned, but Joe Lochren's looking at our options."

"If you'll recall," JoLynn added, "I worked that case in Chattanooga."

"I do." I'd been there, myself, visiting a prison that got damaged in a tornado. "How can I forget?"

JoLynn smiled. "I was invited, because they thought they had something suspicious, so they'd exhumed him. We managed to find evidence of murder in that case, and detectives followed up. But so far, it's unsolved. I got the information about the text in the reports they gave me. Their digital experts couldn't link it to the friend-in-need who'd supposedly texted the victim, and he denied doing it. I used that information to get the next incident further investigated—the one in the flood—and they found a similar text. We haven't taken it further yet, but that's a signature, right?"

I leaned in. "Seems to be, along with fatal assaults associated with extreme weather." I glanced out the window. "And if weather's a factor, we should form a timeline about how often these incidents occurred—"

"Done." Natra pointed toward a whiteboard behind her where I could see scribbles in blue and black marker. "Along with a projection of weather systems over the upcoming week. There are three of concern." She looked at me.

I tapped a pen. "From your expression, I must be in the path of one."

"Maybe," JoLynn said. "Too soon to say but be prepared. Weather-related deaths are rare, unless there's a catastrophe like a Cat 5 hurricane. Stay alert for information in local news about victims. We'll do the same. There's a storm system just passing through Chicago, so we'll be watching."

"How far apart are these murders?" I asked.

"A year between number one and number two," Natra said. "Then six months."

"And when was the third one?"

"In Chattanooga, so several months ago."

"These are just the cases we've identified," JoLynn added. "There could be others. We don't know when this started."

Natra looked at me. "How long will you be there?"

"I don't know, but Judson's fading fast. And I've got a possible murder here, myself. One of my suicide cases has suspicious features. We'll see what Ayden can find. What's the pattern of the three known cases?"

JoLynn shook her head. "No pattern that we can see, except for a weather event being a way to cover it up. Maybe if we identify another one, there'll be more information."

I sighed. "Unfortunately, that's how most profiling works. We hope for an aberrant behavior or a slip-up, always after the fact. Rarely do we get a case where we can anticipate well enough to lay a trap. Okay, look, let me study these documents and think about it. Maybe I'll get an idea."

"We gave Ayden the information, too," JoLynn added.

"Then he'll have ideas. Good work, you two. And let me know what you hear about the weather. I'd like to get out before it gets bad. At the very least, we can drive south a few hours, if necessary."

Natra gave a half salute. "Copy that."

We signed off. I looked at the time. Ayden would be arriving shortly. The staircase would have to wait.

Chapter Nineteen

I felt immense relief when I saw Ayden in the inn's sitting room. He's easy to spot. Tall, blond, and sporting a tan from his outdoor work that most New Englanders never achieve. Also, a wide, boyish grin. I was eager to commence our team investigations. Before I could wave, Kamryn flew over to hug him. Ayden's been a mentor to her for sea turtle care, rose growing, and weather analysis.

"This is so exciting!" she exclaimed. "There's snow, and we saw graves, and Louisa May's house, and ate real clam chowder, and we're getting a storm!"

Ayden laughed. "I can't wait to hear all about it." He looked at me. "What a great area. So many trees! It's dense."

"You can tour later, but first we'll check out where I need the investigation. Remember, you're not a licensed PI here, so please color inside the lines."

"Hope we won't need supplies. I'm lost without my truck."

"You'll be fine. It's mostly figuring out how to find people and getting them to talk. Your usual talents. No campouts, no exhumations. And don't tell me you haven't driven a Tahoe before because I know that's what JoLynn drives."

"No problem, boss. Great room, by the way. The Hawthorne Suite. I'll have to bone up on my American lit."

I knew a deflection when I saw one, but Kamryn was with us, and this wasn't the time to probe. Kamryn chimed in. "I'm reading about him! And you can see his grave. It's right up on the hill with Louisa May." She pointed to her right.

"Did you let Natra know you're here?" I asked.

"Yes, and she said to tell you about a tropical storm in Florida they're monitoring. It's gotten active."

"Hurricane potential?"

"Unclear at the moment, but flooding's likely."

"Okay, we'll check with them tonight. First, let's eat."

We went to dinner nearby. Throughout the meal, I let Kamryn tell Ayden about what she'd learned about Concord. He enjoys being an uncle to her. He appreciates her ability to think along multiple channels, although her quick switches of topic can be hard to follow. Still, I was impressed. She'd clearly absorbed a lot about the area. She also told Ayden about Elyse Teagan, her new friend. "She has a tutor, and we learned a lot from her today about the Minute Men." Kam turned to me. "Am I going back tomorrow?"

I hadn't forgotten to contact Shona. I just dreaded it because I was concerned about her daughter's thefts. I couldn't exactly raise the issue with Shona, since I was sure she wouldn't be pleased that Elyse had told Kamryn the reason for her tutor. But I also knew that leaving Kam with her would free me to take Ayden to Gilly Pond. That piece of business was pressing. "I'll find out tonight," I promised. "I'm sure it'll be fine."

"Can Elyse stay over with us sometime?"

I was unprepared for this question. In fact, Kamryn had never had a sleepover at my house, although she might have at her father's. "I'll have to think about that. We've got a lot of things to worry about right now, so let's put that on hold."

"But she can come over, right?"

"That's okay, as long as I'm there."

Ayden winked at me. He knows Kam can be persistent.

After dinner, I drove Ayden around town so he could see where the inn stood in relation to us and to other resources. Kam wanted to show him where some of the authors had lived, so we drove by each house. It was dark and snow now covered the ground, so I said no to her request to drive into the cemetery. "It's closed after dusk."

When we pulled into Judson's garage, Shona came out. I introduced Ayden to her before I told Kamryn to take him to the guesthouse. I sensed that Shona wanted to tell me something.

When we were alone, she touched my arm. "Dr. Hunter, your grandfather's been taken to the hospital."

I nodded. "I figured it wouldn't be long. Is he in hospice there?"

"I'm not sure. Ms. Duncan is there too. She wanted me to tell you. Your daughter can stay with Elyse tomorrow, so you can do whatever you need to do."

"I appreciate that. She enjoyed the lessons today."

"Elyse likes having someone else there. It helps her to focus."

"I should help pay for the tutor."

Shona held up a hand. "No need. Judson pays for her. You're family. And if anything happens during the night, you can bring Kamryn over. It's no bother. The girls get along."

I found Ayden and Kamryn in the library, looking at books by local authors. I glanced at the hidden door, but it remained securely closed. Unless you knew it was there, you wouldn't notice. I gave Ayden a tour of the house before I asked Kamryn to let us have some time to work. "Shona said you can go back tomorrow, so maybe you want to do some prep."

"Can I use the Internet here?" she asked. "I can look stuff up."

"Of course."

To Ayden, she said, "Don't leave without saying goodbye."

I set Kamryn up for online research in her room. "Please call your father and tell him what you did today."

"I will." She put in her earbuds and gave me a look that said she was respecting our privacy and wanted the same in return. I went down and entered the library with two glasses and a bottle of wine, *Secrets* red blend. The label's keyhole image reflected all the unanswered questions these cases had raised. I poured us both a glass.

Chapter Twenty

Ayden looked at the label. He knows I choose wine to fit our investigations. "Sounds intriguing." He sat in an overstuffed chair before he said, "Natra filled me in. You need records work and some clandestine excursions."

"Yes, but there's more. This has been a long day, and it's not over." I told him about my encounter with Richard Lehr. "I have a deadline. It's this evening. I know a few things, but I haven't been able to learn much about this man. I don't like how he approached me. I don't like how much he knows about me, either, or his veiled threats."

"Gotcha. You need gumshoe and gossip. Sounds like he's used to making people comply." Ayden checked his watch. "When does he expect to hear from you?"

"In about an hour."

"That's not much time, boss."

"I'll need you to stay here with Kamryn. He knows where we are, and I don't want to take her with me. I'm eager to hear his supposed proof that my father's alive, but I'm not striking any deal without knowing more." I told Ayden what Bree had said. "She's lying, I'm sure, but I don't know why. Let's try to stay a step or two ahead of him."

Ayden sat forward. He'd helped me to search for my father. He'd developed quite the network of skip tracers and invisibility experts. I knew what he'd say before he said it. "No way should you go alone."

I held up a hand. "He doesn't want to harm me. In the meantime, I also have a connection for you and a case. First, the case. I discovered that a girl's supposed suicide might've been foul play." On a table, I spread out the documents. "Natra's organized this, so let's decide what to do next. I met Rob Galloway, the reporter who wrote about the incidents and did his own investigation. He knows more than he's put into the articles. A conversation with him might be a good place to start. I'll introduce you when he comes here tomorrow. Maybe he'll give you some leads. I need to know more about the suicide cluster and the area that seems to inspire these acts. I can't do as much as I'd like while I'm looking after Kamryn, especially if Judson dies."

"Think he will?"

"It's likely. He's got hours, not days. I'm glad we rented you a vehicle. I think this Lehr character knows Judson's cars, so you'll have a stealth advantage, at least for now. Plus, you're at the inn. I think he's watching this house."

"I have an idea," Ayden said. "Tell this jerk you're sending your representative to see this so-called proof of life. Until you know it's genuine, you'll make no deal. That'll buy some time and let me size him up. He might not be so aggressive with me."

I considered this. "Not a bad idea. But you might not know how to evaluate what he has."

Ayden held up his phone. "I have a camera. Maybe he'll say no, he won't talk to me, but he'll set another deadline. I mean, it makes no sense that he has to do this before your grandfather dies, because it's not like Judson can talk about it, right?"

"Lehr might not realize that."

"Well, if he knows about Natra, he knows about me, so he won't be surprised you sent me."

I nodded. "That could work. And he seems desperate, so if I hold out the possibility of a deal, maybe he'll play." I patted Ayden's arm. "Glad you came. I feel safer. Let's check with Natra."

The library had a computer hooked up to a large screen on the wall, apparently to accommodate guests who were visiting Judson for business. That worked for me. With our meeting link, she could show us photos and documents.

When Natra came on, she had the look on her face that signaled a warning. I glanced at Ayden. "She's found something."

"Yes, I have," she said. "Be careful of Richard Lehr. He's connected to that business that hoped to develop the Dacretown property."

"Connected in what way?" I asked.

"I think he's a goon, the guy who makes sure deals go through. Won't take no for an answer. He might help people disappear but not as a privacy consultant, not according to our contacts."

I considered this. "So, he's posing."

"Worse, Annie. This guy could actually be dangerous."

Chapter Twenty-One

With less than twenty minutes until the deadline, the three of us discussed a plan. Natra agreed that Ayden's presence might make Lehr retreat, if only for another day. It would also alert him I wasn't alone. I risked Lehr shutting down, but I just didn't have a lock on this guy. Natra showed Ayden Lehr's photo, so he'd know who he was looking for.

"But Ayden's not armed," I said. "Neither am I. Maybe I should just call Lehr and tell him—"

Three sharp raps at the front door startled us. I looked at Ayden. "Shona and Bree wouldn't knock like that. It's not one of them."

"Seems late for someone to come to your door. Think Lehr's watching the house?"

I nodded. "I do. He probably suspects I might not meet him."

Ayden got up. "I'll answer it. You stay out of sight."

"I'll be right behind you." To Natra, I said, "Text Kamryn. She's got her earbuds in, so she might not realize what's happening down here, but just in case, tell her to close her door. Keep her on the phone so she doesn't wander downstairs. We'll call you back."

My adrenaline soared. I could hardly breathe. Why would Lehr come *here*? I stepped to the side, out of sight, as Ayden opened the door. Cold air rushed in, with some flurries.

"Can I help you?" Ayden asked.

"Looking for Dr. Hunter." It was Lehr. He sounded annoyed.

"She's occupied. You can speak to—"

"I know who you are, and you know who I am. I'll speak only to Dr. Hunter."

Ayden didn't back down. He's normally a puppy-dog type of guy, but in protective mode, he's a Rottweiler. "She won't be pressured. If you have something to show her, you can give it to me. She's not going to meet you on her own."

Silence made me wonder what Lehr would do next. I hoped he wouldn't pull out a gun and force the issue. I shivered. Then Lehr spoke in a raised voice. "Dr. Hunter, it's in your best interest to see what I have. I'll show it only to you. You have my number. Time is running out. The next move is yours. When Judson's gone, you'll need me. Don't trust anyone around him. *Anyone.*"

I heard his retreating footsteps and moved closer to Ayden so I could see him. I wanted to stand up to him, but I knew I should let him believe Ayden was my shield. Still, I'd just delayed what might have been a crucial link to my father. It felt as if I were watching Dad's retreating figure. My heart sped up.

Ayden closed the door and locked it. He gave me a big brother look, though he's two years younger. "Annie, this guy's bad news. I don't care what he has, you shouldn't meet with him alone. And I should stay here. If he sees me leave, he might come back, and you've got Kam here."

"What's going on?"

I turned to see Kamryn at the top of the stairs, her pink phone in her hand.

"Nothing," I told her. "We're just discussing whether Ayden should stay here instead of the inn."

"Here!" Kam came the rest of the way down. "This house is huge! There's lots of room. It's a cool place with an attic and a library and a secret staircase. Maybe there's a ghost!" She handed me her phone. "Natra."

I took it and went into the library.

"I heard that," she said, "and I agree. If you've got space, he should stay there."

"I haven't asked Bree."

"Think she'd even check? You told her Lehr approached you. See what she says when you tell her he came to the door. I doubt she'll argue with having Ayden there."

I thought about this. "What *would* she say? She knows something about Lehr and pretends not to. If I tell her he's become menacing, maybe she'll 'fess up. But right now, she's at the hospital with her dying father. Can't really confront her yet."

"So, make the decision. Kamryn's safety is reason enough to have Ayden there. But don't check him out of the inn. It's a suite, right? You can use it for meetings, like the one with Galloway tomorrow. It'll be more secure than the house or a restaurant."

"Good idea."

"And by the way, Annie, there's one more thing to know about Richard Lehr. I've been digging through some news articles about Gregory Hawkins to prepare you for Galloway. I found an article that quotes Lehr. He did know the guy. Did some business with 'im and that guy's now dead. Be careful."

I ended the call and went to the kitchen where Kamryn and Ayden were finishing the apple crisp. Ayden slid a plate over to me. "Saved you some."

"Let's go get your stuff," I said. "You're moving in."

Chapter Twenty-Two

We rode together to fetch Ayden's items and the Tahoe. I passed the Big House to show Ayden where Judson lived. He whistled. "Impressive."

"It's dark inside," Kamryn said. "Kind of creepy. You have to be quiet in there."

"It's a big place for one person," I added. "He has a house manager, a cook, and a maid or two, but still…"

"Bree doesn't live there?"

"No, but she's probably staying there to care for him. His second wife, Bree's mother, left him years ago. Bree has a daughter, but I've seen no sign of her, so they might be estranged. And Bree's husband also deserted her. I guess you could say my father did too."

"One big happy family."

It had stopped snowing, which disappointed Kamryn but gave me comfort. No one followed us that we could see. Ayden drove back in the Tahoe and parked it in the driveway. I told him to take the ensuite on the first floor while I put Kamryn to bed. Then I called Bree to tell her what I was doing. I didn't say why, although I wanted to. Now was not the time.

"It's fine, Ann," she said, "The house is yours to use as you like." She sounded exhausted.

"How's Judson?"

"You were right. He hasn't recovered. Now I'm just waiting. They told me not to hope." I heard her choke. "I can't believe he…"

"Do you want me to come?"

"There's no need. He's pretty much gone now. We have a private room, and I can sleep here. He gave a sizable donation to this place, so they're treating him well."

"I'm here if you need me. I know where the hospital is. And just so you know, I've been asked to consult on a case in the area. Not in Concord, in another town."

"Oh?"

"I've met with some officials. I'd like to use the Range Rover again."

"That's fine. No one's driven it in months. And, Ann, I know you want to ask me about what my father said, but I really didn't understand it. I've no idea what he was talking about or why he yelled out the window."

"Does he know someone named Hawkins?"

Silence told me the answer was yes. "He had some business with the man years ago. It's not the first time he's thought Hawkins was in his room. He said something like that before you came. But the man's dead. He's been gone for years. That's what scared me."

Relief washed through me. Whatever was going on in Judson's subconscious during his life transition, it wasn't about Dad. I tried to offer something reassuring. "Maybe he feels like they have unfinished business, so it's popping up for him now. That can happen."

Another pause. "They did. They had a falling out, but it was a long time ago. He's never talked with me about it."

This was the first time since I'd arrived that Bree seemed more like the person I knew. I sensed she was feeling vulnerable. The burden of this situation fell to her. If she believed, like Judson did, that my father was dead, then she probably felt alone. I wondered if Dad, wherever he was, even knew his father was dying. He should be here. He had the right.

Bree interrupted my thoughts. "There's one more thing. I was thinking about Richard Lehr and what he might want. Years ago, he worked on a project. He had a set of notes, calculations. Maybe that's what he thinks he's owed. If you have an investigator here, maybe he can look into that. If you find it, bring it to me. I can use it to make Lehr leave you alone."

"I'll do that."

"I need to go back in. I'll stay here tonight."

"Let me know if you need something."

I now had more work for Ayden. First, I hadn't mentioned that Lehr thought he was owed something, so Bree knew things she wasn't revealing. Also, she wanted leverage with him. Third, there was unfinished business involving a dead man named Hawkins. Could be Gregory, the accident victim Lehr had mentioned. But then again, according to Jeannette, there was a Hawkins family in the area. I had to learn more.

Chapter Twenty-Three

I found Ayden in the library, staring at his laptop and talking on his phone. He looked at me, then told the person at the other end, "Gotta go." He put down the phone and said, "This house is amazing. It's old, isn't it? The woodwork is so fine. Love all the built-ins." Ayden does renovations when he's not working for me. He notices details.

"This area dates to the 1600s," I told him. "This house is at least two hundred years old. Judson bought up properties decades ago during a recession. Some, like this one, he kept and fixed up for guests or rentals, and others he sold."

Ayden raised an eyebrow. "You comin' in for some money?"

"Doubtful. I'm not even sure why I'm here. He wasn't fond of me. Hasn't even spoken to me in five years. I brought Kamryn up once when she was young. He barely acknowledged her as his great-granddaughter."

Ayden gestured around us. "He let you stay here."

"My aunt did. I'm not sure Judson would've made the same gesture."

"Cheap?"

I shrugged. "Not necessarily, but there were always conditions on whatever he gave, including his love. My dad wouldn't talk much about him, but they didn't have a bond. Still, Judson apparently named me as his executor. I don't know why."

Ayden's eyes grew large. "A family mystery."

"Let's stick to our cases. We need a plan for tomorrow."

Ayden tapped his laptop. "Have you talked to Natra about these weather deaths?"

"Yes, I'm keeping up, but it's too soon to know what we have. Was that JoLynn on the phone?"

Ayden nodded but wouldn't look at me.

I sat down. "Something wrong?"

He glanced up. "No."

"Ayden."

"Annie, I know you don't like me dating her—"

"I never said that. You assured me it wouldn't interfere, and it hasn't. In fact, you two seem to have a lot in common."

He went quiet for a moment before he said, "I'm not at her level, with all her education. There's probably nothing to hope for."

I leaned forward. "Did she say something?"

"No."

I placed my hands on my lap in my best mother pose. Sometimes, that's what Ayden needs most. "She's eager to work with our team. That means she likes working with you, and it was obvious to me during that Tennessee tornado that you two clicked. She's a professional, and she needs her space. Give it some time, and don't overthink it."

He smiled. We both knew that was advice I should heed, myself.

Ayden took a breath. "Okay. I'm ready to work."

That was all I needed to hear. "Is there something more on the weather deaths?"

"No, but it just seems odd. How can one person be traveling to different weather events like this? Has to be a team."

"Maybe. We don't yet know they're linked."

He squinted. "Do you know about the texts?"

"Yes. I'd have to see the full phrasing of both before I'd say they're linked. I agree it seems likely, but I'm not ruling anything in or out. Still, I need your mind on my case *here*. We're under a time crunch."

"On it, boss. We're meeting Galloway tomorrow. I asked Natra to look him up, and she already had a file on him. I scanned it while you were on the phone. You need to know this."

I didn't want more complications. "He's a local reporter. That makes him a source. I'm just asking him for information. I find it strange that he seems bright and educated but has such a low-level gig, like an aspiring reporter's first gig. Still, he's a side note for us."

Ayden turned his screen for me to see. "Doin' my job, boss. Know who you're talking to. We screwed up on that before."

I nodded. We'd made assumptions about sources in two recent cases and that had cost us.

Ayden continued. "He used to be at larger papers, even a stint at the *Globe*. An up-and-comer. Then, things went south. He worked on an expose about corporate leaders being involved in clandestine experiments with gifted kids that exposed the kids to dangerous chemical substances. He alleged that there was a file with information about influential people who supported the program—names, dates, addresses. But he never actually saw the contents. He had only hearsay that it existed. He claimed that cops destroyed it. He wrote about it, anyway, which got him into hot water."

"He never had proof?"

"Just sources he wouldn't name."

"And it implicated powerful people?"

"He said they were in powerful positions, including law enforcement and politics."

I crossed my arms. "Risky. Why would an editor let that through?"

"She claimed she was duped. Maybe she was sleepin' with him."

I nodded. "Yeah, he seems like a persuasive kinda guy. Once she was compromised, he could leverage her. Maybe he faked the sources. But why stick his neck out like that?"

"Maybe warning people in the file he's aware of 'em?"

I leaned back. "If he really had something on powerful people, seems like they'd eliminate him." I thought for a moment. "We need to find out more about Gregory Hawkins and this supposed accident. He's a common factor with Lehr and Galloway. Both knew him. And Judson Hunter, who seems to be haunted by someone named Hawkins, could be in that file if it really existed. We'll have to see if Galloway admits to any of this. Was he fired, then?"

CHAPTER TWENTY-THREE

"Resigned. So did the editor."

"Great. We've got a reporter who takes chances, fudges facts, and might have a target on his back."

"'Cept this was two years ago, boss, and he's still alive and still working as a journalist. Seems odd to me. Did he approach you, or you him?"

"He came to me, but the context made sense, because he covers town meetings. I was in his town to talk with officials about an issue of concern to the public. He requested an interview to get some background."

"Didn't ask you anything beyond the scope?"

Ayden was in investigative mode. It's what I'd want him to do, but it made me sweat. "No. At least, not yet. He listened to my podcast, but that makes sense. And he does have information we may need. He knows people. He can give us names, maybe make introductions."

Ayden looked uneasy. "It doesn't add up. He *accused* people of potentially criminal acts. In a major newspaper. He had details about an experiment with kids. Then he just backed off? Nothing else happened? He wasn't sued?" He looked thoughtful. "Maybe he was bought, paid to keep his mouth shut. That wouldn't be good for us, either. We should keep looking into him."

I gestured. "Be my guest, but don't let that interfere. Whatever else he's done, he's useful for our case, which has nothing to do with his past reporting. I want you to find Marti Fielding's boyfriend, Kip Hawkins, and keep an eye on the status of the boy in the hospital, Owen Kringle. Those two are now our primary focus."

Ayden took a breath. "Copy, boss, but I can do that without Galloway. I don't think I should meet him with you tomorrow. He shouldn't know you have a PI here. It might put him on guard."

I'd never seen Ayden back away from a source. "What's up?"

"It's what you always look for, Annie. What's *missing*? He's reporting on this story here, but he's not pushing. He's not hungry. He doesn't seek out a kid in the center of it all who used to talk to him. Something happened between his ambitious exposé and what he's doing now. It changed him. Think about it. You told him about a possible murder of a girl in his town. Seems like he'd be all over *that*, not this interview with you. He should've put you off for a story that could be his way back to real journalism, but he hasn't. Something's just off about this guy."

"Okay, got it. You're right. Take your Tahoe and do your thing. You'll be more productive than if you're with me. I'll go over to the inn to meet him. Leave the article that disgraced him, and I'll read it myself."

A text to both of us from Natra got our attention. *Sending a photo.*

I tapped her attachment to open it. I saw only a photo of a starfish. Ayden shrugged. I called Natra and put her on speaker mode. "What's this?"

"It's a starfish. It was found next to a guy who died during the storm in Florida today. Car went off a wet road. Names Derek Houde, age thirty-six. JoLynn got it from a contact there in the ME's office."

"There are lots of starfish in Florida. What's special about this one?"

"It was inland, not near a water source. And it's been dead for a while."

Ayden sat forward, his eyes wide. "The tattoo! On the other guy. The one in Chattanooga. It was a starfish on his left shoulder. I saw it." He looked at me. "That's unique. There's your link."

Chapter Twenty-Four

By the time I arrived at the suite to meet Rob Galloway, I was worn out. My team and I had discussed the starfish photo but hadn't known what to make of it. We'd shelved it pending more information.

Then Kamryn had gotten up in the night, anxious about imagined people in the house, and come in with me. Ayden rose early to get started, so we'd had coffee at 6 a.m. My job for the day was to get more background from Rob. I'd skimmed the article with his accusations but saw only what Ayden had described. It seemed a side issue, though it made me vigilant.

The Hawthorne Suite had no spooky Hawthorne vibes at all, save for light gray paint on one wall. It was clean, bright, and modern, with a bed-and-breakfast feel. I'd grabbed some crusty blueberry muffins from the dining area to bring to the room. The galley kitchen had a coffeemaker with all the fixings, and there was a small Early American sitting room with a desk. It would have been a tight squeeze for three to meet, so I was glad Ayden wasn't with me.

Rob arrived. He approved the setting. "Much nicer than a noisy coffee house."

I gestured toward the blue wingback chair that looked comfortable. "Please have a seat. There's an assortment of coffee and tea in the kitchen."

"Had mine, thanks." He sat down. I felt the force of his easy charisma and had no trouble believing he'd seduced his editor into accepting whatever he told her and possibly into more. He was an attractive man in his forties, with a youthful, wide-eyed expression and a broad smile that invited trust.

He dressed well in a navy suit with a patterned silk tie. I hadn't expected such formality. I was in jeans and a sweater. The only formal clothing I'd packed was funeral attire.

We chatted for a few minutes about local lore and Rob's own connection to Concord. "Raised here," he said, "a few miles outside town."

"I spent time here as a kid and came back a few times," I offered. "Love the literary scene."

"It inspires. I assume you've been to Authors Ridge."

"Many times. It was a refuge. Lots of daydreaming there." I held up a pad of paper. "Mind if I take notes?"

"Not at all. I'll ask for the same courtesy. Are we interviewing each other?"

I laughed. "Probably. I need to pick the brain of someone who knows this place."

"Happy to share."

"Thank you." I gestured. "But please go first. You want background for your article. That's important."

Rob tapped his laptop. "Actually, I took some quotes from things you've written or discussed on your podcast. The concept's simple, I think. You gather information about a manner of death that can be interpreted in more than one way to try to help investigators decide the most likely call, usually between homicide and suicide, right?"

"Good summary, although some unclear deaths have also been natural or accidental. But obviously, if it appears that there's been a homicide, it helps investigators to receive the information as quickly as possible."

"Like with Marti Fielding."

"Yes, but that's fresh, and I don't know if what I observed at the site means anything. I spotted some items that seem suspicious. I haven't yet done a psychological autopsy, either. I'd have to interview people she knew."

"Her parents aren't talking to the press."

"I have a call in. They haven't called back, but I'll keep trying. I have the autopsy and police reports from the day they found her body, but there's a lot more to do."

"I don't suppose you can tell me what you found?" The smile lines around

Rob's eyes deepened, suggesting he was teasing. He projected a sense that we were friends, even allies. About *that* feeling, I was wary. Some people cast a spell with their presence. I usually had Natra at my side taking notes and reminding me to be objective.

"You'll have to use your cop connections for that," I said. "Someone's already told you something, or you wouldn't know about the discovery. You just said the concept is simple. It is, but the process can be complicated, especially if people have reason for withholding information. That's when it gets dicey, or if you find out the decedent had a secret, such as a drug addiction or an affair."

Rob scribbled some notes. "Got it. So, you'll do this with our three recent victims?"

"Actually, no. Officially, I'm consulting with the Dunbury officials about protocols in the wake of a suicide cluster, for stopping other kids from being triggered. That's more of a threat evaluation."

"So, a post-incident therapist."

I used my hand to indicate *not so much*. "More like offering expert analysis based on what other towns have done successfully. It's not easy to find guidelines unless you belong to certain professional groups."

"And how did you hear about what happened here?"

I gestured. "Your article. I picked up the newspaper."

Rob sat back. "You're staying here in Concord. You just happened to be in town?"

"Not exactly. I have business here."

Rob raised his chin and narrowed his eyes. "Any relation to Judson Hunter?"

I hesitated briefly. I was sure he noticed. "My grandfather."

"Ah. And he's quite ill, I understand. My condolences."

"Thank you."

His face grew serious. "So, you already know his association with all of this. Is that why you're consulting on our cases? Or *are* you consulting? Maybe gathering information?"

I held up my hand. "Our interview can't be about him. It's strictly about my work and what I do."

Rob looked perplexed. His question hung in the air. Judson's association? I wasn't sure what to say about my family, but I sensed he knew things. I had to tread a fine line. I took a breath. "I don't really know much about my grandfather's business concerns."

Rob nodded. I sensed he wasn't convinced.

I continued. "I lived here for a while as a child, but my father and Judson parted ways. Even when I came on my own years later, my visits were brief. I know Judson deals in real estate, but I haven't been in touch with him or my aunt in some time. Do you know them?"

Rob looked like he wasn't sure what to reveal but wanted to get more from me—exactly how I felt about him. To break the impasse, I said, "How is Judson associated with these cases?"

Rob moved in his seat. "First, I should tell you something about your work here. Yesterday, your discovery halted the momentum of a planned corporate development near Gilly Pond. Some council members who expect to benefit from its completion aren't pleased."

That seemed like an odd shift in subjects. "Because...?"

"Because Chief Blackburn roped off the site and insisted that everything stop, pending an investigation."

"Blackburn? I had the impression she wasn't keen about me being involved."

"Maybe not, but it's her order. She probably doesn't like you showing her up."

"That sounds like the right thing to do."

"And such delays cost investors money."

"For how long?"

"Indefinite."

I shrugged. It wasn't exactly my fault. Then I had a thought. "I know you've developed a theory about the incidents involving these kids, but have you considered that there's no suicide cluster? Maybe something else is going on."

Rob nodded. "I have, especially now."

It felt as if we were facing off. We each had an agenda. The other had information. We both wanted to take away something valuable. Thus, to see where this game would lead, we both had to take a risk.

97

Chapter Twenty-Five

I made the next move. "I think Blackburn should re-examine the first kid's death and also the train incident that put Owen Kringle in a coma."

Rob cocked his head. "Now we have a serial killer?"

"I didn't say that. It could be unrelated deaths that have nothing to do with each other or with Dacretown. That subtracts some color from your articles, but I assume you want the truth."

He cocked his head. "You do know who the primary investors are, right?"

I stared at him. I felt suddenly cold. I knew Lehr had some association but didn't know much more. "The sign over there said it's some kind of institute."

"Hmmm. Okay. Despite your links to this area, I'll give you the benefit of the doubt. You don't know. You're not trying to thwart me from getting to the bottom of this situation."

I sat up. "Sorry? Thwart?"

He leaned forward as his eyes grew more intense. "Briana Duncan is the force behind the development. Her corporation. They've been blocked for years by an association that wants to protect Dacretown as a historic area."

I knew I'd gone pale. "Do you mean the Gray Hollow Group? They were mentioned in an article."

"Them, yes."

I swallowed. "And Gregory Hawkins was part of that."

"So, you do know."

"No, I don't. I've seen the names, and last night I heard that Hawkins was one of my grandfather's associates."

Rob crossed his arms with a smile I couldn't read. "I thought you'd picked this suite as an ironic gesture. Intergenerational conflict, *House of Seven Gables*, and all of that."

I held out my hands. "I don't know what you're talking about, Rob. I came because my grandfather might be dying. I was summoned. But I'm not in conflict—"

"Not *you*." He held up a hand. "I've dug into this for years because they've had so much influence around here. But maybe I shouldn't be telling you your own family secrets."

My racing heart had to be evident in my flushed cheeks. I felt the heat. "What secrets?"

"Judson's partner, Matt Hawkins. What he did." His eyes narrowed. "With Briana."

"*Matt* Hawkins?" I put aside my pad of paper and gripped the edge of my chair. "For God's sake, Rob, who's Matt Hawkins, and what did he do?"

"It was a hell of a scandal at the time, and it didn't come out until years after it happened. But supposedly, Hawkins seduced her when she was sixteen. He was, I'd say, around forty, forty-one. And she was dating his son, Gregory."

I couldn't suppress my surprise. "The man who died in Boston?"

"The same."

Suddenly, I envisioned a network of connections between these two families. I couldn't imagine my formal Aunt Bree as a girl so adventurous she'd get into a racy situation like that. She'd been pretty, but a risk taker? "She said Hawkins died a few years ago. Which Hawkins did she mean?"

"They're both dead. Matt Hawkins was a broken man, thanks to Judson ruining him. He drank himself to death in his sixties. Like I said, the seduction and affair came out years after it happened, so the partnership continued for a while."

"And then Matt's son died in this supposed accident."

Rob nodded. "A tragic family story. And now we have Kip, Gregory's son and Matt's grandson, trying to sort through it all. Now I don't think you can approach him. You're one of the Hunters. He won't talk to you."

Good thing I had Ayden on it. I peered at him. "How do you know all this?"

Rob shrugged. "I investigate. I started when Gregory died. Rumor had him as a member of the Gray Hollow Group. That's what Kip believes. You can see how that makes some sense. Blocking Briana's development as kind of a punishment."

"What's this group? What do they do?"

"It's a conservancy. Among other things, they apparently protect Dacre-town."

"Why? It's reportedly nothing but a bunch of moss-covered foundations and grown-over hollows. What's so important about it?"

He raised an eyebrow. "That's the big mystery. Kip thinks his father figured it out and got killed for it. Thinks his grandfather also knew."

A chill went through me. *This* is the list Rob had allegedly seen, the thing that made him reckless and got him fired. Judson had to be on it, and probably Bree. Maybe Matt Hawkins. But I couldn't ask without signaling what I knew about him.

Rob sat up straight and looked at me askance. "Wait. You must be…Lang Hunter's daughter?"

Just the sound of Dad's name made me shiver. I'd come this far. I felt like I'd found the only stable rock in a rushing stream that was threatening to wash me away. "Yes, that's right."

Rob made a face. "And he told you nothing about all of this?"

"Obviously not."

"Hmmm. And now he's dead too. Or *is* he?" He watched me as if ready to evaluate how I'd respond.

This was too much. I didn't plan to be a character in his story. I stood. I knew it was the wrong move as soon as I did it, but I had to follow through. "I think that's it for me for now, Rob. I need to look into some things before we talk further. I don't want to say anything that might upset my family. I think you have what you need for your article."

Rob rose to his feet, a knowing look on his face. "I get it, of course. Well, you know how to contact me. And I'll extend you the courtesy of not publicly mentioning any of this for now. I'll give you some space. But let me just warn you. Kip and his brothers think your aunt was involved in his father's death. It's a regular family feud."

I felt blood drain from my face. I should have played this out, gotten more information. Too late.

Rob walked to the door. He opened it and turned around. "And one other thing. Again, just a rumor, but I think it's solid. Lang Hunter was also in the Gray Hollow Group. Strangely enough, that might help get your foot in the door with Kip. He might see you as a source for his own investigation. It's fifty-fifty." He made a sweeping gesture. "Looks like us meeting here was ironic after all. Families entangled by scandals and secrets. I expect you'll see a bleeding wall or two before you leave. Call me when you're ready. Maybe we can help each other."

Chapter Twenty-Six

I don't know how long I sat in the chair Rob had vacated. I had to absorb these revelations. He'd blown me away. Judson, at 85, was dying. His children from two different marriages were in conflict over a peculiar piece of property. Judson had partnered with a man who'd seduced his daughter. The son of that man had aligned with Dad, and he'd died just before Dad vanished. That had to be related. And Judson had refused all my requests to help find Dad. This aligned Judson with Bree. Yet there was something prickly between them as well. He clearly had not liked her in his house yesterday. My head was spinning.

If Rob had guessed correctly from the links he'd made, this put sibling rivalry on a whole new level. I began to understand why my mother had been so unhappy being part of this family. It had to have been a perpetual battlefield. But it couldn't just be that Bree had succumbed to the seduction of an older man over three decades ago. There had to be more.

Why had my father told me nothing? Certainly, if the GHG was committed to historic preservation, I'd have carried the torch for him. I'd have helped, especially now, with his father dying and him flicked out of the picture. He could've prepared me.

My text alert pulled me back to the present. I grabbed my phone. Ayden. *Call when you can.* I took a deep breath, sat up, and called.

"Your meeting's over already?" he asked.

"Yes."

"Did he admit—"

"We didn't get to that. Other things came up. Tell you later. Find something?"

"I went to the hospital first to check on the train victim, Owen Kringle. Police cars were there. Not sure why, but something happened where his room is, so I didn't get close. No one would talk. I think his parents were there, and it wasn't a good time to approach them, so I didn't stick around."

I had no doubt Rob would find this out. "Did you get to the pond?"

"Again, police presence. No one allowed past the tape. Fortunately, others were there, so I didn't stand out. I took some pictures of the general area but didn't want to raise suspicions."

"Good decision."

"Then I saw a guy there, watching. Seemed the right age to be friends with these victims. He went back to his car—driving a silver Outback—so I followed him and watched where he went."

I got to my feet. "I wonder if it's Kip or one of his Skeleton Crew. We need to get a photo of him and anyone else who might be part of his group or club, or whatever it is."

"Natra's on it. Should have some shortly."

"Did you say anything to him?"

"Not yet. Watching for an opportunity."

I suddenly realized I needed to alert him. "Listen, Ayden. If it turns out to be Kip or one of his friends, don't mention my name."

"Boss?"

"There's a situation…it's complicated. Just…see if you can buddy up and get him talking without saying why you want to know. You're good at that. I'll tell you later."

"Copy that."

"I'm heading to the hospital here to check on Judson. I want to make sure Kamryn's okay, and then I'll try to meet you wherever you are. I'll text you."

I had no idea what I'd say to Aunt Bree. She suddenly looked different to me. More than just the heir to a wealthy businessman and a CEO in her own right, she'd been against my father and possibly had fractured Judson's partnership. She might even be involved in another man's controversial death. And she most definitely did not want me to see Judson's business records. I was beginning to understand why.

At the hospital, a nurse escorted me to the light green wing that housed the private suite where they were treating Judson. Large vases of fresh bouquets sat on wall shelves. I breathed in their fragrance to prepare myself. My escort touched my arm in a kind way and told me, "Your grandfather's transitioning. It won't be long. He's not in pain." Then she left me to enter alone.

I stood outside the closed door and wondered what I should do. I couldn't confront Bree. I couldn't ask her anything about what I'd heard today, not while she was holding this vigil. I knew she didn't want me here. I wondered if Judson had named me his executor to torment her. This was his parting shot.

I heard what sounded like crying. I froze. The door opened, and a nurse came out. She stopped and asked, "Are you family?"

I nodded.

She cocked her head. "I'm sorry. He's gone. He's at peace now."

I moved past her and entered the spacious room. It smelled like soiled sheets and Lysol. Bree was bent over the bed, holding Judson's hand and weeping into a tissue. Judson lay still, his mouth slightly open and his eyes closed. Machines still beeped as if trying to detect a vanished heartbeat. A nurse across the bed from Bree dabbed at Judson's mouth with a cloth. She nodded to me, picked up some crumpled tissues, and withdrew. It was odd to see a man who'd once seemed so portentous reduced to this pale, shrunken corpse. Blue veins stood out against his stark white skin.

I put a hand on Bree's shoulder and felt her wracking shudders. Whatever issues she and her father might have had, she seemed genuinely bereft.

Bree looked up with reddened eyes. She blinked, apparently surprised to see me.

"I came to see how he was," I offered. "I'm so sorry. Please let me know how I can help."

To my surprise, Bree straightened up, rose to her feet, and said, "I'm fine. We'll just get on with this now." Her hand gripped and kneaded the tissue. She wasn't fine.

"I can call Shona—"

"Ann, I'm fine. I've been expecting this. It's just…done."

She was Judson's daughter, no doubt about that. All business and no time for weakness. I wonder if she already knew I was responsible for the halt to her development plans. Surely not, as she'd been here since last night. But she had a phone. And Lehr knew her, possibly had once worked for her. If he was her goon, she knew.

Bree turned away. "Please, just leave me alone with him. I'll speak to Shona. She knows what to do."

"Of course."

I walked out, relieved to be dismissed. I'd come into something I wasn't really part of. Still, I felt numb. In the car, I texted Ayden and Natra: *Grandfather passed. Busy now. Will be in touch. Please proceed on case.*

Both knew better than to send condolences, but Natra texted a hug symbol. No matter what Bree said, I intended to talk to Shona. She'd have to get things ready for guests and possibly for a wake. I might also need her to watch Kamryn.

I pulled into the driveway of Judson's house and sat in the car for a moment. The darkening sky seemed to match my mood. I wasn't sad, myself, since all I'd known of Judson was his inability to embrace his own son. He'd been no grandfather to me, and he'd barely acknowledged Kamryn. But there's still something about a death in the family that feels somber.

Movement at a window on the second floor made me look up. I leaned forward. Someone was there, but the curtain moved back into place. Then Shona opened the front door. So, the person upstairs hadn't been her. Someone I didn't know was in my grandfather's house, possibly watching me.

Chapter Twenty-Seven

I met Shona on the porch. Her expression told me she knew about Judson. She reached to console me, but I held up a hand. "I wasn't close to him. I'm not grieving. He lived a long, very comfortable life. But he snubbed my father, and I don't forgive him for that. I'm just relieved that I can conclude this business, finally."

Shona nodded and stepped back. "Of course."

"Are the girls over here?"

"They went to Lexington with Jeannette. They wanted to see where history happened. There's a Welcome Center there and a trail. I hope that's all right. They're staying there for lunch."

"It's fine." I wished I were there, too, exploring with my daughter. "So, have relatives arrived? I saw someone upstairs at the window."

Shona's face paled, but she said, "Most of those who might attend a wake already live in the area. No one will stay here at the house. Judson owns— owned—several guest lodgings we can use. I've already prepared two."

"I'm sure I saw someone at a window."

"Maybe the maid? I believe she's upstairs."

I sensed from the tension in her expression that it wasn't the maid, but I didn't press. For all I knew, she'd snuck in a lover. Bree had been gone overnight, after all. "Yes, maybe the maid."

Shona looked as if she was about to say something else. Then she seemed to change her mind. "Please let me know if I can help in any way." She turned to go back inside.

I returned to the guesthouse. It felt empty. I texted Kamryn to tell her I knew where she was and to encourage her to have fun. I loved that she was so excited about learning something. She sent back a ☺. I was about to call Ayden when I realized that, with Kamryn away, I could get into the hidden staircase. I felt just violated enough by Bree's behavior to forget my guilt. It had been my hideaway once. I grabbed the key and went upstairs.

The lock at the top of the staircase didn't yield easily. It took some twisting before I heard the click. This door opened inward over a small landing. I'd sat on that landing many times.

I pushed.

The door resisted.

I placed my hands flat against it and pushed again.

It yielded. I nearly fell over, but I was in. I clicked the light switch. The staircase remained dark. I clicked it several times, but the dim light I remembered didn't come on. I used the flashlight on my phone and saw that there was no bulb. Rats!

I flashed the small beam down the steps. Too dark. Retreating, I turned on the hall light and ventured down. The stairs seemed narrower than I remembered. I went halfway down to my beloved cubbyhole. The light worked here. I stepped into it and lifted the hinged seat on the bench. I'd half-hoped I'd left something from my father behind. To my surprise, I saw a couple of 8-by-11-inch envelopes. I couldn't imagine who'd leave something like this here. They both felt stuffed. I took the envelopes to the bottom of the stairs and pushed against the door. It stuck but moved, so I pushed harder. It opened.

Now I had light from both sides. I took the envelopes over to a table. There were no markings to indicate ownership. I hesitated. It was one thing to open a locked area but quite another to rifle through someone's possessions.

They weren't sealed. I had to see.

I opened the top envelope and saw what seemed to be a stack of prints of photos. To my shock, one was an image of my father standing in a rugged landscape that looked like the Scottish Highlands. There appeared to be a dozen from the same area. My father was in some, but most showed people

I didn't know. They seemed to be exploring something. Dad looked around fifty, so this trip occurred before he'd vanished. I knew about his trips to the Celtic areas. He was looking for *thin places*, areas where the veil between life and whatever's beyond grows thin enough to have a paranormal experience. Some people go missing. Dad was obsessed with figuring out how these portals worked. I'd visited some of the places he'd explored. He'd even made an app that supposedly helped to detect the energy shifts. I'd used it, but I'd come no closer to finding him.

I went over and closed the staircase door. I considered locking it but decided to leave it for now. Should Shona ask about the key, I didn't want to give it back and then be unable to replace the photos. I stuffed them back in the envelope and took both envelopes to my room upstairs. Then I closed the top door of the staircase.

I opened the first envelope again and spread the photos across my bed. There were multiple landscape depictions, and a few showed some deteriorating properties. I wondered if these were from Dacretown. Why not? Dad was part of the GHG. But a series of photos of a modern building suggested it had to be elsewhere. Nothing was written on the back to help me ID the location.

One set of three photos startled me. They showed Dad with me. I was young, maybe four or five. I'm not sure who would've taken them. But I looked happy to be with my dad. My eyes watered. I missed him. It looked like we were at North Bridge, so this was taken in Concord.

I let myself cry. All the pressure of being in this house again released a surge of grief. I wanted those days back when Dad would take me with him, wandering the cemetery or looking at historic sites. I hated that Judson had driven him away. But these photos brought him close again. They had to belong to Bree.

A firm knock on the door downstairs startled me. I couldn't imagine who'd be there without calling or texting me first. I looked at my phone. I had no new messages.

I shoved the photos back into the envelope and placed both on the top step of the staircase. I expected to come right back and place them in the bench. The person knocked again, this time with the knocker. Then the doorbell rang. I went down and opened the door.

Richard Lehr stood on the porch, his face red with fury.

Chapter Twenty-Eight

"Why are you talking to that reporter?" Lehr demanded. "Did you tell him I approached you?"

I hardly knew how to respond. "What business is it of yours?"

"Believe me, it is. Don't tell him *anything*. These things don't concern him. He thinks you're his way in."

"Excuse me, Mr. Lehr. If anyone's butting in, it's you. And if you don't know it, Judson's—" I caught myself before I said it.

"Of course, I know! He'd dead. And now you're too late. You could've gotten what I needed. So simple." He stepped closer to put his face near mine. I wasn't about to back away. "You'll wish you'd heard me out." He took a step back. "Your whole family's gonna wish you'd talked to me yesterday. Now I can't stop what's coming. This is on *you*."

He turned and went down the steps. He didn't look back. His departure seemed decisive, as if he'd dismissed me. My stomach dropped. I wanted to know what he had. I should've said, "Okay, I'll help," and then seen his so-called evidence. And he was right. If he had something definitive, I might've shown it to Judson while the old man was still alive and persuaded him to fund my search.

I stood at the door until the cold air pushed me back inside. The temperature seemed to have dipped, with the wind picking up. That wasn't good. I closed the door and locked it. Lehr had shaken me. I didn't know how much he knew about the Hunters, but I was glad Kamryn was in another town. The weight of all these secrets just kept growing.

I called Natra by video. She was out on the balcony outside my office. It was 72 degrees there. She turned her tablet to show me the blue sky and calm ocean. I heard Mika bark nearby. I wanted to be there.

As I described Lehr's confrontation, I walked from window to window to be sure he wasn't lurking outside. His forceful presence remained with me like a shadow I couldn't escape.

"Is Kamryn there?" Natra asked.

"No. She's in Lexington, a few miles away. Lehr hasn't said what he wants from me, but apparently, Judson's death just shifted his plans."

"What's the deal with the reporter?"

"Galloway? That meeting didn't go well, either. Both of these guys seem to know things about my family that I don't. They also both know Gregory Hawkins, and so does Bree, and she's in this up to her eyeballs. Lehr's worked either with her or for her. To make things worse, it feels like that weather front's coming."

Natra nodded. "Oh, yeah. I've been keeping track. Hope you have boots. This storm could stretch from Maryland to Maine."

"It can't be that bad. It's cold but not freezing. Many trees are still in leaf."

"It's coming off the Mid-Atlantic coast. The Florida storm went out to sea, then made an unexpected turn. It's heading your way. In fact, rain started just north of here, and cold is pushing in. I expect it to be in the fifties here tomorrow."

"I thought it was coming from the Plains. Slowly."

"There's one there, too, and a ridge over Canada that could advance. You better hope they don't all meet. If you get snow, it'll be heavy and wet. There was a system like that in 2011. Snowtober, they called it, and Shocktober. There's already talk in New Hampshire and Connecticut of plows and salt and shelters. There could be widespread outages."

I shook my head. "Damn! And I can't get out of here now. Judson's wake will probably be in the next day or two."

"Not to mention, this storm could create a large area to monitor for the weather deaths. If weather is the trigger, you'll have the brass ring."

"Oh, God, just what I need. And what's happening with that?"

"One fatality in Chicago that's questionable, but we're not sure it's part of this."

"If it's linked to the others, this can't be one guy. He'd have to be traveling at the speed of light. This is like those Smiley Face murders of all the healthy young men in different towns who supposedly drowned in mysterious circumstances. In some cases, a smiley face was posted nearby."

"Had the same thought. And those are unsolved. JoLynn and I think it's a team or even a network, something related to the starfish symbol. We've researched things online but haven't found anything yet."

"Have you asked Joe? Maybe he can look at the darknet. That's where I'd expect to see an organized effort involving murder. It's a marketplace for demented connections."

"He's looking."

"And has Ayden checked in? I need to find him."

An image came onto the screen. It resembled the dark-haired young man I'd seen on the bench in Dunbury the day before. Natra came back. "That's your guy. Kip Hawkins. That's from a high school yearbook about four years ago, so it's outdated, but he's probably about the same. Found one in a newspaper from when his father died, but it's blurry. Ayden's found the Skeleton Crew's clubhouse, or whatever they call it. The Crypt, I think. He gave me the location. He'll stay there till you come."

Chapter Twenty-Nine

I pulled into a parking space near the Tahoe. I'd texted Kamryn that I was going to shop for a heavier coat and some boots for her. She sent three happy faces and *get a pink one!*

Ayden had found the Crypt on the other side of Gilly Pond, close to another part of the Dead Line. I got into the Tahoe's passenger's seat so we could talk. The moss-covered stone building was small, with a steep, capped roof that made it look witchy. A chimney blew out smoke.

"Great find, Ayden. And someone's home."

"You okay, boss?"

"If you mean my grandfather's passing, I'm fine. It's just bad timing. What did you discover?"

"Seen a couple guys go in. They're wearing caps, but one could be Kip. Tall and thin."

"Could be. Now that I've seen his photo, I know he's the guy who was watching me yesterday."

"Want me to go knock?"

"Let's think. Ordinarily, this would call for a nuanced approach, but there's no time, and it probably won't work. This Bone Head has a bone to pick with my family."

Ayden glanced at me. "What?"

"I've had a day full of nasty surprises. To summarize, my aunt once hooked up with my grandfather's partner, a.k.a., Kip's grandfather, Matthew Hawkins, father of the late Gregory Hawkins. Gregory was dating Bree at the time. She was sixteen, so when the affair was discovered, it was quite a scandal."

"A father and son were both—"

"Yes. Years later, Gregory died. Maybe an accident, maybe not, but it was right after he was about to meet a source who had significant information for him for an exposé. And there's this cursed property, Dacretown, in which my dad *and* Gregory had some stake. And now Kip's GF might've been murdered near it."

Ayden stared at me. "That's pretty screwed up." He glanced up and gestured. "Isn't that Dacretown over there?"

"It is, and yeah, that's a twisted bit of history. And that's not all. If I can believe Galloway, my aunt is the force behind the development that's slated to erase Dacretown. The Institute of Mentalistics. And *my* discovery of evidence near Gilly Pond has delayed that, which is making a lot of invested people mad—at me. Somehow, this Lehr character is part of it, but I haven't figured that out yet. He came to the house and told me Judson could've enlightened us all while he was alive and now it's too late."

Ayden's expression turned to alarm. "Lehr was there again?"

"Yes. He yelled at me about meeting with Galloway. So, I've got loads of family secrets I knew nothing about, we're about to be blasted with a storm, I have to address this suicide cluster—"

Ayden held up his hand. "About that."

I looked at him. "What?"

"There's a twist. I told you there were cops at the hospital, so I watched the local updates. The cops were there for that kid, Owen. I think someone tried to kill him."

"Kill him?"

"Tampered with his oxygen. Maybe to silence him. Like, he was 'sposed to die under the train but didn't."

Neither of us spoke for a moment. Then I said, "So there's no suicide cluster."

"Or there's a fake one."

"What do you mean?"

Ayden gestured toward the Dead Line. "Well, there's this legendary place with a curse and some earlier suicides, so that could set up faking an echo cluster. Only one target didn't die, and they didn't count on an expert spotting problems." He gestured toward the hut. "I'd guess those guys know something about it."

I sat back. I could barely comprehend this. In all my suicide research, I'd never heard of faking a cluster. That would take a lot of planning and a devious crew. But if ever there was a perfect place for it, Dacretown fit the bill. "So, who'd have a reason to do that? Not someone trying to develop the property. They'd engineer the suicides away from it."

"But they'd lose the narrative."

"True. Then maybe someone with an investment in protecting the curse?"

Ayden shrugged. "It's not like there's an entrepreneur running tours. This area's not a tourist destination, not compared to all the other historic spots around here. Natra says there's not much solid information online about Dacretown, either. Most of it's from ghost groups making stuff up."

"That suggests a local, then." I looked at the Crypt. "Like…a skeleton crew. But why? And would Kip kill his girlfriend?"

"We need more intel about this Mentalistics development. Seems like they could find a less troublesome location. And now that you've said there's this father-versus-daughter thing with Judson and Bree, that's where I'd start."

I looked out the window. "I have a feeling this goes further back. If my father's involved, there's sibling tension, too. They're seven or eight years apart, with different mothers, so it's not like they were ever close. I think I need you to investigate my family."

"Annie…"

"I mean it, Ayden. Something's deeply wrong with all of this, and whatever it is, it feels like it has a long history."

"What if it implicates Lang in something? I mean, you think he faked his death. Maybe he did something illegal. Or violent. Didn't Hawkins die around the same time—"

"Yes." I crossed my arms and sat back. My heart thumped. Finally, I said, "No matter what. I need to know."

Ayden tapped the steering wheel. "You're Judson's executor."

I looked at him. "I am, yes. And maybe that's why. Maybe he wants me to know something. Bree seems determined to reverse his decision. She's frantic about it. But I won't see the will till the funeral formalities are over."

"Or you can just go to the attorney and ask. Why wouldn't he show you?"

I nodded. "You're right. When we get back, I'll call him. But first, let me tell you some things about my family. I don't know a lot, but I know some things that will get you started. You'll like this. There's ghost lore involved."

Ayden gestured toward The Crypt. "Nothing's happening here. We got time. And a dark sky. Let's hear it."

Chapter Thirty

I hugged myself, as if to ward off spirits. "I told you once that I have an ancestor, Merrick Hunter, who was among the scientists involved with William James at Harvard who were studying psychic mediums. The American Society for Psychical Research. Recall that?"

"I do. The ASPR had ties with some group in England."

"Yes. They all believed that science could answer the question of how certain people seemed able to access current but remote events—ESP—and also get messages from the dead, like from automatic writing. They identified a few seemingly authentic mediums and spent years putting these people to the test. One woman was tested here in Boston. They uncovered a lot of fraud, but they couldn't refute a few. They were also never able to explain how these people accomplished it."

"'s'that where your interest came from?"

"Mine's more about being open to these things. I mean, I've heard stories from my father. You know he experimented with automatic writing. He tried to get me to do it, but I was dismal at it. He was disappointed, I think. I'm willing to give things a try, but I'm more concerned than he was about real proof."

"Didn't he make an app? You used it, right?"

"Yes, and yes. He used large language artificial intelligence models, but his pool consisted of automatic writing samples. He used this to create his AWAI app. Automatic Writing Artificial Intelligence. Kind of clever because he was looking for people who'd gone *away* and then communicated through a medium. He used the app to locate thin places."

"Here?"

"I don't know. Maybe he experimented here. Dacretown's supposedly a negative vortex. Maybe that's why he was in the Gray Hollow Group. He devoted his life to studying these anomalies."

Ayden nodded. "So, maybe he found a portal and went through?"

I shrugged. "That's a big leap for me. I don't know what to make of a reality that buckles in some places so people can slip through. I used his app in areas like Yeats' tower in Ireland, and some places in Scotland. Celtic lore has a bunch of thin places where you can supposedly encounter strange entities."

"What happened when you used it?"

"The app seems to detect energy shifts, but that's a long way from proving there's a vanishing hole."

Ayden stretched his back. "Why'd your dad think it works like that?"

"The lore, I guess. That fairies take you to their lair, or that mysterious beasts won't let us discover their secrets. Merrick was his great-grandfather, so maybe he passed along some tales. But, if I'm honest, it could just have been a broken heart. Dad was involved with a woman on his research team, and she apparently disappeared. He thought she went through a hole. Maybe he was just reframing her rejection, but I think he's been looking for her."

Ayden nodded. "I get that. When you find someone…"

We were getting off track. I got us back on. "Anyway, Merrick Hunter was a member of the ASPR. He came here from Scotland to be part of it, but I think he didn't stick with it, because his name's not in any published ASPR accounts. He settled in Concord. Judson's house was once Merrick's. There were a series of family losses, like illnesses and bankruptcy, even a poisoning attempt. Judson stabilized things with real estate ventures just before a boom. He rebuilt the wealth."

"Still…" Ayden said.

I looked at him. "What?"

"It's not like you're one big happy family."

I nodded. "Right. We're fractured in multiple ways. And look at Judson's personal losses. First and foremost, his son. Then Bree's daughter—my cousin, Maisie—seems to be out of the picture. Bree's husband split. Judson's wives left him, and his business partner betrayed him."

Ayden raised an eyebrow. "Sounds like a curse to me. Still want me to investigate?"

"I do. And check with Natra about—"

"Boss!" Ayden had gone alert. I followed his line of sight and noticed a young man striding away from the Crypt.

"He's heading to a vehicle," I said. "When he drives away, follow him."

"Without you?"

"Yes. Now, move! I'll keep watch here. Text me when you can."

Ayden started the engine, and I slid out. He pulled away. His expression said he didn't like splitting up. I stood near the Range Rover and took out my phone to text Rob. The reception was poor. I stepped away to improve it and typed in: *Heard about cops at the hospital. Related to my case?*

Behind me, I heard the crunch of dried leaves. I turned. A young man in a black hoodie stood ten feet from me. Aside from an angry frown, I could barely see his face.

But I saw his gun.

Chapter Thirty-One

yden was too far away to have seen this. He wouldn't circle back. I held up a hand. "There's no need for that."

"What're you doing here? It's private property." From the little I could see, this guy looked to be in his late teens, still enduring acne and a cracking voice.

"That's right," I said. "It belongs to my family. What are *you* doing here?"

He looked momentarily confused. My ploy had worked, though I was operating on rumors. I kept it up. "I came to check. I've heard that kids've been doing things out here where they shouldn't be. It's dangerous. I'm looking for a place to put up a barrier. And I've already called the cops."

His mouth formed a hard line. "No, you haven't. I watched you. Who are you?"

"I'm Dr. Hunter. I'm investigating the incidents here. I'm authorized to be on this property. What's your name?"

He raised his gun. "Jesse James."

I took a step backward.

"Stop!" he ordered.

I shook my head. "You won't shoot me. There's a collection of cop cars not far from here. If they hear a gunshot, they'll be here so—"

"Shut up! Turn off your phone, turn around, and walk." He gestured toward the Crypt.

I was sure this kid was one of the Crew, and he might lead me straight to the person I wanted to see. Or he might take me to some deep pit in Dacretown where no one would ever find my body. I might have the right to be here, but he probably knew the territory. I felt a pinch of panic when I shut down my phone, and he took it. I turned around.

We arrived at a wooden door with peeling black paint. Across it was a hand-painted sign, *The Crypt*. The sodden wood was bare in spots, and I smelled mildew. I didn't want to be locked into a moldering dungeon.

"Just tell me what you want," I said.

He reached around me and knocked in a pattern that sounded like a code. Then he ordered me to open it.

I turned the metal knob. The door opened inward to warm air. I took several steps in, with the gunslinger behind me. To my surprise, this wasn't a nasty little place full of moss and mice. Someone had made it livable, with classy furniture. Some pieces looked like antiques. Chair rails, contrasting green trim, and stylish woodwork gave the impression of a master craftsman. I saw another young man at a table near the fireplace where a woodworking project sat on newspapers. He watched me with wary brown eyes from a face almost too delicate to be male. He resembled the yearbook photo Natra had shown us—the head Bone Head himself, Kip Hawkins.

He squinted. "You. Saw you in town."

I stood as tall as I could. "That's right. You did. I'm no danger to you. Now, will you tell your bodyguard here to put down the gun?"

Kip looked at him. "Why'd you bring her here?" His accent grounded him firmly in the metro-Boston area.

"She's watchin' us. Outside."

Kip frowned.

"Yes, I was," I said. "And so was my PI. He knows where this place is, and if I don't show up within an hour, he'll be back here looking for me. So, let's just reduce the stress. The gun, please."

Kip made a motion with his head, and I heard "Jesse James" breathe out as if unhappy about the order. He dumped my phone on the table and retreated. But I remained guarded. I suspected they didn't care for intruders, especially not those who might tell someone what kind of place they had here. I watched for a way to escape. I figured the kid behind me still had his weapon ready. I looked directly at Kip. "I've been looking for you. I need to talk to you."

His frown deepened. "'bout what?"

"I'm investigating the death of Marti Fielding." I saw blood rush to his cheeks. "I understand you knew her pretty well."

Kip's nostrils flared, but he remained silent, so I continued. "I know you're Kip Hawkins. I've learned some things about you. Maybe you already know I found some indications near the pond that suggest that Marti didn't kill herself."

Kip rose to his feet, his eyes alive with anger. He was tall, over six feet. Despite his slender build, he felt menacing. "What the hell?"

I stood my ground. I might be petite, but I could enhance my stature with authority. "I saw things, and I alerted the police. That's why they're over there right now."

He swore. It wasn't the reaction I'd expected. He glared at me. "Are you accusing me of something? Is that why you're here?"

"No. I'm telling you something important and I want to ask you some questions. I'm a psychologist, not a cop. I'm assisting the town officials here to devise a plan for dealing with the recent deaths. Like Marti's."

Kip looked over my right shoulder, his eyes bright and his jaw tight. I assumed he was silently communicating with his associate. Then he crossed his arms. "I know who you are." He jutted his chin. "'s'the old man dead yet?"

I realized he was referring to Judson. "Yes. This morning."

Again, Kip looked past me. This time, he gestured with his head toward the door I'd just come through. I heard scuffles behind me, and the door opened and closed. The gunslinger was gone. I looked around but saw no one else, though a closed door on my left suggested there was more than one room to this place.

Kip didn't invite me to sit down. Instead, he planted his feet and asked, "Why should I tell you anything?"

"I assume you want to help find out what happened to Marti."

His mouth formed a hard line. He shook his head. "You'll never find out. They won't let you."

"Who?"

"They're all paid off, everyone you talked to. I know who was in that meeting. You're s'posed to just do what they want and go away. They're not gonna let you screw things up. *Especially* not you."

I wanted to press him on this. "The chief of police has already stopped the development, if that's what you mean."

Kip sneered. "Oh, Emmie'll go through the motions, make it look good. She'll find a way around it."

"I don't think so. Marti was there in cold weather with no coat. She got to that remote place in someone's car, not hers. I also found footprints near an earring that might be hers. Someone was with her."

"I wouldn't have thought you'd be naïve."

This seemed like a strange remark. "Do you know me?"

He crossed his arms. "Let's just say I know people who know you."

I made a quick mental calculation of whom he could mean. "I've never met your father."

He looked me over before he said, "I've met yours."

I caught my breath. Blood rushed to *my* cheeks. "When? He hasn't lived here or even visited since before you were born."

I saw a flash of alarm before Kip's face tightened. He shrugged.

But I intended to pry it out of him. "How do you know my father?"

"I'm not answering any of your questions. Could be a trap."

Kip suddenly seemed young and vulnerable. I had to remember he was just out of his teens. He thought his dad had been set up and killed; now I was telling him about the possible murder of his girlfriend. That made him a target. If I wanted him to cooperate, I had to think from his perspective. "Can we just talk?"

He took a step toward me, flushing with anger. "I'm telling you *nothing*. You can't just come in here and think you know what's going on. You don't! And don't come back here." He cocked his head. "If I decide to talk, I'll find you. I sure as hell know where *your* family lives."

I reached for my phone, but he grabbed it. "Put this in your pocket. Don't turn it on until you're away from here. We're watching you." He handed the phone to me.

I slipped it into my pocket. I was not about to let him intimidate me. "You'll call me, Kip, because you did care about Marti, and you do want to know. Just don't wait too long or you might end up as a suspect."

He snorted. "I already am, thanks to you. They *want* to arrest me. If you'd left it alone, there'd be no investigation. They'll make it go away, no matter who takes the fall. This works even better for them. Thanks a lot! You've just made everything harder."

Chapter Thirty-Two

I called Ayden from the parking lot of a store where I could buy Kamryn some winter gear but told him only that I'd been delayed. He gets upset if he thinks he left me in a dangerous situation. The encounter with Kip still stung, so I wanted to process it before I discussed it with my team. The things I'd told Kip shouldn't have made him so angry, and now I'd lost him as a source. He was right. I *didn't* know what was going on.

"Got some intel, boss," Ayden said. "I followed that car. Went straight to the hospital."

"Hmmm. That suggests there's a connection between Owen and the Crew. I'd say he's a member. Galloway seems to think so."

"I couldn't see which room the kid went into, and he didn't stay long. I followed him to another address, which I gave to Natra. She got a name. He kept looking at my Tahoe, so I left. He mighta spotted me before."

"Well, I encountered another kid. He took me to meet Kip. I'll tell you about it when I'm back. Where are you now?"

"Nearly to Concord."

"Let Kam know. There's a book of menus in the house. Can you two decide on something for take-out for dinner?"

"Copy that. Everything okay?"

"I'm fine. We've made progress. But this whole thing's more complicated than I anticipated. We'll sort it out later. Good work today."

I sat for a moment to think about what had transpired with Kip. Almost as soon as he'd made his parting shot, I realized that if these town officials were as corrupt as he believed, arresting him could kill two birds with one stone.

They'd thwart him as a Dacretown guardian and remove the impediment he posed. I'd given them a perfect fall guy. I hoped he had a solid alibi. I feared he might just pack up and run. I understood why he was upset. Still, he had to be curious about what I'd found and what it meant. I thought he'd call.

I purchased winter clothing for Kam and myself, then drove back under thick gray skies. The roads were sloshy, with some icy spots. I reminded myself to check the weather. There'd been no messages from Bree. I expected she'd been busy getting Judson's body moved to wherever she'd hold the wake, probably the Big House. I called the lawyer but got only voice mail. I left a message that I needed to see him as soon as possible.

When I arrived at the house, I heard girls giggling in the library. I found Ayden in the kitchen on his computer.

"What's going on?" I asked.

He looked up. "We thought we'd get take-out from—"

"I mean, the girls."

"Oh. Kam asked if she could show her new friend the library. Thought it was okay. It gave me a chance to catch up with the starfish investigation."

"Yeah, sure, of course. Anything more on that?"

"No."

"Ask Natra to look into Matthew Hawkins."

"Boss?"

"Just trying to put some pieces together. I've already got her on Gregory."

"Copy."

I took the coat I'd just purchased to show Kamryn.

"Mom!" she shouted. "Look what we found!"

To my shock, the door to the hidden staircase stood open, and the girls had pulled out the packets of photos. They'd opened both envelopes and arranged the contents on the coffee table. My stomach dropped.

"Elyse showed me how the stairs work," Kamryn said. "The door wasn't even locked. I think it was just stuck. And we found all these pictures!"

I swallowed hard. It wasn't exactly Elyse's fault, but Kam wouldn't have opened a door or an envelope without asking first. And I'm the one who left the doors unlocked. When Lehr arrived and yelled at me, I'd forgotten to put everything back. I'd never imagined they'd try to get in. To prevent Kamryn from noticing my distress, I gave her the bag with her new coat and boots.

She pulled the coat out and squealed at the dark pink color and white fake fur lining. "I love it!" She tried it on, pleased that it fit, and ran to show Ayden.

I turned to Elyse. I wanted to be calm, but this girl spelled trouble. I figured she knew the signs of someone preparing to scold her, so I took a different approach. "Thank you for letting Kamryn be part of your lessons. She's really enjoying it."

Elyse smiled. "She's a blast. She makes it a lot more fun. She even showed me how you meter a room. That's so cool! And tomorrow, we're learning guitar. Can she come again?"

I leaned down to collect a photo off the floor. "I'll discuss it with your mother. I'm not sure what we're doing tomorrow." My level of restraint surprised me. I wanted to lecture the girl about this hurtful violation. She'd handled photos of my father. She'd had no right. But I reminded myself that she was just a kid.

Kam ran back in, hugging herself in her new coat. "I can't wait for it to snow!"

I took the pair of snow boots from the bag. "These should fit, too."

She tried them on and did a little dance. I loved watching her joy, despite my concern about what she'd just done in the staircase. Then she seemed to forget her new clothes. She went to the table and grabbed a small stack of photos. "Mom, you have to see these. They're your dad!"

This felt like someone had opened the door before I was clothed. Elyse should not be part of this. "Okay, but right now we're getting ready to order dinner."

"We did it already." She shoved a photo at me. "Look!"

I couldn't do this in front of Elyse.

"Let me walk Elyse back to her—"

Kamryn looked at me. "Can't she stay for dinner?"

Elyse held up her hands to indicate she wouldn't ask. "Don't worry about it. Mom told me not to stay long. Maybe I'll see you tomorrow."

I felt guilty at not welcoming her, but I had to get my world under control. The fewer people, the better.

Elyse put on her coat and boots, and I told Ayden I'd walk her back to Shona's.

"Maybe I should?" he asked.

"No, she knows me, and it's not far. Shona might have some news for me. I'll be right back."

The slush was now ice. "Please be careful," I told Elyse. "I hope you're not taking another trip tomorrow."

"No, we'll be here. I heard your grandfather died."

I nodded. "Yes, he did."

"He was pretty crazy, always yelling out the window. Oh, sorry. Was that mean?"

"That can happen to older people, Elyse. They think they see someone who's not there."

"Oh, someone was there. A man. I saw my mom talking to him."

I stopped. "There was someone outside the house? When?"

"Yeah, ask my mom. And that old man would shout things."

"Like what?"

"They're here. Leave. Get away." She shrugged. "It was always about staying away."

That sounded rational to me, but I wondered what he meant. "Did you ask your mother about him?"

"She just said not to worry, but it seemed like she was."

"Elyse!" Shona came out and crossed the yard. She hugged her coat close. "I've been waiting for you. Supper's ready."

Elyse waved to me and ran to their house. Shona kept coming toward me.

I waited until we were close enough to talk. "What's happening with the arrangements? Bree hasn't told me anything."

"It's been taken care of. She's moving it up because of the weather. She hired a professional to handle it."

"Where's she now?"

Shona gestured with her head toward the Big House. "Inside."

"Shona, has someone been hanging around the house?"

She cocked her head. "Have you seen someone?"

I wasn't about to snitch on her daughter. "I understand that Judson's been yelling at someone on the property. I saw him do this, and my daughter heard it. What he said made no sense, but I've noticed people following me ever since I arrived. There's a guy named Richard Lehr. He claims to know Judson and Bree." Shona's eyes widened slightly. "He insists that Judson had something of his, and he wants it back. Have you heard of him? Bree knows him. And look at the way she's treating me, keeping me from seeing Judson, leaving me out of arrangements."

Shona pulled her coat tighter. "Ms. Duncan's private. She doesn't like having anyone here."

"But she called me."

"Mr. Hunter insisted. He kept asking if she'd called and she kept telling him she had. But she hadn't."

"Why not?"

She hesitated. "Have you spoken to Mr. Hillman yet? He has something for you."

"Shona, what's going on? I have the impression my aunt doesn't want me to see something that Judson wanted to show me."

"It's not for me to say, Dr. Hunter." She took a step back. "I need to see to Elyse."

"Okay. I'm sorry to make this awkward. I just need some answers."

"I understand. Ms. Duncan and Mr. Hunter, they…they didn't agree on things."

I narrowed my eyes. "But she's here taking care of him."

Shona glanced at the Big House. "He didn't want…didn't need that. I should get back. We hope to see Kamryn tomorrow. I expect you'll be busy." She gave a quick nod and walked back to her house.

That was weird. But she'd given me a clear message. Judson had not asked his daughter to care for him. Shona wasn't divulging secrets, but the attorney would. I looked at my watch. There might be a chance of seeing him today, especially considering Judson's death. I texted Ayden. *Going to the atty's office. BRB.* Then I headed to the garage. The fob was in my coat pocket. I had no purse or license, but the office was close. I just had to pray I wouldn't slide on the road and hit another car.

I drove slowly past Peter Hillman's office and saw a police car. I parked nearby, uncertain what to do. I watched for activity but saw nothing. Finally, I decided to walk over. I had business here. A cop exited just before I got to the door. He didn't notice me. I went into the building. Hillman's door stood open. I entered. A CSI person inside was dusting for prints. Hillman sat at his desk, his round face an ashen mask of distress. When he saw me, he rose and came over. I introduced myself, but he seemed to already know.

"Dr. Hunter, I'm so sorry I didn't return your call. I intended to." Hillman hustled me into the hallway. "There's some bad news. I'm afraid there's been a break-in. They went through my files and took some items."

"Judson's will?"

"No, no, I have a digital copy. Don't worry about that. But I don't have a copy of the note he wrote specifically for you. He insisted that it remain sealed until I could give it to you. When I heard he'd died, I took it from the safe and put it in the desk drawer. I was going to deliver it to you, myself, on my way home." He shook his head. "I'm so sorry. I'm afraid the letter's gone."

Chapter Thirty-Three

I must have looked dreadful when I returned. Ayden's eyes widened and Kamryn halted her passionate story mid-sentence. I waved off their concern. "It's icy out. You know how much I hate to be cold."

Ayden understands my code. I had things to say that Kamryn shouldn't hear. With wary eyes, he gave a quick nod.

I tapped the table. "Food here yet?"

"Soon." He removed the cork from the remainder of last night's wine and grabbed a clean glass for me. The label, *Secrets*, caught my eye. That one was truly appropriate. I hadn't anticipated its ominous warning when I'd purchased it. Now, secrecy dogged every step.

I turned to Kamryn. "Did you put those photos away?"

She shook her head. "I wanna show you some. I picked them out for you." She pointed toward the library.

"Let's go see." I gave Ayden a look that said I'd find a diversion for her.

In the library, Kamryn grabbed a pile of photos. The top one wasn't familiar, so I assumed they were from the envelope I hadn't yet opened. As I looked through them, I saw images of my father in various places. I fought to hide how my stomach clenched. Seeing Dad felt remote, like rejection.

"Look at this one," Kamryn said. "Is that me?" Dad held a small, dark-haired child. Both were laughing.

I nodded. I'd taken this one and shared it with Bree. "That's you."

"Can I have it?"

"I have a copy at home. We can't take these. They belong to someone."

Dad looked so vital in some. Had he ever imagined the dark turns his life would take? He seemed unaware in some shots taken from a distance outside that he was being photographed. Several were in the cemetery. There were a few of Bree as well, also walking. I'd suspected these photos were hers, but now I wasn't sure. It looked more like someone was following her.

I walked over and closed the door to the hidden staircase, pushing it to ensure it was firmly shut. I glanced at Kamryn. "Let's leave this alone for now, okay? It's steep and dark, and I don't want you to get hurt."

"Is it okay that we opened it?" Her worried expression told me she sensed something not quite right.

"I wish you'd ask me first. This isn't our home." Kam seemed confused, so I added, "Yes, these photos are our family, but we should get permission to look at them. There might be private things in these envelopes that their owner wants to protect."

"Elyse said it was okay to look at them."

"But they don't belong to her. She can't give you permission."

Kamryn shrugged.

I reached for a stack of photos clipped together.

"Not those," Kam said. "That's just trees and stuff. I picked out these." She thrust another photo at me. "This is the ghost place we saw yesterday, isn't it?"

The scene was dark, as if clouds muted the sun. Dad stood near a *Keep Out* sign attached to a thick yellow post like those that I'd seen at the Dead Line fence. He looked over his shoulder, frowning at the photographer. Next to him, turned away from the camera, was a slender form in a black hoodie. I stopped breathing. A white image was printed on the back of this hoodie that resembled a skull. The guy looked as tall as my dad, who was six feet. I looked for a date or description on the back of this photo but found nothing. My heart beat faster. Kip had said he'd met my father. That figure in the hoodie had Kip's build. Here, he and my father seemed like allies. Maybe they'd more than just "met."

"Are there others like this?" I asked. "With a guy in a black sweatshirt?"

Kamryn produced another one. My dad wasn't in it, but another guy was. Still, no faces. In another, it looked like the same guy was with a female, but it was too far away to show their identities. Who was taking these, and why? I had to talk to Kip.

"Mom?" Kamryn's voice brought me back to the library. "Ayden said dinner's here."

"Okay. Please go wash up. I'll help him set up."

Kam cocked her head as if she didn't know what I was asking, but she left the room. I waited for her to go up the steps before I packed the photos and hid them behind books. Then I took the photo that featured Dad and the slender guy with me to where Ayden had set out plates. My hand shook when I handed it to him. "Look at this."

Ayden took it. "Dacretown? I saw signs like that."

"I'm sure it is. That's my dad and maybe one of the Skeleton Crew. Put it in your room. I don't want Kam to know I took it. But let's see if we can figure out exactly where this sign is. If that's Kip, then my dad was here." I glanced toward the steps. "We'll discuss this after she's in bed, but here's the gist. I had a brief encounter with Kip. He's angry that I stirred things up about Marti, thinks it'll come back on him. He could be right. He said he'd met my father but didn't tell me when or how."

"Maybe he can explain the photo."

"I'd like to show it to him. If this is him or one of his crew, either he was sixteen in this photo, or my father was here during the period he's been missing. If it's the latter, here's my proof of life. Maybe this is what Lehr meant to show me. I don't know who took these photos, but it could've been Lehr. They were left here, so maybe he gave them to Bree. I could see her wanting photos like this. There are some of her as well."

"Let's go back tomorrow."

"Kip said, 'Don't call me. I'll call you.'"

"Not promising. But I can try. He doesn't know me."

"Yes. Or I can ask Bree."

"What about the attorney? Did Hillman tell you anything?"

"Oh, yeah. Someone broke in and stole several items, including something in an envelope from Judson for me. Whatever Judson wanted to tell or show me, it's gone now." I sat in a chair. "Had to be important for someone to risk arrest. I wish Judson had just said it when he saw me."

"That's why you looked so numb."

I nodded. "I was that close to discovering something that could've solved some of our mysteries."

Ayden snorted. "Only one person could be behind a theft like that."

I heard Kamryn's door open upstairs before I whispered, "I can think of three. Bree, yes, but also Richard Lehr and Rob Galloway. There's something Lehr wants that he thinks I can help him get, and Rob's a snoop with an overly keen fascination with my family. We don't know what his goals are, either."

"D'you tell your aunt?"

I shook my head. "I'm not sure what to say. Maybe she doesn't even know about the photos."

I picked up my phone and opened the text feature. I thought for a moment before I decided to just say it straight. *Theft at Hillman's office, including an envelope from Judson for me. Do you know what it is?*

If Bree had orchestrated the theft, she'd wonder if I suspected her. I was curious how she'd respond.

Kamryn entered the dining room. She'd brushed her dark hair and changed into a long-sleeved T-shirt that was so large she'd had to roll up the sleeves. It bore the image of Thoreau.

"Where'd you get that?" I asked.

"Elyse gave it to me."

"Ah." I made a mental note to ask Shona. Kam's attachment to Elyse worried me. She'd been led into things she wouldn't ordinarily do, but she also now had an interest in the work of someone she'd probably never have considered. There were pros and cons to this relationship. I just hoped the pros carried more weight.

I desperately wanted to go through the other photos, but that had to wait. I'd put them off limits to Kam. I also didn't want her asking questions I couldn't answer. It was bad enough I didn't know much about Judson and Bree. I also knew little of my father's history. It had never made much sense to me why he'd stepped so abruptly out of his life. Something had happened here in Concord. He'd *been* here. But when?

I kept my phone on the seat of the chair next to me. If Bree texted back, I wanted to know at once. Ayden and I engaged Kamryn in a conversation about her lessons that day. She was absorbing history through the land around her. It pleased me to see her so eager to know more. Her rendition of the battle at Lexington was filled with engaging stories. Despite the swirl of concerns the day's events had raised, I focused on her. So did Ayden. It felt good to put aside everything else.

"Did you tell your father about your tutor?" I asked.

"He said he wishes he were here to see it with me."

In a way, I wished Wayne were here too. He's in law enforcement. He might make some inroads for me with the local cops. But he'd also try to control what I did—one reason we'd split.

When dinner was over, I urged Ayden and Kam to go look at weather forecasts while I cleaned up. Ayden's a weather addict and Kam loves learning from him. They were both eager for snow. I'd be a Debbie Downer in that conversation.

I checked the phone but had no message. Aunt Bree might have turned in early after her difficult day. She was grieving. I had to be patient. I wanted to send another text or just call her, but I forced myself to wait. I hadn't liked hearing that Bree had called me only because Judson insisted, but it explained her avoidant behavior. She didn't want me here. Still, we were heading for a clash over the will. I was the executor, and Judson *had* wanted me here.

I joined Kamryn and Ayden in the library. They had a local weather channel up on the TV screen that showed blue, pink, purple, and green bands for areas likely to see different types of precipitation. The brunette weather woman in a tight orange dress pointed out four different models from which we could choose. I focused on the most conservative one.

"Snow tomorrow, Mom!" Kam shouted. "I can use my new coat and boots."

I sat down. "How much?"

"Five inches, maybe," Ayden said. "It's still unclear. Most heavy in the evening."

"So, we could get out before it gets bad."

"If your business wraps up tomorrow, I'd say yes."

"I guess it could, if the wake is tomorrow and the attorney can show me my part. I'll have to come back to complete it, but I'd rather make another trip than get snowed in. Let's see if we can get a late flight."

"No, Mom," Kam protested. "I wanna stay here."

"I have to get you back to school."

"I'm learning stuff. This is better than school."

I'd already told Wayne that I'd extended our stay so he could alert her teachers. I considered sending her home with Ayden, but I needed him here. I could take her and come back alone. I just needed some information from Bree about the arrangements for Judson.

My text alert sounded. I looked at my phone. Bree had responded. *The note was an apology. Let's talk tomorrow.*

I showed it to Ayden. He frowned, looked at me, and shook his head. We both knew she was lying. I just didn't know why.

Chapter Thirty-Four

Once Kamryn was in bed, we brought up Natra on the TV screen. I needed my info manager. She has a knack for streamlining our cases so we can brainstorm effectively. Mika snoozed next to her on the couch.

I sat down. "First, let's go over what's happened here. I know you got some from Ayden, but I need to get it mentally organized. I've asked Ayden to investigate my family, because they might be associated in some way with the Dunbury incidents. As you know, Judson has passed, so I'll have to show up for some things, like a viewing. I'll be watching Bree. We think she might have orchestrated a break-in at Judson's attorney's office, which resulted in the theft of a private message to me from Judson."

Natra gasped. "No!"

"Bree says it was an apology, but Judson was alert enough yesterday to have said that to my face. He was also functional when he gave the note to the attorney, so he could've called me if he was feeling end-of-life remorse. We believe Bree's lying. But the break-in could also have been Lehr, who's been watching me and who warned me away from Galloway. He seems to have an association with Bree, which she denies. And we've discovered that Kip Hawkins' father and my father might both have been in this Gray Hollow Group. Ayden located the Skeleton Crew's hangout, the Crypt, as you know, and I've talked briefly with Kip. He says he's met my father."

Natra sat up. "That's great!"

"Not great. He gave me no details, and he's upset that I've directed cop attention to Marti's death. And he has other reasons to hate my family.

Unless he contacts me or I can find a way to approach him again, he's a closed door for now. But Ayden followed one of the crew to the hospital, where an attempt was made this morning on Owen Kringle's life. So, we think Owen might be a crew member. The fact that someone apparently wants him dead suggests it wasn't a suicide attempt. We haven't yet made a firm link among these kids, but I doubt there's any suicide cluster here."

Ayden leaned in to get Natra's attention. "I sent you an email with a list of things I need, if you can dig up the info."

"I got it," she said. "I've been trying to learn more about the Gray Hollow Group, but they're heavily insulated. I'd guess there's money behind it. Someone knows how to hide a business operation. They seem to have roots in Boston, and possibly overseas. It's no ordinary conservancy group with public records. Maybe not a conservancy at all."

I folded my arms. "Look, I want both of you to pull no punches with what you learn. Something's going on that involves Judson and Bree, and maybe even my ancestors. I know only about Merrick Hunter, my great-great-grandfather who worked briefly with William James in Boston before settling in Concord. That was spooky stuff, but I don't know of him doing anything else like that. He had a son, Harrison, who was Judson's father, but I know little about him. I believe he died in his thirties."

Natra held up a hand, palm out. "I thought of the ASPR, since you'd told me about Merrick before. I dug up an archive where one of the members described a rift between the established group and a newcomer from Scotland. Didn't name him."

"A rift?"

"Philosophical differences, apparently. The group focused on observation and testing of mediums, but this Scotsman wanted to take it further. He hoped to create conditions in which intellectually gifted people could be trained toward developing super-minds that could penetrate other dimensions. It was the age of mentalism, after all."

I sat up. "The Institute of Mentalistics! Has to be related."

"It could be. That business wants to develop the abandoned asylum property that borders Dacretown."

"And Briana is involved in that, as is Lehr, and the developers tried to purchase Dacretown as well. But you're saying this all dates back before them."

Ayden held up a finger. "Two of our victims were high achievers. Maybe they knew something about this Institute, something they shouldn't."

I considered this. "And isn't that legend about the Dacretown relic related to enhancement? The Scotsman must be Merrick Hunter. I'll bet Rob Galloway knows this. He's kept track of my family. He was also doing an investigative exposé on some scam about an experiment with gifted kids. That's what led to his disgrace and resignation. I shouldn't have stopped that interview."

"Oh, about him," Natra said. "I've located his address. He lives close to Concord, in a house much nicer than he should be able to afford from his current gigs. It's not from family inheritance, either. He's come into a lot of money, somehow. That's as far as I can legally get."

I nodded. "I need to get him back in my circle." I looked at Ayden. "Anything else?"

"We need more about Dacretown."

"That's a hard one," Natra said. "I even have Joe digging around on the dark web. I've got land transfer records dating back as far as they go, but almost every transfer since 1903 is shielded by some veil, usually corporate. The last recorded legal transfer was over fifty years ago, and it went to a Boston-based group that has since dissolved or evolved. I'm working on tracing the remnants."

"Great. So, someone or some organization owns it, and their records might not even be digitized."

"That seems likely, but I'll keep looking."

I thought of something. "Wait! When did the Gray Hollow Group officially register itself? Do you have a year?"

"It goes back a ways, but its history has gaps. Like it was started, then restarted. The most recent one has been in existence about three decades."

Ayden focused on me. "Boss?"

"I don't know what it means, except that my family is part of it. Maybe they founded it." I looked at Natra. "Let's probe the lore, whatever you can find. I need to know more about the group that protects that property. Sometimes things show up between the lines."

"What I've found, you already know," said Natra. "Some Scottish brothers arrived there with an item their father stole, a relic of some kind. They founded a community that suffered nasty setbacks before it was all abandoned. Same for another community that tried to settle there, so the place seemed cursed. That's how the Dead Line got its name. One account says the brothers buried the relic somewhere there—"

"Wait!" I considered this. "Buried? Someone said there's been digging in Dacretown. Maybe they're looking for it. But it's too much land to dig randomly, so they must have an idea of the right place. And Lehr said Judson has something that belongs to him. Maybe these people believe the lore. They want the prize, whatever it is."

"Bet your dad knows," Ayden said.

I narrowed my eyes. "Why?"

"The Gray Hollow Group's protecting *something* there, right? They don't care about a bunch of old buildings, and it's not like they're using the place for some high-minded purpose or for tourism."

"He's right, Annie," Natra chimed in. "Its location makes it valuable, but only if it can be used. That's why your aunt's making a grab for it. That's a lot of acreage close to Boston to be sitting vacant."

"Okay, I get it. And for us, it seems like all roads run through that place. And we have a photo of my father there with a kid in a skull hoodie. Since it's in a stash of photos in this house, I think the photographer could be Bree, or even Lehr. I need to find Galloway, see what he knows. Maybe Lehr as well."

Ayden held up his right pointer finger. "Not without me."

"Ayden, I'll be fine. We have to split up the work."

"Copy, boss."

I turned back to Natra on the screen. "We need to work fast because that weather front's coming in. Sounds like it's raining there. I can hear it."

"Yes, and it's cold. This system's already traveling up the coast. It's in southern Virginia, with winds picking up."

"We're watching it," Ayden said. "Could move off the coast."

"Maybe, but I suggest getting some supplies. Power outages are common up there."

"Not a bad idea," I said. "So, what's going on with the weather deaths?"

Natra changed out the chart on her screen for a different one. "Believe it or not, we've had some tips on our chat. I ran your podcast episode featuring an interview with JoLynn on forensic meteorology and weather-related murders. Some of these tips are intriguing."

"Like we've hooked a starfish?"

"Not that lucky, but maybe someone who knows him. Too soon to say. JoLynn's picking up some files. We think we have four potential cases, dating back a few years. Two happened on the same day in different areas, so if they're related, it's gotta be organized. More than one killer. We've got a line symbol drawn on a post near one incident that has five points, so Joe's searching that case for digital footprints."

"What could this even mean?" I asked. "Any ideas?"

"In the lore, a starfish symbolizes the ability to regenerate itself. It's an immortality symbol. Also, their eyes are at the tip of each arm, and they see only light and dark. Some have more than five arms, even up to forty, which suggests an organization that radiates in many directions from a center."

"Do the victims have anything in common?"

"Working on that. We need access to their digital records, which is tough, especially if they're linked to dark web activity."

Ayden tapped his fingers on the table top. "What about the tipsters? Any way to connect with them?"

"One was helpful. Didn't want to reveal himself but said he knew a guy with a starfish tattoo who created video games. He's working with Joe. A few tips directed us to deaths that had investigative errors. We always get those, but I'll follow up, Annie. I'm making my charts."

I nodded. "Good. Any tip could unexpectedly pay off, even if some lead us down rabbit holes. Has JoLynn seen those cases?"

"She's in New York right now tracking something down."

Ayden perked up. "She is?"

"Went up today. She—"

My text alert chimed. I thought it might be Bree again. It wasn't. The text was from an unknown number. I read it, looked at Ayden, and showed him what it said. *Kip Hawkins arrested.*

Chapter Thirty-Five

Ayden paced while I tried to think of a plan. It was late. I was annoyed. There wasn't much we could do besides be ready to act once things opened in the morning. That would be Ayden's task. He thinks best on his feet.

I tried texting back to get more details, but the person didn't respond. Natra looked up the number. It appeared unattached to a name or address. "Must be a burner."

"This is just weird," I said. "The items I found aren't sufficient for an arrest, not even if Kip's boot print is the right size. There's been no time to process anything for DNA."

"Or they don't need it," Ayden said. "Remember, he figured he'd be a suspect. There might be something we don't know about."

"Will you go see him at the jail?" Natra asked.

I took a slow breath. "We need to be careful. What if this is all part of the orchestrated aftermath of Judson's death? If Bree's his heir, she now controls a lot more than she did before, including people. Kip told me there's corruption, including Dunbury's police chief. I just hope Kip has the means to get a good lawyer."

Ayden stopped as if he'd just thought of something. He bent down and sorted through my files. He pulled one out. "We should look at this other kid, Ralph Steiner."

I frowned. "How's that related? We've already decided there's no cluster."

"Don't know, but something about it's been bugging me. Marti and Owen are linked to Kip and his club, but is this kid an outlier? Or another member?

We haven't looked at him closely. We need to figure out what's common."

To Natra, I said, "I sent you the file the cops gave me. Did you notice anything?"

"Just a sec." She brought up a chart drawn with red, green, and blue lines. Each color represented one of the victims. "Ralph was a year older than Marti. The cops collected cellphone records, social media posts, and some journal entries. Worked as an aide in a hospital. He jumped or fell from a volcanic bluff. Blunt force trauma. They decided it was likely a suicide based on dark themes in his poetry."

"Yes," I said, "near the asylum property, right?"

Ayden stared at the screen. "Weren't there death scene photos?"

"Two were in the file."

In moments, we were looking at the body from atop the two-hundred-foot bluff, splayed out face-up and drenched from a recent storm. He wore jeans, a T-shirt, and a light jacket. The second photo was a close-up of the head, the skull fractured by hitting a rocky surface on the ground.

"Go back to the first one," I said. I waited for Ayden's response. He studied it. "The autopsy said he jumped rather than fell due to how far out he landed, but does that look like a position he'd land in if he jumped?"

I glanced at the screen and back at him. "What're you thinking?"

Ayden gestured toward the photo. "Natra, can you turn the photo to a vertical angle?"

She did so.

He folded his arms. I sat up straight. No one spoke until I said, "That's some coincidence." The death pose, with arms stretching away from the body, resembled the five-point starfish pattern we'd been looking at in the other cases. This decedent had been posed. "Do we have his cellphone records?"

Natra turned away to look through the paperwork. Mika raised her head as if she sensed a change in the air. She's always ready to work. Natra held up a paper. "Just times and numbers. We have a call on the day his parents said he left the house."

Ayden turned to me. "Like two others who got texts and went out in bad weather before they died."

I heard the click-click of keys while Natra typed. "I've got the weather for that area for that date. In the report, they said only that the rocks were slick from rain." She looked up. "But it was a lot of rain. Three inches in a day, with wind and flooding."

Ayden breathed out. "Who goes out in a storm like that?"

"Can you get Joe on the line?" I asked. "We need him."

While we waited, Ayden looked at me. "You thinking what I'm thinking?"

"Probably. We might've had a starfish right under our noses, camouflaged in a cluster that turns out to be no cluster at all. Without the context from the others, we wouldn't have seen it."

"What's next, boss?"

"Time to pivot. I need to talk to Kip, see if Steiner was part of his group… but how do I get to him?" I snapped my fingers. "Jesse James, his bodyguard. He's gotta be upset by the arrest. Maybe I can convince him I can help."

"He had a gun?"

"Yes, so I'll need to be cautious. Problem is, I don't know his real name." I thought for a moment. "Galloway will. I'll ask him."

Joe came on the screen. We rarely see him on a video chat, but it's always a pleasure. He has the kind of softened masculinity that casting directors look for in TV cops they want for heroes. He'd been a detective before moving on to cyber security, and he misses the heat of an investigation. That's good for us because he gets invested in our cases. He's saved us more than once with his research and his knowledge of shady online practices. He and Ayden work together on inventions that benefit us, though they flirt with legal gray areas. I don't ask questions. In our most recent case, Joe had used a darknet device to assist with an identification and tracking. It worked, and fortunately, no one in law enforcement had called on us to show our hand.

"Hey, Joe," I said. "Are you up to speed on our investigation?"

"Pretty much. I've been digging around. I didn't find tracks online for the two victims we have cellphone records for."

"Well, now we seem to have another one. Maybe it'll offer leads."

"Got it, and I have a connection with someone who works for a large search engine. He could query searches in a specific location, but that's kinda dicey if you think this could end up in court."

"It could," I said. "That's likely. Let's avoid anything a defense attorney could challenge."

"I have an idea about what could be happening, if you want to hear it."

I blinked. "You do?"

"A network?" Ayden asked. "That's what we think."

"Sort of, but not like people working together. It's more like strangers all doing the same thing in an organized way, maybe working toward a reward."

Ayden glanced at me, then at the screen. "Like a challenge? Eating Tide pods and all that?"

Joe nodded. "Yeah, sounds dumb, but this has the marks of one."

"But that stuff's innocuous," Natra said. "Some are dangerous, like igniting yourself or getting high on Benadryl, but no challenge incites murder."

"None yet. Internet influencers are always pushing the envelope, moving toward extremes. And this seems based in the dark web, where we see the most repulsive human proclivities."

"Let's not forget the choking game," I said. "Kids were urged to choke each other till one passed out. Nearly two-dozen kids died doing that."

Joe put up his hands. "Can't prove it yet, and I don't know who launched it, because there'd have to be a gamemaster. But the behavior patterns you've shown me do suggest it."

I nodded. "Now that you say that, I see it too. And we've had some suicide games, like the Blue Whale Challenge."

"What's that?" Ayden asked.

"It was supposedly a game that appeared on social media platforms in Russia in 2017, named after whales that purposely beach themselves to die. Over the course of fifty days, players were to engage in behavior each day that grew increasingly more dangerous. They had to put themselves in harmful positions, like listen to high volumes of music that could break their eardrums, or do something that fractured their bones, or ingest something toxic. The final task was to commit suicide in a public setting. They'd make videos of themselves doing these things or get someone else to record them. The payoff was to accumulate followers. Obviously, unstable people got involved."

"Did anyone die?"

"Yes, in several countries, especially when triggered by media reports about the challenge, but there turned out to be less actual contagion than reported. In fact, no such game existed, despite a guy saying he'd started it and even going to prison for it. He said he was cleaning up the earth or something like that. But the idea hit the chat boards, and it swelled into something that some kids tried to follow." I took a sip of wine before I asked Joe, "Are you telling us that someone has created a challenge to go out and kill people?"

"Possibly, Annie. I'll keep digging, but I found a game scenario that uses weather to camouflage crimes. It's a short step from there to creating a murder challenge in a similar format just to see if anyone will do it. The challenge might be to play it out and report in. If so, there will be an influencer at the core."

"What's the starfish, then?" Natra asked. "That seems to be part of it."

"That could be the badge. That's what suggested to me that players are working toward something in the game. They're all connected to a common idea or goal. They're contributors."

I held up my hand. "Sorry. I need to be clear. You're saying that there's a dark web-based challenge that dares people to exploit a weather event that lets them stage a murder as an accident. A hit-man challenge."

Joe nodded. "Pretty much, Annie."

"I can see it as a video game, but why would anyone actually do it?"

"There's gotta be a payoff," Ayden said. "Something big and worth the risk. Like, who wants to make a million bucks? A scenario like that would account for the cellphone contacts right before the person died. They're luring their victim out. The killers don't know each other, so no one's connecting the incidents."

"And those texts were spoofs or hacks, or from burner phones, so probably untraceable," Joe added. "I'm just throwing out an idea, Annie, but so far it explains what's going on."

I shook my head. "It's bizarre, but people do some sick things. We've seen that in these other games. And we might have one of these incidents right here."

Joe rubbed his chin. "It's possible that players who succeed without getting caught would do it again, especially if a second murder advanced them in the game, like to the next tier. I can see how someone who's fantasized about murder might think it's an opportunity."

I crossed my arms. "This gamemaster's a psychopath. How could we possibly identify him? And who would issue such a challenge? It's gotta be risky for that person too. The more people you engage, the more likely you'll attract a leaker."

"Can I share my screen?" Joe asked.

Natra made a maneuver until we saw Joe's computer screen. He'd created a visual for us. It looked like a game board in the form of a starfish, with a center that radiated outward.

Joe pointed at the center. "We put the person or group that created the Starfish Challenge in the center." He ran his finger over an arm. "Each of your events is on an arm, separate from the others but connected to the core. And we don't know how many arms there are or how many starfish. It might even have started in another country, like the Blue Whale Challenge."

Ayden nodded. I was having a harder time with this notion.

"I have some ideas about tracking down the instigator," Joe said.

I cocked my head. "Such as?"

"Covert operations."

"Legal?"

"Fine line, Annie."

"I don't want you, or us, getting into—"

Bam! Bam! Bam!

Ayden and I both jumped. Someone had rapped on the front door.

Chapter Thirty-Six

Ayden looked at me. "It's late. Who could that be?"

"You got me." To Joe and Natra, I said, "Excuse us. Ayden, come with me."

At the door, I switched on the outside light. Through a peephole, I saw a young man dressed in what looked like a uniform. I shook my head. "I don't know who it is."

Ayden gestured for me to stand aside while he opened it. The young man offered up an envelope the size of a UPS Express packet. "Delivery," he said. "Sorry for the lateness. Just need a signature."

I stepped into view. "Delivery from whom?"

"Attorney," he said. "Kathleen Gardiner to Dr. Ann Hunter." I saw his white van at the curb, still running. Dark letters on the side spelled out *Quik Courier*. I signed for the envelope, and he walked away. In the shadow of a large tree, I spotted a dark Lexus SUV parked across the street. I figured it was one of Lehr's spies. I stood long enough to show I was aware of them before I stepped inside and closed the door. Ayden slid the bolt.

The envelope showed the Concord address for Kathleen Gardiner, Esq. Mystified, I took it into the library and waved it at my team. "From some attorney. It's been a day full of mysteries." I ripped off the tab and opened it. A sealed 8x11 brown envelope was inside. I looked at Ayden and pulled it out. Only my name was written on it. I opened it. Inside was a letter on legal letterhead stationery addressed to me and another sealed packet. I read the brief note out loud. "Mr. Judson Hunter employed this office to ensure that you receive the enclosed package upon news of his death. He asked that you keep this document safe, pending further instruction. Our office has a copy on file. Please contact us after receipt."

"What is it?" Natra asked.

"I don't know. Maybe it's Judson's explanation of why I'm his executor. But I've never heard of this attorney."

Just then, Kamryn came into the room. She wore her new coat over her pajamas. "What's going on?" she asked. "I heard someone at the door."

I set the envelope down and went to her. I hugged her, and she leaned into me. She'd been scared about intruders, and I wanted to reassure her. "Nothing's going on. We're just getting some legal documents. We have to prepare for tomorrow."

She looked up at me as if to check for deception. Then she saw Joe on the screen. He was her digital forensics mentor. She smiled and waved. "Hi, Joe!"

"Hi, Kamryn."

I turned her around. "Let's go upstairs." To the others, I said, "I'll be right back."

Kamryn waved at Natra on the screen. Mika barked, which made her giggle. All good. That would help to settle her. I went with her upstairs and tucked her back into bed.

"Everything's fine," I told her. "You know your great-grandfather died today, and now we'll have to do some things to honor him. People will come to the door with messages, maybe with other things. Are you okay with that?"

Kamryn nodded.

"Good. I'll be in meetings with attorneys tomorrow, and we'll get this wrapped up so we can go home."

Kamryn touched my face. "Are you sad?"

"No, Kam, I'm not. He lived a long life."

She frowned. "Will we have to move here?"

"Absolutely not. Aunt Bree will inherit his house. We're here to pay our respects, that's all. Please don't give it any thought. I need to complete some business, and then we go back to normal."

"Before the snow?" Kamryn looked pouty.

"Probably not."

She smiled.

"Now go back to sleep. It's late."

Kamryn pulled up the covers. "Okay, Mom."

I noticed a book on Thoreau on her nightstand before I turned out the light.

"Don't close the door," Kam said.

I returned to the group. Ayden's expression told me he was bursting with curiosity. "It's probably the letter that was stolen," he said. "Maybe he gave it to two attorneys to be sure you'd get it. Didn't trust his daughter, did he?"

"We don't know what happened at Hillman's office, or if Bree was involved."

"Annie," Natra said. "The suspense is killing us. What's in the envelope?"

"Okay, okay." I could hear my heart beating fast. I was nervous. The idea that Judson didn't trust Bree had also occurred to me. Maybe he hadn't said anything when he saw me in his room because she'd been there. Like there was something he wanted me to know that he was hiding from her.

I took a breath. Ayden handed me his pocket knife. When I gripped the envelope for leverage, I felt the hard outline of a key. I slit the seal. The key fell out. Ayden picked it up. The envelope also contained several folded pages of a document on legal-size paper. I paged through it and saw Judson's distinct signature at the end. Then I read the first paragraph. I blinked and read it again. I turned to the last page, which was a copy of an old surveyor's map.

I shook my head. "I don't believe this."

"What?" Ayden asked. "What is it?"

"It's a property transfer." I looked at Joe and Natra on the screen. "I think I just inherited a curse."

Chapter Thirty-Seven

That night, I couldn't sleep. My heart raced. Kam was in my bed again, deep asleep, but I remained awake as I tried to understand what had happened. I'd risen several times to reread the deed and study the map, as if I'd find an escape clause I'd missed. I kept thinking it was all a dream—a bad one. But it always looked the same. It was the strongest transfer the state offered, a warranty deed. The acreage was guaranteed free from encumbrances. A note from the attorney of record, Kathleen Gardiner, said she'd assist to get it properly registered. All fees were paid, including legal fees. The property was a gift. The key would open a lock on the northern access gate. Gardiner awaited my call. Cryptically, she urged me to "be discreet."

"There's your *mortmain*," Natra had said, "the dead hand. Your grandfather's posthumous control."

Ayden had given this a twist. "So, hex marks the spot."

"Glad I'm here and not there," Joe had added, "in case it's contagious."

None of this was amusing to me. If I accepted this gift, creepy cursed Dacretown, the negative vortex, was mine. That was enough to cause nightmares.

I scrutinized the map. Rather than straight lines for the boundary around the eight-hundred-acre plot, it had an irregular pattern, jutting up on the north side into more of a point. People had been murdered there or gone mad or killed themselves. And my family had owned it, maybe as far back as Merrick Hunter. Maybe he'd moved to the area for that reason. He'd been part of the spook hunters' society, so he might've been drawn to a reputedly cursed place. Maybe he'd heard about the relic. Could be he'd come to see if the lore was true. Something about the property had seemed worth purchasing. Thus, it had passed down to Judson, and for some reason he didn't want to give it to Bree. Seemingly, my father had been a member of the protection crew. Bree had made a failed grab for it. Now, she'd failed to inherit it.

Seemed like Dacretown came with a load of issues.

During my 3 a.m. stroll, I looked up *mortmain*, the term Natra had used. It meant more than just a decedent's property control. It was a metaphor, too, for an oppressive influence from the past. The dead hand gripping us. Indeed, it was. And now it was *my* problem.

Whoever had broken into Hillman's office must have believed that Judson had placed the deed there. Clearly, Judson had been wary. But why would he entrust it to me at all? I hardly counted as a worthy descendant. I hadn't been part of any of this. And what was I supposed to do with it? There was no chance I was going to caretake a moldy ghost town.

I'd discussed this unexpected transaction with my team, but we didn't know if anything we surmised was true. We'd wondered what was so important about this eerie place that required this cloak-and-dagger approach. My father clearly had known but had revealed nothing to me. Even my mother couldn't have known, or she'd have told me. The Dacretown deed had to be what Lehr wanted. He probably believed my father had it. And, certainly, Galloway would be intrigued, based on what he'd learned about the Gray Hollow Group. And that Skeleton Crew, with their Crypt on the Dead Line, they knew something too.

Before going to bed, I'd confirmed with Ayden that I wanted him to pursue the investigation of my family. "Maybe we'll get some answers about this place."

"We should go there tomorrow," Ayden had said. "Walk around, see what's still there."

"First, I should talk to this attorney. She might know how this all happened. It goes back to Merrick, it must. Why did he come here, specifically? What did he know? I need you to find out."

"No matter what?"

"No matter what."

I didn't say what we were both likely thinking: Dad's departure could be related to Dacretown and to the murder of Kip's father. Maybe Judson had given it to me to protect Bree from repercussions. That possibility left a sour taste.

I'd also asked Joe to work with Natra and JoLynn—carefully—on the starfish cases. With the startling interruption, I'd forgotten to ask him about his suggestion for our investigation, but I knew Natra would follow through. I was tempted to call Wayne to come and collect Kamryn, but the approaching storm nixed that notion. He hadn't liked our extended trip, but he'd understood my need to be here another day. Kam would be pleased, especially at the idea that she and Elyse could play in the snow.

At 5 a.m., I went downstairs for coffee. The lights were on. I encountered Ayden in the kitchen. He wore his coat. I gave him a quizzical look. "Planning to flee before the curse gets you?"

"Not a chance, boss. Bring it!"

"So then...?"

"Picking up JoLynn from the airport."

"JoLynn?"

"She launched the starfish case for us, and she wants to come. Her dime. She grabbed an early flight from New York. She's a forensic meteorologist, after all, and with the death here possibly related we could use another investigator. You still have that suite, right?"

"Ah, yes, that's fine. She can stay there. She'll like it." I peered at him. "You didn't sleep much, did you?"

"Neither did you."

"Be careful about driving, especially if that storm rolls in."

"Copy."

"Shall I take your overnight kit to the inn?"

Ayden looked away.

"I know you're in a relationship. At least you'd have it, if you decide to stay there. If you don't, then you can bring it back."

He nodded. "Thanks, boss."

Just before Ayden opened the door, I said, "Wait." I handed him the key fob I'd been using. "Take the Range Rover. I just gassed up. I'll use the Tahoe."

He looked surprised. "You sure?"

"Take it. She'll be impressed."

Ayden blushed slightly before he thanked me. "Just so you know, I'll be in Boston this morning. Got some stuff to look up in an archive. Not sure how long it will take."

I knew he meant "stuff" about Merrick. It made my empty stomach churn. "Okay. Keep in touch, and I'll let you know what I learn from Galloway. He's first on my list, after the attorney."

"Copy that."

When Ayden left, I looked outside. Some snow had fallen, but the air looked clear. I didn't realize I'd been tense until I breathed out in relief. I had a packed day ahead, not the least of which was to learn what Bree would be setting up. Shona had said she'd moved it up, but I had no details. Judson was already a ghost to me, penetrating my life in a way I'd never wanted. Maybe the best move would be to accept his "gift" and then hand it over to Bree. She'd be happy, I'd be unburdened, we'd all win. Except the *dead hand*.

I pulled up the weather report. We'd get snow. An unseasonable cold front chugged along from the Midwest toward us while a rainy system came at us from the south. A low-pressure area had developed off the coast down south, and wind speeds were increasing. Winter storm warnings had been issued from Virginia to Maine. Snow had already accumulated in Maryland and Pennsylvania. I felt cornered.

Next, I reread the article that had gotten Rob Galloway in hot water. I now believed his exposé centered on people in my family. He'd written about a file full of information about people supporting a program that trained rising young stars in advanced cognitive development. He described the Institute of Mentalistics as the program's location, identifying several pending government contracts. That was Bree's organization, and Rob was now in Concord, apparently awaiting her next move. Rob implied that the program was a sham operation. She had to be livid. But why hadn't she sued him? She'd had every right. That remained a mystery.

Now, I had a better sense of how Rob crossed paths with my family. Lehr had yelled at me about meeting with him, and Lehr had been involved with the Institute. They'd tried to buy Dacretown, and that process seemed linked to Gregory Hawkins' death and my father's disappearance. Lehr had even alluded to it in a threatening manner. I now thought Rob had known before we met that I was Lang Hunter's daughter. Then there was his untethered prosperity. Maybe someone was paying him to keep digging, or he was blackmailing people from the alleged list.

I grabbed the envelope of photos to look at the landscape depictions. I believed they were of Dacretown, my unwelcome acquisition. Some showed just trees, which meant nothing to me. A few were close-ups of large holes, confirming the rumors of digging. Stone walls and overgrown building foundations completed the set. If Bree had shot these, she was likely looking for development areas.

The map showed me the north gate relative to roads that would take me there. I saw what looked like main roads that cut through the property and counted five entry points. I suspected there were 'keep out' signs posted at all of them. It looked like there might be a large building in one area, perhaps a secret development already in process—that modern building in the photos. I'd have to check that out. I considered hiring a drone service to give me aerial photos, but that, too, would have to wait until the storm had passed. Ayden was right. I should go look at the place.

My text tone sounded. I picked up my phone to read it.

Hawthorne Suite. 9?

Galloway. Perfect.

Chapter Thirty-Eight

Bree wanted to expedite Judson's wake ahead of the storm. It would run for several hours in his mansion, going into the afternoon. It would be more of a viewing, I learned, where mourners could come and go than a structured fête of his life. Bree was offering a private luncheon to some business associates, and the public could come in the afternoon. Shona invited me on Bree's behalf to a private "purvey," or afternoon tea. That typically happened after a Scottish funeral, but Bree wanted to ensure that visitors could get out before the storm. Judson was to be cremated, and his ashes interred in a vault, so there would be no graveside ritual. Bree seemed in a hurry to get this over with.

I didn't know much about Judson, but one thing I recalled: he had a deep fear of fire. He'd never let us light the fireplaces in his house. I didn't think his final wishes included cremation. But once you're dead, you lose control over such things.

The arrangements gave me time to get things done. I told Natra my plan, then got Kamryn over to Shona's, which freed me to meet Rob. I could also visit Kathleen Gardiner, the attorney. She had a satellite office that put me on the road to Dacretown. I'd be engaged with Judson's *mortmain* while others communed with his corpse. I'd be back in time to have a last look at him.

I assumed that Bree didn't know I'd received the deed. I felt secretly powerful. I controlled an area that drew everyone's focus. They all knew more about it than I did, but they'd have to get past me to complete their ambitions. I was the gatekeeper. Maybe I'd soon meet a Gray Hollow guardian or two.

I arrived at the inn a few minutes before nine. Rob was outside the Hawthorne Suite door with two lidded paper coffee cups. He held one toward me. "I suspect you're a fan of a good latte. Has chocolate sprinkles."

I accepted it, impressed again by his professional appearance. Slightly more casual in a sportscoat and heavier shoes, he still wore a tie—and his charming smile. I now had more information about his fixation on the secrets of the wealthy and powerful. He might suspect I'd looked him up and learned about his past, but I'd play it like I'd had no reason to do so.

Rob cocked his head. "Condolences this time?"

I waved my hand. "I had no deep connection to Judson."

"Fair enough."

I was bursting with questions, but Rob had initiated this meeting, so I opened the suite and placed myself in a listening mode.

He went to the same chair as before and sat down. He wasted no time on chitchat. "Heard there was a burglary at Judson's attorney's office."

"I can't be a source, Rob. You'll need to call your cop friends."

"Thought you'd say that. And they did tell me one thing. If you're looking for Kip Hawkins, he's been arrested."

I decided to pretend ignorance, but his statement eliminated him as the mystery texter. "For what?"

"For being implicated in Marti Fielding's death."

I squinted. "They think he killed her?"

"More like assisted her."

"Assisted? As in assisted suicide?"

"Pretty much, yeah."

So, Blackburn was going for a lesser charge but still serious for Kip. "I've heard of kids doing that, but do the cops have reason to believe that's actually true?"

Rob lifted his chin. "Why wouldn't they?"

I had to be careful. He was hunting down info as much as I was. "I heard something about agendas. You told me people were expecting to benefit from the new development. Maybe Kip's just in the way."

Rob placed his coffee cup on the table. He looked so directly at me I thought he was going to blurt out, "So, who owns Dacretown now?" He didn't. Instead, he said, "Yes, it could be a set-up, possibly a way to thwart you from snooping any further while they also remove a hindrance to their development. To my mind, it's no coincidence that they arrested Kip once Judson was dead."

I couldn't hide my surprise. "Why?"

"I think Kip knows something that could hurt people. His father and grandfather were associated with the Hunter family, and both were the worse for it."

"Do you mean Matthew's affair with Briana?"

"That's how it started. The rift had a significantly negative impact on the work they were doing."

"When did they actually discover it?"

"Not when she got pregnant. It was a few years later. She gave the story that a classmate had knocked her up. I think Gregory's the one who discovered the truth and told Lang." As Rob talked, he watched me. I knew he was looking for a revealing reaction.

"I wonder if it was before or after I lived here. I remember Briana being married then." I thought about this. "Or separated. Hmmm. Maybe that's when things soured, and my dad left Concord. But you're saying that the Hawkins and Hunters were aligned for years. Must've been hard to dissolve their various interests."

"I don't think they did."

"Meaning?"

"The Gray Hollow Group continued. Your father—and Kip's—were supposedly in it. I think Kip knows what they were really doing. Maybe the Skeleton Crew is the new generation. They keep an eye on the Dead Line, and they've been in Dacretown."

I nearly said I'd seen Kip there, but quickly pivoted. "Does Kip have an attorney?"

"I'm sure he does. His cousin's married to one. But he'll need bail money." Rob waited.

"If that's your way of trying to find out if I'm the surprise heir to Judson's fortune, I assure you he's never been generous with me." I wanted to say, *but I've heard that you have money.* I didn't. Instead, I decided to hold that card and show another. "You know, a man named Richard Lehr approached me, rather aggressively. He seemed to think my father had something that belonged to him." I saw a flash of annoyance on Rob's face. "You know this guy?"

"He's a troublemaker. He was in the group too."

I sat back. "In the Gray Hollow Group?"

"Yes. I have a theory…I probably shouldn't say…"

"I think he's dangerous."

Rob's expression shifted too fast for me to read, but I sensed he'd changed what he'd been about to say. "I think you're right. Some believe he was… well…that Lehr knows that Gregory Hawkins didn't die by accident."

Silence hung between us. Then I asked, "You think he orchestrated it? Or even killed him?"

"Like I said, I don't really know, so I won't say. I don't want to falsely accuse someone."

I wondered if he meant Dad. "Did Lehr have something on my father? Was there some kind of deal?"

Rob snorted. "There's always some kind of deal, but that group's been tough to penetrate. Their secrecy is well guarded."

"Do you know how many members it has?"

"From what I can tell, Dr. Hunter, it's something *your* family formed."

"No. It goes back further than my father."

Rob raised an eyebrow. "You've done some research. So have I. Your family's been here for several generations. There used to be a file that listed names of people financially involved in their operations."

We'd arrived. I tried not to react. "Used to be?"

"Apparently, the file was discovered and exposed. It had names of influential people who'd made contributions to some clandestine activities that were likely both harmful and illegal."

"What activities?"

"Training programs that used unorthodox methods. They were exclusive. For child prodigies. Wealthy people signed up their kids, who got screened for intellectual and mental fitness. If they made the cut—which most didn't—they got the training."

"And then what? Where do they run these programs? Where are the graduates now?"

"You got me."

"Really? That's all you discovered? What happened to the file?"

"Conveniently lost or destroyed by law enforcement. Seems it contained some high placed officials' names. Lots of journalists have tried to track it down, me included, but no one's figured out who's seen it or how it got lost."

"How do you even know this?"

"I used to have connections. I nearly got killed for knowing things. So, I work on low-level stuff now."

"And you think Gray Hollow Group members were named in the file?"

"I think they *made* the file. Do you know the group's original purpose?"

I shook my head.

"It was formed to explore the Dacretown property. They weren't guardians. More like looters. They were looking for something."

"Did they find it?"

"Apparently not, because the group then became protectors to prevent anyone else from exploring it. Pirate versus pirate, so to speak."

I frowned. "My father wasn't a pirate."

Rob gave me a look like I wasn't getting it. "Then maybe he was just the sacrificial lamb."

I felt as if we both knew something neither wanted to say. I took a sip of coffee before I said, "I wouldn't put it past Judson to have done something like that to him."

Rob tapped his cup. "I would've laid odds that he'd target Briana for that, given how she tarnished the family name."

"Well, they must have made up, because she's been taking care of him." I knew better, but I said it anyway.

"Hmmm. Has she?"

I blinked. "What's that supposed to mean?" Then I realized. "You think she hastened his death? Like, poisoned him?"

"She had a lot to gain from it and a lot to be angry about, especially with you in the picture. She hasn't welcomed you, right?"

I was beginning to see this situation in a different light. Shona had hinted at some discord as well. In fact, Judson had seemed upset with Bree. And she was cremating his body, posthaste.

Rob leaned forward. "I assume she wasn't happy about being expelled."

"Expelled? From what?"

"The Gray Hollow Group."

His phone alert sounded. He read the text. He looked pleased. "There's been a development. Sorry, I need to move on this tip. Can we meet later? I'll be at the viewing."

"Why?"

"It's public and it's news. Besides, Judson would hate having me there. Maybe I'll bring Kip. They're about to release him. That should be enough to make the old man turn in his grave before he even gets there."

Chapter Thirty-Nine

I entered the office of Kathleen Gardiner in an agitated state. Kip was free. Someone had posted his bail. I wanted to go find him. Maybe he'd refuse to see the person who'd inadvertently sent cops his way, but I thought I could persuade him.

Dad, Bree, Gregory, and Lehr. It was beginning to come clear. I believed Merrick had come to this place to find the fabled relic and attain whatever powers it conveyed. As a member of the ASPR, he was primed for the paranormal. Somehow, he'd had the means to purchase the Dacretown property so he could freely explore. Apparently, he failed to find what he was looking for, but maybe his mission had motivated successive generations—such as Bree's Institute for Mentalistics.

As Dacretown was passed down, the Hunters and Hawkinses formed the Gray Hollow Group to protect its secret. I couldn't see how Lehr fit in. He must have brought something the group needed. But then they'd splintered, with Bree expelled, Lang absent, and Gregory dead. As a Hunter, I should've been told about this legacy. Instead, the mission had gone into Hawkins' hands.

Or had it? I was about to complete forms that would give me control of the land.

Gardiner's young secretary, a red-haired college-age girl named Sara, ushered me into a small but comfortable room and offered a beverage. I declined.

"Ms. Gardiner will be with you soon."

Moments later, I heard the outside door open and close. I looked out the window and saw Sara drive off in a green Kia Rio. Then, a voice behind me got my attention.

"Dr. Hunter." A tall, slender woman who looked to be in her mid-thirties strode toward me and held out her hand. Her dark brown hair was perfectly cut in a long bob to brush her shoulders and frame her delicate face. "I'm Kathleen Gardiner. Please call me Kate. I'm sure you're wondering why I had that packet delivered so late last night."

I shook her hand. "Among other things."

"I apologize if it startled you. Let's go in my office."

She led me across the hall into a spacious room with floor-to-ceiling bookcases that were loaded with law books. I breathed in the comforting smell of leather covers. It reminded me of the home office of a lawyer I'd been seeing. I took a seat in a leather chair near the large oak desk. Ms. Gardiner had it all.

"I'm so sorry for your loss," Kate said.

I nodded my acknowledgment.

Kate picked up a large brown envelope with my name on it. "I have some things for you to sign so we can get this deed properly—"

I held up a hand. "Wait. I don't want this property. I didn't ask for it. Is there any way to refuse it?"

She looked confused. "Judson was quite firm about it going to you."

"He told you that?"

"Yes. Just last month."

"Why didn't he tell *me*?"

She hesitated. She knew. But she said, "I'm not sure."

I doubled down. "He has an attorney, Peter Hillman, who's handling his will and even my part as the executor, which also surprised me. Why did Judson come to you for this other transaction?"

Kate put down the envelope and clasped her hands. "Forgive me. I assumed you were aware of all this. I'm associated with Judson through the Hawkins family. I was Gregory's attorney. I'm married to Gregory's nephew. He runs our family's restoration business. He's worked on Judson's properties."

"And how does this relate to the Dacretown deed?"

"Judson thought his daughter, Briana Duncan, might try to bribe Hillman, so he entrusted the document meant for you to me. You were supposed to get a note that he gave to Hillman to come here to pick up the packet, but I heard there was a break-in yesterday." She shrugged. "Maybe there was, maybe there wasn't. My instructions were to get you the document. I figured I'd initiate the contact in case you never received Judson's note."

I squinted at her. "Was Judson healthy when he saw you?"

"Well, he was eighty-five and used a cane. He was frail, but he met me on his own power."

"And he didn't trust his daughter."

"That's my understanding."

"So, he's not trying to protect *her*. He's trying to protect the property."

"I believe so."

"What's so important about it? Why is it just sitting there, undeveloped? I've heard it's cursed."

Kate waved her hand. "Those are silly stories. Surely you don't believe them. The way I understand it, something valuable was buried there a long time ago, but no one knows exactly where."

"Why not just excavate the place?"

She cocked her head. "Have you seen it?"

"Just through the fence."

"Well, it's yours now. It's sizable acreage. I suggest you go out and have a look before this storm rolls in. There was a key in the packet I sent last night. It's to the lock on the gate off Gray Hollow Drive—"

"There's a Gray Hollow Drive?"

"Yes. It's just a lane, but you can find it. It's the northern access route to the property." Kate gave me more specific directions before she added, "It's better if you don't tell anyone where you're going. Some people at the viewing will be wondering about its status, including the attorney who doesn't have a certain document he probably expected. Briana will pressure him about it."

I crossed my arms. "What's all this secrecy?"

"Go look at it. Drive around. Then we'll talk."

I had a thought. "Did you bail out Kip?"

She blinked at me as if I'd just violated some invisible boundary between our families. Then she looked at her watch. "He'll be out soon if he's not already out. My father's a judge, and there's no evidence to support the charge. I understand that you're looking into these unfortunate deaths around Dunbury. I'm sure you'll find it's all just small-town concerns."

I'd just been handled. Nicely, but definitely handled. I rose. I had to find Kip. I sensed Kate wouldn't help. But who better to guide me around Dacretown? "I need to know more about this place before I make any formal declarations. The last thing I need is a fallow piece of land with bad juju."

"You should get this deed on the record. The paperwork's ready. Everything's paid."

"What's the rush?"

Kate glanced out the window before she said, "You have competition."

"I have the deed."

"I think you should let me get the paperwork properly filed."

"I'll tell you again, I don't want the burden of this property."

Kate picked up the packet. "Okay. Judson told me something to pass along to you if you resisted."

"What's that?"

"Dacretown's a gift from your father."

Chapter Forty

Tears kept blurring my vision as I tried to watch the road. The sky had darkened considerably since I'd left the guesthouse that morning. The purplish clouds looked ready to birth a significant snowfall, and wind gusts battered the Tahoe. Thoughts raced through my brain. How could this be a gift from my father when he'd never told me anything about the place? Never passed to me the Gray Hollow torch. Never left me a note about Judson's guardianship or his half-sister's aggression. And why would Judson give it to me? I didn't know what seeing the place would achieve, and Ayden would never forgive me for going without him, but I had to. Something about putting my feet on that ground, cursed or not, would bond me to Dad. Maybe I'd realize why he'd done this. The place had mattered to him. And something was *there*.

First, I wanted to find Kip. The Crypt was on the way. I drove to the spot where Ayden and I had surveilled the Skeleton Crew's hangout. To my surprise, the green Rio that Kate Gardiner's secretary had driven away was parked there. I drove past it to get a look. Two people were inside, apparently arguing. I turned and found a place to park where I could watch without being obvious.

The passenger side door opened. Kip Hawkins emerged. He leaned back in and yelled something, then slammed the door and stalked away in the direction of the Crypt. Sara got out and ran after him, shouting, "Kip! You're not supposed to go over there!"

He ignored her, so she ran past him, turned, and raised her hands to try to stop him. She caught sight of my parked SUV and froze. Kip turned in my direction. He raised his chin in a defiant way.

I got out, held up my hand, and said, "Wait!" A sudden gust of cold wind sucked the word from my mouth. Kip remained where he was. When I reached him, I saw him shivering. His sweatshirt and bare head and hands were no match for the frigid air.

"Come in my car," I said. "It's warm. I'm driving into Dacretown. I need a guide."

Sara shook her head. "He can't! He's s'posed to stay out—"

Kip turned on her. "Go back to work, Sara. She's got business here. She'll give me a ride."

"You shouldn't do this, Kip. It's trespassing. They're watching you."

"I'll take responsibility," I said. "It's my property."

Kip glanced at me, eyebrows raised. Then he said to Sara, "Go. I'll come by later. Tell Kate."

With a sour look, Sara returned to her car. She glanced at us once but got in and drove away.

Kip cocked his head. "So, you're the heir."

"Just of this deed."

He narrowed his eyes. "You know what's here?"

"I have some ideas, but you're gonna tell me what *you* know. I'm tired of all this secrecy."

He pointed toward the Tahoe. "Let's go."

In the car, I turned up the heat. Kip rubbed his hands together. "Nothing like a night on a hard, stinky bunk in the local clink. Thanks for that."

"Not exactly my fault."

"You gave Emmie the idea."

"I didn't name you."

He looked at me. "Aren't you scared to go into the Devil's Den with a killer?"

"I heard it was manslaughter." I glanced at him. "That about right?"

He turned away and gazed out the window. Then he pointed. "I'll show you a way in."

"I have a key to the Gray Hollow gate."

"That's the easiest one. They'll be watching it."

"Show me the way, then. And while we're driving, you can tell me how you know my father."

Kip frowned. "He never told you about us?"

"Us?"

"The Crew."

"No. Nor Dacretown, 'though I think he took me there when I was a kid. I didn't know what it was, but I remember some things."

"He knew my father, like I said. And my grandfather."

"Right. They were in this Gray Hollow Group, with some mission to guard a piece of property that has some kind of buried treasure."

Kip snorted. "Treasure?"

"That's what I heard."

"Better for you just to see it. And don't get out of the car."

"Kate told me—"

"Kate doesn't know."

"What're we heading into? Jurassic Park?"

"Just…don't. I'll show you when we get there."

He directed me down a narrow road, then onto a rutted dirt road that was partly stone and told me to stop. In front of us was a *Keep Out* sign on a thick yellow post. I stared at it. Then I looked at him. "You were here. With my father. I have a photo."

Kip's face paled.

"Who took it?" I asked.

He looked out the front.

"Kip."

"I told them about Marti. I shouldn't have said anything. Marti had it, just like they thought, but then it hurt her. She couldn't take it."

"Are you telling me she did kill herself? And you were there?"

"I was too late."

"So, you struggled with her?"

He scowled. "No." He opened the door and got out. I watched him go to the gate and fiddle with the lock. The guy was so evasive. If he didn't struggle with Marti, then who pulled off her earring? I had to get him to trust me. I heard a car drive up behind me. I checked in the rearview mirror. A cop car. I looked for Kip, to warn him, but he was gone.

I got out.

Chief Blackburn strode up to me. She looked annoyed. "Dr. Hunter. What are you doing here?"

"I came to check on my property."

"*Your* property? I don't think so. I've had word this place is going to the developers, 'long with those nasty nut houses. Good riddance to it all. We need something more positive around here. I was just checking the entry points, making sure they're all secure."

"On whose orders?"

"Not at liberty to say. And glad I ran into you. Now that we know Marti Fielding isn't part of any suicide cluster, like I said, we won't need your services. We can assure all the concerned parents that there's no taint effect, or whatever you called it. We'll take it from here. You'll get official notification."

I realized she hadn't seen Kip. "So, you have proof of a homicide?"

Her face went hard. "That's our concern, not yours."

"I still have business here." I dug in my pocket for Kate Gardiner's card. "Please call this attorney. I just left her office. She sent me here. She'll tell you I'm within my rights to enter this property."

"Got a key?"

"I do."

Blackburn glanced at the gate. "I think you're at the wrong entrance. This one doesn't take a key."

"I know how to get in."

The chief narrowed her eyes. She made a gesture that I should go ahead and show her.

I was on the spot. I walked over to the gate as if I owned the place and looked at the lock. It was a combination padlock on a hefty chain, still closed. I felt the chief watching me. She lifted her phone and started talking. Hoping Kip had unlocked it, I grabbed the lock and pulled. It opened. A common trick. I figured the Skeleton Crew rigged it to look locked so they could go in and out undetected. Relieved, I removed the chain.

Blackburn came over to me. She looked displeased. "It seems we have a conflict. Gardiner supports your claim, but another attorney says someone else has a deed. I can't let you go on the property till it's resolved. If you're not the rightful owner, you're about to trespass."

Chapter Forty-One

I called Kate. She confirmed what she'd told Blackburn.

"Well, she says another attorney—probably Hillman—is claiming someone else owns it."

"Oh, I was afraid of this."

"Of what?"

"A forged deed. They probably didn't know Judson had a backup plan. If I hadn't been proactive and sent you the deed, you'd never have known about it, and no one would think the forged deed was fake. That's why I wanted to get the paperwork done. Wish you'd—"

"So now what? Briana owns it?"

"Not legitimately, and she's probably assigned it to her businesses to obscure the trail."

I took a breath. A snowflake hit my face. I looked around. Others were falling. Just what I needed. "Look, fine. She can have it."

"No!" Kate's voice was so sharp it startled me. Then she softened. "Please come back. We'll get this done. Then we can contest whatever claim she might make. She'll back off once she knows what I received from Judson. You have the authentic deed, I promise you. I have a recording of him giving it to me."

"I can't understand how this land could be from my father since Judson thought he was dead and refused to help me find him. Judson would've known I'd be startled by all this. And now I can't even go in and look at the place."

"I'll see what I can do, Dr. Hunter. But you'd be in better legal standing if you'd get it recorded ASAP."

"I'll think about it." I ended the call and told Blackburn, "Don't worry. I'm leaving."

She went over to the lock and clicked it shut, twisting the combination dial. "Just so I can report that I found the lock secure."

I didn't want to abandon Kip, especially with him having no coat, but mentioning him risked getting him rearrested. I hoped he had resources. I could try sneaking back, but I figured Blackburn would post an officer here.

I backed out and drove away. When I thought I could pull over, I took a moment to look at the map that came with the deed. I needed another way in, an entry that cops wouldn't be watching. I saw the main roads from the five entry points. I also noticed a couple of thin lines that appeared to be old logging trails. I called Natra to have her look at the map she'd found of the area.

"I'm assuming Kip knows the place like the back of his hand," I said, "but I can't just leave him out there. Have you heard from Ayden or JoLynn?"

"Ayden sent me some reports from an archive. I haven't read them yet."

"Okay, he might still be in Boston. By the way, my gig with Dunbury was terminated. Since there was no suicide cluster, they don't need my services. But send them a bill."

"Will do. And that's good because we'll need you here. We think we found an early starfish murder, maybe the first one. Remember those tips we got from the chat? One paid off. The note directed us to an incident a few years ago, and it has similar markers."

I caught my breath. "Where?"

"Down near Hatteras. A drowning in the Pamlico Sound."

"That close to us? That seems bizarre."

"Thought so too. I'm driving down today to meet with the family, maybe get some records."

"A tipster gave you this?"

"Yes. And we can't contact them back. Whoever it is knows how to anonymize. Yet they gave clear details and seemed to know the victim."

"A secretive tipster. Even worse. Why do you think it might be ground zero?"

"Joe found something on a darknet site that corresponds to this one and makes it sound like the launch of a game. He's looking into a method that provides private access to hidden databases."

"What's the victim's name?"

"Lee Bandisi. Older guy, fifty-three."

I searched my memory. "Sounds familiar. Maybe I heard about it when I moved there."

"This happened before you moved in."

"That long ago? Does JoLynn know?"

"She does."

"Okay, we'll all gather later to pool our discoveries. Now I *really* want to get back home."

"We miss you. Just don't bring that curse with you."

I felt left out. They were all working on a serial case that I wanted to be part of, while I was merely entangled with my family demons. I didn't even have my suicide cluster case anymore. I had to get my business done here and go. Dacretown could be caught in a legal battle for some time.

I texted Ayden. *Find anything good?*

He didn't respond. That could mean his phone was off.

I texted JoLynn. *Are you two still in Boston?*

No response.

I checked on Kamryn. She sounded excited. She said they were making a New England-style lunch. "I'll save you some pudding!" I told her we'd be attending the wake this afternoon, and I'd come and get her.

"It's snowing, Mom! Did you see?"

"I did, yes."

"We're gonna play in it."

"Have fun."

I drove back to the Crypt, just in case. If Kip had a phone on him, he might've called someone to come get him. Still, I'd try to find someone here. I understood why he'd run. I hoped he didn't think I'd set him up.

Near the Crypt, I parked and walked over. It looked dark inside. I knocked.

No one answered. Where was Jesse James when I needed him? I walked around outside to look for tracks. I found only mine. It seemed that no one was there. I looked over at the Dead Line. I figured the logging road crossed it somewhere, but the snow was heavier now, and I didn't have footwear for traipsing around overgrown property. I came around a corner to return to the Tahoe when I saw a polished maroon G-Wagon parked next to it, motor running.

Richard Lehr got out.

Chapter Forty-Two

I realized he must have followed me, probably tracked me. The Tahoe had been parked unsecured at the guest house. Lehr could've put a device on it. If so, he knew I'd been to Gardiner's office and at the remote Dacretown gate. He might've spotted Galloway near where we'd met at the inn. I braced for another show of his wrath.

He stood waiting, as if my approach was his due. I took a breath and strode over.

To my surprise, he wasn't mad. He wore an I-told-you-so expression, but he merely said, "Consider me your guardian angel. Now you *really* need my help."

I stopped ten feet from him. "Why is that?"

"Because I know things you should learn before you get hurt. Have you gone in there yet?"

"No."

He gestured toward his imposing SUV. "Hop in. I'll give you a tour."

This seemed like the kind of thing the next victim in a horror movie would do. "The gates are all locked, and they won't let—"

"I know a way. And they won't stop me."

When I didn't move, Lehr said, "The proof you want's in there." He pointed toward Dacretown. "Don't you want to see it?"

This sounded like a trap. But he was getting to me. "What's the price?"

"Only what I was promised. As Lang Hunter's daughter, you represent his interests until he faces his responsibility."

"I don't know what you mean. I can't give you what—"

"Come with me. I'll show you. Then you can decide for yourself what I'm owed."

A deal that seems too good to be true could hide something bad. "Just tell me what—"

"A box. A particular box."

Not what I'd expected. I looked toward Dacretown. "If it's in there, why don't you just go get it? You know your way."

"It's not in there."

"Then how am I supposed to give it to you?"

He pointed. "Dacretown first."

"I need to get back to Concord before it—"

"This won't take long. Your rental will get you back. Tires are good."

I thought this comment was a veiled message: he'd been close enough to inspect them. My spine tingled. "The cops are watching."

Lehr patted the hood of his G-Wagon. "This'll take us where they can't go. You game?"

I weighed my options. Lehr seemed utterly confident, as if it was just a matter of time before I'd cave. He might be a narcissist with no sense of his limits, or he might really have something that would blow me away. I had a child here, which concerned me. I was taking a risk. I knew Ayden would take care of her should something happen to me, but I shouldn't even get into that position. Yet Lehr was promising proof of my father's continued existence, maybe a way to find him. I seemingly owned the property where this proof was located. I had every right to go there. Natra knew where I was.

"I'll follow you in my—"

"You'll wish you hadn't. You could get stuck out there."

He had an answer for everything. I felt cornered. I sensed he knew he had me where he wanted me. Plus, I'd abandoned Kip. I had to get back in there. I relented. I glanced back toward the Crypt, grabbed my phone from the Tahoe, locked the vehicle, and got into Lehr's G-Wagon.

"Seatbelt, please, Dr. Hunter. This will be rough."

He wasn't wrong. Lehr drove like he talked, blunt, aggressive, and with little regard for how jarring he was. He drove right up to the fence that marked the Dead Line, and I braced for him to barrel through it. But he stopped and said, "Wait here." He got out. That gave me an opportunity to text Natra and Ayden about where I was and what I was doing. *Heading into Dacretown. Off the grid.* I turned off my phone volume so their responses wouldn't register. I couldn't even be sure the texts would send from in here.

The fence appeared impenetrable, but Lehr moved a post and rolled the wire fencing like it was a cardboard façade. This guy was strong. I saw ruts that marked a pathway in. Someone used this route quite a lot. Probably him. While Lehr was busy, I scanned the G-Wagon's interior for ropes, a hit-kit, anything that would signal that I should get out and run. It was immaculate, which I'd have predicted from his controlling manner. The leather-wrapped steering wheel looked built for a racecar. There were buttons and dials and screens of all kinds—all the bells and whistles for a high-end all-terrain vehicle. I was dealing with someone well above my pay grade. But I saw nothing that set off alarms.

Lehr got back in and drove through, not bothering to stop and repair the opening. I almost told him I had a key, then realized I should keep my access to myself. Even if he knew my movements, he didn't know what Gardiner had told me.

Lehr stepped on the gas so hard I jerked back against my seat. It *sounded* like a racecar, purring then revving up when he pressed on the gas. I tried to spot landmarks I could use as breadcrumbs to find my way back should I decide to jump. The trees, thin and thick, blurred together. I noticed that a swath of red marked some trunks. Here and there, I spotted what looked like crumbling old buildings, but they sped by. I hung onto the support handle on the dashboard I'd used to climb in.

Lehr stared ahead and talked as if I weren't even there. "He's been in and out. Don't know his mental state yet. The thing picks and chooses. It watches!"

"Are you talking about my father?"

He hit a bump. I jerked forward.

"He's living here. I'll show you. But don't touch anything. They're crazy, they just lost it. Wasn't my fault. I didn't know."

"Who's crazy?"

Lehr zipped under a moss-covered stone arch. Snow hit the windshield and made it difficult to see. He put on the wipers. He seemed to know his way, but he still hit every hole in the road. I tried to keep balanced in the seat but couldn't anticipate his quick swerves. He went off the track and ran over fallen limbs and humps in the ground. In a couple spots, the lane smoothed out, but my relief was short-lived. I saw a path among the overgrown shrubs.

"Too bad you didn't listen to me," Lehr said. "You should've come here before Judson checked out." He swerved hard around something, and I hit the passenger side door.

I straightened up. "Why is that?"

"Could've told you things." He glanced at me. "Things about your father, your whole family. He knew it all. You could've confronted him. You'll never hear it from your aunt. They don't even know how it got to them. The thing infects you, then hides. Infect and protect."

I swallowed hard. "Infect?"

He nodded. "That's what it does." He glanced in my direction. "Sell this place to me. Be done with it. I'll give you a fair price. You don't want to get caught here. They don't understand it, but I do. Lang should've given it to me."

So, he hadn't forged the deed. That narrowed the suspects.

I gripped my seat. It seemed that Lehr himself was infected. He was jabbering like someone possessed. I realized what a mistake I'd made getting in this SUV. Some psychologist I was. I made a living observing and interpreting behavior, and still I'd gone with this lunatic into a place I knew nothing about.

I looked out the window to my right. On a dark day like this, the place was creepy. Trees were overgrown with ivy and other vines, and some were storm-ravaged. I spotted a broken stone wall, a set of stone stairs going up a hill, and the hollow window of a stone building that looked to date back more than a century, maybe two. Weeds grew thick and tall in places.

Lehr drove into a shallow ditch, throwing me forward before zipping up the other side.

As we came over a rise, I noticed a graffiti-stained two-story concrete building. I'd seen it before, in those photos in the packets. I suspected this was our destination.

Chapter Forty-Three

"So, what's this proof?" I asked.

"You have to see it."

The intensity in Lehr's eyes was all I needed to see. This guy was psychotic. Driven. Obsessed. I began to think that moving past the Dead Line had just exposed me to the curse. If I had an opportunity to jump out, I'd take it. I thought I could find my way back, though it had to be over a mile. I'd just follow the tracks we'd left.

Lehr drove up to the building and stopped. He turned off the motor. "Judson's father built this place," he said. "Years ago. You know about Harrison?"

"No. Not really."

"Crazy. Attacked his own son. They locked him up." He pointed. "This place here, it's the Proving Center." He drew a square. "It's the barrier, goes around like a moat. To protect it." He snorted.

I regarded the dingy walls and darkened windows. The storm-heavy sky made it look grim. "Proving Center?"

"The testing site, where they brought candidates. Guinea pigs. Care for a tour?"

Kip had warned me, *don't get out of the car*. Not to mention, I didn't want to go into a rundown old building with a crazy man. "I don't need one. Just tell me what you want to show me."

I *was* that idiot in a horror movie. I'd end up hanged and flayed in some monster's dungeon. I had to stay alert, not turn my back.

Lehr stiffened in his seat. I watched where he was looking and saw the flash of a figure in dark clothes sprint toward the building.

"That's him," Lehr said. "That's Lang."

No way. I knew that lanky form. Had to be Kip, but I wasn't about to tell Lehr that. I reached for the door handle.

"Wait!" Lehr opened a compartment near his seat and pulled out a gun. Looked like a Glock. He got out. I followed him, bracing against the harsh wind. I had nothing on me that could work as a weapon. I had to keep my eyes open for something inside.

Lehr went to the front door and tested the handle. It didn't budge. He went to the side where we'd seen the figure. I followed. He opened a side door. Lights were on. He gestured for me to go in before him.

My heart raced. I was tempted to run. Instead, I went in. It felt warmer inside, but I stayed near the door. Lehr came in and stood still. I looked down the hallway. From where we stood, as far as the light reached, I saw graffiti from floor to ceiling. Among scribblings that were difficult to read were skulls, bony hands, devil's faces, reddened eyes, and images of dripping blood. The work of kids. I wanted to take pictures of this but didn't dare.

Somewhere in the building, a door slammed.

Lehr raised his gun.

I looked for the door we'd come in.

He whispered something. I leaned closer to hear.

"It gets into the nerves...don't touch...in here. Amplifies perception... amazing at first. You see...vivid colors, textures. You feel great...like you're a god. Some can't take it...but they can't..."

Lehr strode down a hall. I wasn't sure what to do, so I followed him. If Kip were here, I had to warn him.

Another door slammed. I heard a shot from down the hall. I ducked and reached for a wall. Then I recoiled. *Don't touch.* Still bent over, I curled my fingers into my palm.

Lehr took off, yelling, "I've got you! I've got you now! Show yourself! Your daughter's here. I brought her. Show yourself!" He disappeared into the darkness. I heard his footsteps as he rounded a corner.

I stepped closer to the door until I heard another shot. It couldn't be Kip.

He'd just been picked up from his brief detention. He didn't have a gun when he fled from the spot where Blackburn approached me.

To my right, someone ran toward me. He saw me and pivoted. It was Jesse James. He ran right into Lehr, who grabbed him and slammed him against a wall.

"Stop!" I shouted. "He's okay. Don't hurt him."

The distraction was enough to give the kid leverage to kick Lehr hard. Lehr swore and let go. Jesse sprinted past me. "Run!" he shouted, then exited through the door. Lehr followed. I waited. No one came back.

I had the opportunity I was waiting for. There were doors all the way down this hallway. I could find a place to hide. I knew this would show Lehr he scared me, but if there was proof that my father was living here, I could find it myself.

I used the flashlight on my phone to light my way. There were sticks and leaves in the hallway but nothing else to stumble over. At the end, I opened a door. It led to a staircase going up. Rusted metal strips lay across the stairs and cold air blew into the stairwell from a broken window. I went up. Outside, I heard another shot.

I came out to a long hallway. Two, in fact, because I was at a corner. Both were dark but dim light from overhead windows helped. I had to choose which way to go. I looked for a light switch, then realized I shouldn't signal to Lehr where I'd gone. I heard a door slam downstairs. Lehr called my name. I had to hide.

Chapter Forty-Four

I held up my phone to find my way. The hallways were long but too dark to estimate. I saw twenty or so doors. Some were closed and locked, a few rooms had no doors or broken doors, and some doors stood open. I looked inside one for a hiding spot but saw nothing promising. With only two floors in this place, Lehr could find me easily. He yelled again. I considered going outside to run, but I'd leave tracks. I had to stay inside.

I entered another open room. It had some desks and broken chairs, and even a large cabinet. But no, Lehr would look there first. I stopped to listen. I heard steps just outside the door. Then, a whisper. "Follow me." It wasn't Lehr. I emerged and saw a slender, hooded figure trot down the hall away from me. He turned and beckoned. I flashed my light at him. Kip. He gestured to cut the light.

I followed him to the corner and turned down another hall full of doors just as I heard Lehr emerge on our floor where I'd come in.

Kip opened a door and pulled me inside. He closed and locked the door, raising a finger to his lips to shush me. He pointed toward a door across the room that looked like a closet, then motioned for me to go over to it, then lock it.

I shook my head. Too obvious.

He moved his finger emphatically toward it.

In the hall, Lehr yelled, "Why are you hiding, Hunter? There's no place to go. You won't get back without me! Come out, or I'll leave you here. You won't like being here alone."

I went to the closet door and turned to look back. Kip was gone.

The sound of a shot in the hallway made me open the door and slip into the closet. So much for not touching anything. It had a bolt lock that worked from this side. I turned it to lock myself in, then hunkered down in the dark.

Lehr yelled again, closer. I held my breath. If he figured out where I was, or just shot randomly through the wooden door, I was a goner. Heavy footsteps sounded nearby. I tried to make myself smaller.

The doorknob twisted. I leaned back in case he tried shooting the lock. The wall behind me gave way. I caught myself before falling, but I was sure he'd heard the noise.

Farther away, Kip yelled. I stayed still. The footsteps moved away. I used my phone flashlight to see this space. The closet had a fake wall. Someone had made a living space, cramped but large enough to move around. In the hidden cubicle, I saw a narrow cot with a crumpled sleeping bag and a pillow. On a table was a thick book, a lamp, and a laptop. My heart raced. Was Lehr right? Is this where Dad was staying?

But this wasn't proof.

I looked at the book. Neurobiology. Not what Dad would read, not that I'd ever seen. Under it was a set of papers bound with a clip. I grabbed a latex glove from my pocket and used my pocket knife to lift the pages. It contained a handwritten ledger that showed dates, formulas, initials, and what seemed to be shorthand. The last recorded date on one chart was from a decade ago. The handwriting didn't look like Dad's. Another list with ten items seemed more recent, but it was just initials and dates. A scribbled label, "Released," was the only context.

I opened the laptop. I couldn't get it to turn on. Maybe no one had lived here in a while. The place smelled stuffy. Under the cot I found a pair of muddy boots Dad's size, but this was too generic for proof. I saw no place to store clothing, no suitcase or dresser. This seemed to be nothing more than a sleeping space.

I wanted to believe I was close to finding Dad. That made me prone to seeing what I wanted to see, especially with Lehr's comments about proof. But I was mad at Dad too. He'd left without an explanation, putting me through hell. And he'd burdened me with this wretched place.

I heard an engine start up. I unlocked the closet door and ran into the hallway. No one was there, but I smelled the acrid scent of shots fired. I ran to the stairs and descended. The engine noise receded. I found a window to look out. Lehr's SUV was gone. He'd threatened to leave, and now he had. I looked at my phone. No one had answered me back. Then I realized I had no reception. The place was too remote.

I had to find Kip. Then I had to find a way to connect with Kamryn and my team.

Kip hadn't returned to the room with the cubical. I called for him. No answer. I ran down the hall to the corner. "Kip!" The echo made the place feel empty. I'd heard multiple shots. Had Lehr killed or wounded the Bone Heads? I realized that he could drive out, report it, and pin it on me.

I went outside. Lehr was truly gone. His tracks were still clear, but snow had begun to cover them. I took photos, just in case. I wouldn't have returned with him, but I didn't like being left behind. The whole place felt colder. I shouted again, but no one answered.

I walked deeper into the woods and found one set of footprints. It seemed clear that Kip, at least, knew this place and was probably faster than Lehr. And Lehr wasn't the only one shooting. Someone else had shot *at* him, probably Jesse James. The tracks ended where an SUV had been parked. That vehicle was gone too.

The warmth inside lured me back. I walked down each hallway, downstairs and up. I found no bodies. So, where was Kip? He knew I was here. He'd protected me. He wouldn't abandon me. Through a window, I spotted a large propane generator, which explained the heat and electricity. But why was it on? Who paid for that? What were they doing out here?

I peered into several rooms. Each had a stripped mattress, a bathroom, and a small kitchen. One looked recently used. Sheets and a blanket were on this bed. I spotted a girl's coat draped over a chair. I thought of Marti.

Even with my glove on, I used a rag to open the mini-refrigerator. It held a few transparent plastic containers, but the food in them looked dried out or rotted. Maybe a week or two old. I saw a few strands of long hair in the bathroom. Blond but too long and dark for Dad.

I had to make a plan. For all I knew, Lehr would return. I couldn't be here if he did. I could follow Lehr's track until I reached a spot that had reception and call for help.

I heard a noise. A vehicle outside. He was coming back. I listened, ready to return to my hiding place. But no. It wasn't Lehr. The engine sounded louder. I went to a window on the second floor. The snow had diminished to flurries. I saw a set of lights and backed away from the window. When I heard the vehicle stop out front, I peeked again.

Just below me was a light gray Jeep Wrangler coated in mud and missing part of the front bumper. A guy emerged, then reached in the back. He brought out a rifle. I gripped my arms. What now? Then the passenger door opened, and another guy got out. A slender one in a black hooded sweatshirt.

Kip. He'd come back.

He said something to the driver and pointed into the woods. The driver stayed where he was, seeming to keep watch, while Kip entered the building.

I strode back to the room where he'd left me. When he entered, I confronted him. "What's going on? Why did you run? Is this where my father's hiding?"

Kip ignored my questions. "We need to leave."

"There's some writing in here I want to grab." I pointed toward the closet.

"Did you touch it?"

"With this." I held up my gloved hand.

"Take it off!"

I did.

"Drop it! We have to go."

"But the papers—"

"No. It's not safe."

"He left."

"Not him." He pointed down. "This building…it's not safe."

Chapter Forty-Five

Kip had me take the front passenger seat while he climbed in back. It was an older Jeep with scratched and blurry vinyl side windows. Someone had smoked dope in here recently. A tear in the back let in cold air, 'though the heater ran on high. I realized the driver was the kid, Jesse James.

Kip gestured toward him. "You've met JJ. My brother."

JJ made a quick nod at me before he revved the Jeep and pulled onto a bumpy lane away from the building. The wipers scraped a dry windshield, but without them, there was no visibility.

I leaned toward him. "Jesse James, you said. What's your real name?"

"That's his real name," Kip said. "Jesse James Hawkins."

I turned toward him. "So, you're Frank?"

"Nope. That's our brother. I got an outlaw name no one knows. John Kinney. Billy the Kid shot him. S'all he's famous for. JJ got the cool name."

JJ snorted and glanced back at him.

"Well, whatever outlaw gang you two are in, can you please explain what's going on? What's that building for? Why's it dangerous?"

We hit a bump, which nearly sent me through the windshield. I grabbed the seat.

"Sorry," JJ said. "It's rough out here."

Kip leaned forward. "What about you tell *me* something? What're you doing with that crazy asshole? Thought you could read people. Can't you see he's nuts?"

I wasn't about to admit how right he was. "Richard Lehr? He said he'd take me to my father. The cops were blocking me, so I grabbed the opportunity."

Kip shook his head. "No one's out here."

"I saw beds and food and the place was heated. Someone's been in there."

"We go in and out. No one lives there."

"Why does Lehr think my father's here?"

"He's crazy. One day, he's gonna blow."

That I didn't doubt. "He thinks I owe him something. It's in a box. Any idea what?"

Kip narrowed his eyes. "He didn't say?"

"No. He said Judson could've told me, and apparently my father's the one who promised it to him."

Kip shrugged. "Wouldn't know."

JJ gave me a fierce look. "You really own this place?"

"Apparently."

"You kicking us off, then?"

"JJ." Kip's tone was a warning.

"Why?" I asked. "What d'you do on this property?"

"We're the caretakers. We rehabbed it. We've marked—"

Kip cut him off. "You gonna keep it?"

"I don't have a plan yet. You seem to think it's toxic, but no developer would touch it if that were true. Do you know something others don't?"

"Oh, they know. All of 'em. They don't want anyone else to know."

"Lehr said something about a Proving Center. There were candidates and some kind of bad results." I recalled the exposé Galloway was working on. "Is this about experiments with prodigies?"

JJ's face tightened. He glanced in the rearview at his brother. I looked at Kip.

"That's what happened to Marti, if you wanna know," he said. "They got to her. Your aunt. It's in those papers."

"Briana Duncan? Got to her? You think she killed Marti Fielding?"

"They bullied her. She was scared. She was hiding."

"So, we should go get those papers. She asked me to bring something like that to her."

Kip shook his head.

I persisted. "Was that Marti's coat in there? I thought the place was toxic."

Kips mouth tightened. "They did things out here. Trainings. Lehr was a trainer. He wasn't gonna show you anything. He wants you outta his way. Probably thought he could make it look like you snooped into something and had an accident. Those things happen out here. D'you tell 'im you own it?"

"No, but he might've seen me go to an attorney this morning." I leaned toward him. "*Your* attorney, actually. Kathleen Gardiner. She had the Dacretown deed."

"And that cop's in on it," Kip said. "She's paid off. She knows what's out here. She won't let you ruin everything."

JJ sat up straight. "Someone behind us!"

I looked back. It was a large SUV, coming fast, lights bouncing. "It's Lehr."

"Go, go!" Kip shouted. "Take the north route."

I grabbed my seat again as JJ sped up, bumping us hard over something underneath. Kip picked up the rifle and turned around.

"Do not shoot at him," I ordered. "You'll make it more dangerous."

Kip ignored me. "Get down. Keep outta the way." He steadied the rifle against the back seat and aimed through the rip in the vinyl.

I leaned down. Lehr had the superior vehicle. He'd catch up. He was also armed.

"Head to the main entrance," I told JJ. "The cops are there. It's the safest place for us."

"Not for me," said Kip.

"Can't trust 'em," JJ agreed. "Frank's ready. We head there."

I had to let them do their thing and pray we survived. JJ seemed to know how to maneuver this Jeep well enough to get us through what seemed to me impassible places. I just hoped we wouldn't get stuck. His smaller vehicle gave him an advantage, but Lehr was gaining. His SUV was made for the most rugged cross country.

JJ made a fast right and passed between two close-standing trees that jarred the Jeep as one tree bent the passenger side mirror. I flinched and pressed my arms together. Kip swore at him.

I looked back. Lehr's headlights receded. JJ's move had worked. The trees had thwarted him. He'd have to back up and go around, which bought us time. JJ took a left turn and sped so fast into a gully I nearly lost my lunch. I held my breath, but he seemed to find his way. Then he drove up onto flat ground. Lehr was nowhere to be seen. Kip laid down the rifle and picked up his phone. He called someone.

"We're close," he said to the person on the other end. "Cover us."

I checked my phone. It was nearly noon. I had multiple messages. I picked Ayden's first. As I typed a return text, Kip leaned over and put a hand on my phone. "Not yet. Turn it off."

"I just—"

"Off."

I complied.

When we neared the stone arch I'd seen on the way in, I knew we were near the Dead Line. We'd soon exit this property. As long as no one started shooting, I thought we'd make it out alive. We passed a thick tree, and JJ waved. A young man stepped out who looked about JJ's age. He took a position to watch the road behind us.

"*That's* Frank," Kip said.

JJ drove us to the Crypt and parked. He kept the motor running. I got out, stepping ankle deep into snow. Kip followed. He left the rifle behind.

I held up my phone. "Now? It's not like Lehr doesn't know about this place."

"He knows. Let's go inside."

Chapter Forty-Six

I glanced at the Tahoe. I wanted to get back to Concord, but Kip had answers I needed. He strode toward the Crypt while JJ pulled away. I surreptitiously turned on my phone so I could be located. Ayden was likely frantic over me going off the radar. To avoid pings, I silenced it. Then I followed Kip.

"Is your Skeleton Crew all your brothers?" I asked.

"Just the Bone Heads. You have to be a Hawkins to be a Bone Head."

"And you're the head Bone Head?"

"Maybe. My cousin was for a while, but he kinda stopped."

"What about Owen Kringle?"

Kip shot me a fierce look. "What about 'im?"

"He's a member, right?"

Kip turned away. He opened the Crypt's door and held it for me. When I went in, he bolt-locked it.

"The others aren't coming?" I asked.

"They'll keep watch. But the asshole won't do anything here. He knows we have surveillance and that we'll shoot."

Kip went to the galley kitchen and opened a cabinet. He grabbed a bottle of alcohol and a roll of paper towels, then gestured for me to come over. Mystified, I did. He soaked a towel, grabbed my right hand, and rubbed it.

I reacted to the strong odor and tried to pull away. "What're you doing?"

He held on until he finished. "Other hand, please."

I curled my left hand into a fist. *What are you doing?*

"Detox. Then I'll explain."

"I didn't touch anything."

"You probably did. Added protection won't hurt."

I hesitated, but he looked so intense I gave him my hand. When he was done with me, he wiped his own hands and also his face. He gave me a clean towel and suggested I wipe my face as well. "You should consider a shower as soon as you can."

"Am I contagious? Like to my daughter?"

"No. This is for you." Kip went to the refrigerator and took out a brown two-liter glass bottle. He poured some liquid into two shot glasses and gave one to me. He drank down the other one.

I sniffed it. "This smells like…I don't know…rotten leaves?"

"Just drink it. Fast. My dad figured out what works." He offered a half-smile. "My family's kind of the antidote to yours, 'cept for my grandfather."

I tossed it down. It burned my throat and left a nasty taste on my tongue. I coughed. Kip handed me a water bottle. I drank deeply before I said, "This is awful! Couldn't you put some cherry flavor in it? I think I just poisoned myself."

"Don't eat for an hour or two."

"Don't worry." I held up a hand. "I need to tell my daughter I'm okay. I'll just text her. Then I want to hear what's going on."

Kip shrugged. I took that as assent. I sent a quick message to Ayden and Natra: *I'm safe. Heading to Concord soon. Details later.* To Kamryn, I texted, *Be there shortly. Hope you're having fun in the snow.*

Kip went to a window and pulled aside a closed curtain. He moved to the front door, opened it, and looked out. "That's your Tahoe."

"Yes. I came here to tell someone you were out there without a coat. No one was here, but Lehr followed me. I got in his SUV right there." I pointed.

Kip walked across the room to open a door and check inside a darkened room. I saw enough to realize it was a bedroom.

"Someone live here?" I asked. "Like maybe my father?"

He turned and looked at me.

I crossed my arms. "I wish you'd just tell me! Dad left this place before you were born, so obviously he's been back. When was he here? How did you meet him? He never told me he went to Concord."

Kip went over to a sturdy wooden dining table and leaned against it, facing me. "Maybe he didn't want you to know what they were doing here. Wasn't something to be proud of. But he's been other places. So've I. In fact, I first met him in North Carolina."

It disturbed me to think some of this vexing mystery had spilled over into *my* house, even though at the time, it was Dad's. I had a hundred questions, but the main one burst through. "He's alive, isn't he?"

Kip rubbed his chin but remained silent.

I stepped toward him. "You're protecting him."

Kip gestured for me to sit.

"Tell me!"

"It's complicated."

I remained standing. "Is Dad alive? Everything I've seen and heard since I've been here says he is. He vanished from my life, and I want to find him no matter what he's done. You lost your father. You must understand. Have you *seen* him?"

Kip cocked his head and squinted at me. "How close are you with your aunt?"

"My aunt? She's barely spoken to me since I got here. Before that, I hadn't talked to her in several years."

"So, she hasn't told you why she wants what's out there…the danger zone?"

"Dacretown? No. I didn't know she wanted it till this morning." I stepped closer to get in his face. "Stop deflecting. Is my father, Lang Hunter, alive? I want an answer. I know you know. What if your dad was here and no one would tell you? *Is Dad alive?*"

In a voice so quiet I barely heard it, Kip said, "He is."

Chapter Forty-Seven

A chill raced through me. My knees buckled. I backed up and sat down hard. I shook like I'd stepped into ice water. I'd wanted an answer so desperately and now I wished I didn't know. The reality hit hard. I put my face in my hands.

All this time I'd been looking for him. Worried about him. Fighting with Judson over him. Making excuses for him. Frantic that he needed help. Lost without him. And now I realized. He'd decided to leave, to abandon us. Just like that, as if he had no daughter or granddaughter. As if we didn't matter.

My throat tightened with anger as I wept. Dad had let me grieve in deep anguish over him, believing he might be dead. He'd let me waste time searching for him in Scotland, France, and Ireland. In this moment, I hated him for what he'd put me through. No reason could adequately explain it. He had to know the impact on me.

I sensed Kip standing next to me. He touched my shoulder. I flinched and shook my head. Through sobs, I choked out, "Where?"

He handed me a tissue. "Concord."

I gasped and looked up. "*Concord?* Now? He's that close?"

Kip ran a hand through his hair.

I sat up, blew my nose, and wiped my face. "He came for Judson. Right?"

He shrugged.

"Why? He avoided the man most of his life. Why now?… Ah!…Judson *knew*. He lied to me too. He knew Dad was alive. That's who he yelled at to stay away. That's why he wouldn't help me find him."

Kip frowned.

"So, they conspired to foist this poisonous property off on me. Why? What am I supposed to do with it?"

Kip looked at the floor. I'd put him on the spot, but I didn't care. He could've told me this when I first met him before Judson died. Then I could've asked the old man myself. Kip flung his hands into the air. "It's all a mess! They thought they could contain it. They just made it worse. He hurts too! He doesn't want you to see him, to see what's happening to him. My dad had it too."

I couldn't grasp this. The room felt cold. "Like what? He's deformed?"

"In a way." He pointed to his head. "He gets manic, kind of crazy."

I stared at him. "What are you saying? Can't you just be clear? I don't care if you took some vow of secrecy." I stood up, hands on hips, and glared at him. "Spill it!"

Kip folded his arms, a protective gesture. "I don't know what to say, except that Dacretown is…just…*bad*. Like, radioactive. It infects people."

"The place?"

"The dirt. It's in the dirt, and in some of the trees."

I remembered trees with red marks. "The dirt? It kills you?"

Kip breathed out. "It would be better if it did."

I went over to the sink to grab a paper towel. I wet it and wiped my face. For good measure, I ran it over my hair.

"He's protecting you," Kip said.

I turned on him. "And he couldn't have just told me? Instead, he told *you*?"

"I'm…a guardian. The Skeleton Crew…we're the shields. Like the Gray Hollow Group. My dad—"

"My dad was in that group too. Why didn't he pass the mission to *me*?"

Kip took a step. His mouth formed a hard line. "We *took* the mission. *My* family. My dad was murdered. You weren't here. We are. And we want to prevent more…" He made a gesture of futility.

"Like Marti?"

Kip nodded. "And Owen, and others."

"So, Owen and Marti—they were candidates?"

Kip's eyes narrowed.

"Lehr told me. There was some program and a proving ground."

Kip nodded. "Owen was just too inquisitive. He confronted people. Marti was a candidate. There were half a dozen candidates I knew of, some of them in the program for years. Like an exclusive school for gifted kids. Marti wasn't my girlfriend—way too smart for me—but I was trying to get her out of it. We hid her out there since she was already infected, but she was threatened. She couldn't take it. She did kill herself. She was coerced into it."

"You saw her do this?"

He blinked. "I came...after."

"I don't think she did, Kip. Girls don't yank out their own earrings. I think she struggled with someone. She was out there in the cold without her coat or her car. She couldn't have walked, not even from that Dacretown building. Someone took her there. Who bullied her?"

His eyes widened as this sunk in. "She wouldn't tell me. She thought it would put me in danger. What happened to Owen scared her."

"And now someone's just tried killing Owen in the hospital."

"What?" He pushed his hair back. Discomfort. Hiding something still.

"He apparently knows something, and someone doesn't want him to tell. I'd guess the same was true for Marti. Don't let them hang this on you. The more you tell me, the easier it will be to help you. So, the issue with Dacretown is about contaminated dirt? Not about some stolen relic, like the lore has it?"

"It's that, too. That's how it started."

I crossed my arms. "You believe in this curse?"

"It's not a curse. It's...the necro-preservative."

"What? Necro...like a corpse stabilizer?"

"Exactly. It's a neurotoxin but they thought it was a neurotrophic enhancer. The brain gain, they called it. You think it's a good thing, even miraculous, so it draws you. Like those big white flowers that entice you to sniff them so they can drill into your brain and scramble your memory."

Lehr had muttered something similar. *You feel great...like you're a god.* I shook my head and sat down. "Start over, Kip. Pretend I know nothing.

Give me the nutshell version because I need to get to Concord soon."

"To see the stiff?"

"To get my daughter. So, let's have it. What's the brain gain?"

Chapter Forty-Eight

Kip leaned back against the table. "Started in Scotland, on the west coast, couple centuries ago. A great healer died. The clan sealed his body in a cave. After decades, they found it still fresh, so they formed an immortality cult around him. Then this guy, Henry Dacre, broke into the cave and stole the body and the dirt around it."

"The whole body?"

"Yes. He cut it into parts and packed them in boxes with the cave dirt. The big deal was the left hand, the one used for healing. Supposedly, it channeled spirits. The clan discovered the theft. They tortured Dacre, but he buttoned up, so they hanged him. His sons got scared. They brought the boxes here by ship. When they settled Dacretown, they sifted the dirt together with soil from the land and spread it around the property to get good crops. Like they thought the healer's contact with the dirt had transformed it into a magical substance. They didn't know about preservatives in the soil."

"So, the body was naturally mummified, like the bog bodies." I peered at Kip. "And the ritual seemed to work. Dacretown did have prosperity for a while, right?"

"For decades, apparently, and the place attracted more settlers. But that soil and the food they grew gradually twisted them. People started seeing creatures in the woods and hearing voices. Some turned violent or just wandered off. Even those who tried to move away ended up in bad shape. It was like OCD on steroids."

"I've never seen anything about the soil in the lore."

"Because back then, a curse made more sense. No one knew about neurotoxins. Your ancestor didn't."

"Merrick?"

"Right. He bought the abandoned land because he thought it held secrets about the afterlife. He discovered that some of the parts had been dug up and sold to an oddities museum. Merrick bought what he could find."

"Does anyone still have these parts?"

"Judson used the tissues from them for the experiments. Pretty much used them up, so they excavated to find the rest. They found a cache, but the boxes had crumbled, so the parts were mostly just bone.

"Left hand too?"

"Not that. No one would've dissected that. But by then, my dad was finding problems among people exposed to the preservative. He discovered it was a neurotoxin."

"How?"

"He went to the cave."

"In Scotland?"

"Yes. Then he took Lang." Kip gestured toward me. "And that was the worst thing they could've done."

"Why?"

"It got them. It took a while. It's slow. Takes years because it works in stages. At first, they experienced euphoria and mental clarity. They thought they'd been endowed with some sixth sense, some clairvoyant gift. They thought Merrick was right. It energized them. They designed and invented things, like your Dad's app."

I nodded. "I remember that. Dad was so passionate about his work. But I didn't know anything about a sixth sense."

"Really? Because he said he tested you. You don't remember? We were all tested to see if we were candidates for the program."

I closed my eyes. The memory was vague, but I did recall it. Dad had tried several times to get me to do some automatic writing. I'd been abysmal at it.

"I wasn't eligible," Kip continued. "Not smart enough. Even expensive boarding schools couldn't make me the savant they wanted. That's what saved me." He gestured around the room. "I restore things. Stonework.

Carpentry. Nothing that inspired my dad's associates. They'd gotten this weird notion that they had to find prodigies so they could hone the most discerning vision that had ever existed."

I snorted. "Why?"

"That started with Merrick. He thought a highly attuned person could locate the missing parts. He wanted the healing hand. He persuaded his son to help, I think, but when that guy tried to kill the whole family, Merrick withdrew. Nothing much happened for years, decades even."

"Wait. That was Harrison. He was locked up."

"Right, yeah. So, there was a pause. Judson grew up and inherited Merrick's house. He found Merrick's writings and boxes that contained the relics. He restarted it all. He called it the Perfect Perceiver Project. My grandfather, Matthew, was part of that. He was a decade younger than Judson, so he looked up to him."

"That was the Gray Hollow Group," I said.

"The first one, yes. Matthew was a geological surveyor. He went into Dacretown and located the original town square. He tested the soil. Harrison had started a building in that spot, and Judson finished it. They figured the most fertile soil was in that area. They grew things there. Then they looked for candidates for their training program. They thought the stuff in the soil could be cultivated to enhance giftedness. They mixed it with things that made it even worse."

"But Judson wasn't infected."

"He managed his part mostly from an office. My grandfather was on the property. It got to him. He died a depressed alcoholic."

"I was on the property as a kid."

"Maybe not enough to be affected. Your dad didn't get it as bad as my dad because he left. He also didn't ingest things like the stuff they gave the candidates. My grandfather and father lived on the property for extended periods."

"That Matthew…he was involved with my aunt."

"Yes. And they had a child. A daughter. And they subjected her to this program."

"No, no, Matthew was kicked out of the group when the affair was discovered."

"He was. But Briana kept the girl. She turned out to be the kind of kid they were looking for. The group focused on this girl."

"Wait." I leaned forward. "Do you mean Maisie?"

"Yeah."

"She was a year younger than me. She was smart but nasty. I thought she left." I stared at him. "You know where she is?"

Kip rubbed his face and looked at the floor.

"Oh, no. Did they harm her, like...?"

"No."

"Did *she* do something?"

"She's locked up."

"Why?"

"Tried to kill people. Got involved with a guy in the program named Seren, a candidate. He started out well, like, really promising. Their star, my dad would say. Helped them with biological research. But then he went sour. Not just hyper but also paranoid. He thought they were stealing his work. He persuaded Maisie to help him push everyone out so he could take over and do it *his* way. She set fire to the building—the one you were in—and three staff members were critically burned. Judson paid some psychiatrists to get her committed rather than sent through the courts."

"When did this happen?"

"Years ago. She was an adult, though. I don't know much about her, not even her current name, because they legally changed it. I tried finding her once. Couldn't."

"What happened to Seren?"

"He denied any involvement and left. Don't know where he went. But other savants who'd shown promise started to flounder too. The Gray Hollow Group wondered if they'd misjudged the brain gain. My dad had studied affective neuroscience. Know what that is?"

"How the brain processes emotions."

"Right. His area was about reward, so alertness, anticipation, stuff like that. I studied it, too, to try to understand what happened. But he'd already guessed, based on the shift he'd seen in Seren and Maisie and even in himself." Kip squinted. "Dad created some genetically encoded sensors to map out the neuromodulator activity and dissect what was happening. The stuff poisons the brain, but you don't know it's happening."

"Anosognosia," I said. "You're crazy but don't know it."

"Like Richard Lehr. Didn't you notice how jumpy he is?"

"Yes." I shrugged. "I figured he was just that way."

"He wasn't always. He had it together. He was part of the Gray Hollow Group. He's your family, too, by the way. Some kind of cousin to your dad. He worked with Briana. But then he took the injections."

I leaned forward. "Injections?"

"Yeah. They thought the process was taking too long, so they distilled the magic. Instant giftedness. Your dad thought they were making a mistake. By then, he'd been to the cave."

"He was digging in Dacretown when I lived here."

"Looking for the left hand, still missing. He wanted it for his own experiments. Briana wanted it, too, later, when my dad told her it could heal the damage to her daughter."

"She's too smart to think that."

"Not the supernatural part. It's the cells. My dad thought the way the preservative interacted with the cells would show them how to reverse it. He cared about Maisie too. She was, you know…his half-sister."

I stopped to consider this. "That's why Bree wants Dacretown so badly. But how can she possibly find it? That hand's probably disintegrated by now."

Kip went across the room to look out the window again.

"Wait," I said. "Where's this cave?" Suddenly, it hit me. "Is it near an area called Morvern?"

Kip turned around. The look on his face confirmed it. In a flash, I realized that Shona, from Morvern, had come to the Hunter household for a reason. Maybe she'd also befriended me for a reason. I could hardly breathe. I had to get back.

"I need to go," I said. "Come with me. I'll get you back here, but I must leave *now*."

He looked confused. "Why?"

"Just come. You're in this, too, and I'm not leaving you here alone. Anyone who knows this stuff is vulnerable. Tell your brothers to get off the property and go home. Let's just keep everyone safe."

Kip retrieved a black leather jacket. I looked outside for any sign that Lehr was close. Falling snow prevented me from seeing very far. That made me uneasy. We went out. Kip locked up. A loud car horn startled me. Kip started to unlock the door to let us back in when the horn made three quick taps before a shout, "Annie!"

Chapter Forty-Nine

yden came toward us.

I ran to him and beckoned to the Range Rover he'd just parked. "Let's go. We need to move. You drive. I'll get the Tahoe later." I gestured toward Kip. "This is Kip Hawkins."

We got into the Range Rover, Kip in the back seat. It felt pleasantly warm on heated seats.

Ayden looked grim as he pulled out. I knew he was upset with me.

"I have a lot to tell you," I said, hoping this might lessen his ire.

He glanced at me. "Me too. A *lot*."

"Where's JoLynn?"

"Medical examiner. She made an appointment, and I dropped her there before I got your message and came looking for you. Why was your phone off?"

"No reception in Dacretown. I didn't know that going in, but I texted as soon as I could."

"You didn't—"

"She was protecting me and my brothers," Kip said. I appreciated his attempt to help. Ayden glanced at him in the mirror.

To Kip, I said, "Ayden's my PI. He's been helping me figure this out."

At a stop sign, the SUV slid. My heart raced.

"Roads are icy," Ayden said. "We'll take it slow."

Something rolled against my foot. I reached down and felt a paper bag covering something round and hard.

"For you," Ayden said.

I picked it up and slid the paper bag off a bottle of wine. I snorted at the label. *Troublemaker.* "Forewarning?"

"Yes."

I leaned forward as if I could move the car with mental force. "I need to get Kamryn." He looked at me. I could tell he understood. He pressed on the gas.

I told Ayden the gist of Kip's narrative about the cave and Dacretown and what his father had learned. Kip filled in gaps. Then I turned to Kip. "When was the photo taken of you and Dad at that *Keep Out* sign where we tried to enter?"

He shrugged. "A year and a half, maybe two years ago."

"Two years ago?" Ayden echoed. "Then—"

"Yes, my dad's alive. He's in Concord."

Ayden's eyes widened. "You saw him?"

"Not yet. Kip knows him." I looked at Kip again. "Do you know this woman, Shona Teagan, Judson's housekeeper?"

"She took that photo. But I haven't talked to her in a while."

Ayden glanced at me. He knew Kamryn was with Shona.

Kip continued. "She knew my dad. He met her there. I think they had a fling. She's the one who showed him the cave. Anyway, when she heard he'd died, she came to help us figure out what happened."

"Is she infected too?"

"No. My dad discovered the clan's biological shield—the ones who lived around the cave. They had some kind of immunity. She can handle the stuff without it damaging her. At least, I think so. My dad made something that blocks it, so my brothers and I aren't affected either. I know how to make it. That's what I gave you, that stuff you didn't like."

"Shona helped you figure out who killed your father?"

"He was going to Boston to meet someone who said he had information that would help expose Judson's program. And they were going to tell it all to a reporter. We think Lehr killed him."

"Why hasn't he been arrested?"

"Can't prove it. But he was working for Briana, and she made that list."

"What list?"

"The one in the closet you saw. Just dates and initials but it's her handwriting. Marti's initials are on it."

"The list titled 'released'?"

"Yeah."

"Wait. So those *are* the papers she wants. She asked me to look for them. She said she could get Lehr to stop harassing me if she had them."

Kip snorted. "Probably just protecting herself."

"What does 'released' mean?"

He shrugged. "Some of the initials match candidates I knew, so maybe released from the program."

"Not necessarily sinister, then."

"Don't know. Marti's dead. I haven't checked on the others."

I cocked my head. "I doubt Briana would send me to find her list of murder targets."

"You're the shrink. But you wouldn't know it's hers unless you heard it from me. She could say it's Lehr's."

"Does he know you're aware of this?"

Kip looked at me like I was missing the obvious. "I'm still alive, right?"

"Why don't we tell this reporter, Rob Galloway?" The look on Kip's face stopped me. "What?"

"Don't talk to him!"

Ayden looked at me.

To Kip, I said, "He seems to want to help."

"Helping *himself*. I used to talk to him. Seemed like a good guy. But he wants to write some epic exposé about us, all of us. Two corrupt families going back generations."

"He doesn't really know—"

"He does! He knows a lot. Don't trust 'im. He knew my dad was in Boston."

"You think he set your dad up?"

Kip's eyes blazed. "He knew my dad was there. Told cops my dad had a file with incriminating details about some powerful people. He said one of 'em probably killed him. I used to think he was trying to help till I realized he was just squeezin' me for information he could twist."

"Wait, Kip. Galloway said he's never seen the contents of that file. If he knew your dad had it, then of course he's seen those names." I recalled Natra's uneasiness about him. "Was Galloway blackmailing people? Like Judson?"

Kip looked out the window. "Ask him, yourself. Your dad said you're good at reading people, 'though I can't say I agree."

Ayden stiffened as if preparing to defend me. I gestured for him to stand down. I'd just hit a brick wall and had to pivot to something less prickly.

"Back to Shona," I said. "If she's here to help you, why is she Judson's house manager?"

"She wants the parts, to take back to Scotland. What better way to search for his hiding spots?"

I nodded. "Right. She has keys to his properties. But she hasn't found anything, has she?"

"She got some things. She burned them and put the ashes in a jar. But she still wants the thing everyone else wants."

I flashed on her pottery urn. "Which is?"

"The left hand."

"As if it actually has power?"

"They need it for the cells. Different people want it for different reasons."

"Do you still talk to her?"

He shook his head. "I saw her talking to Galloway, so I avoid her."

Some pieces were falling in place.

"Maybe I should tell you what we learned today," Ayden said. "We got some important stuff. Might explain some things."

"Okay," I said. "Skip the starfish stuff. Tell me what—"

"Starfish?" Kip sat up. "What about it?"

I looked at him. "What do you know about a starfish?"

"Just...that guy. That one who got Maisie in trouble."

"Seren?"

"Yeah. He had a starfish tattoo. He said his name means *star*."

Chapter Fifty

Ayden drove past the coffee shop in Dunbury where I'd first talked with Galloway. My stomach churned over things I'd told him. But I couldn't think about that. Kip had possibly just linked my family's work with our starfish murders. That wasn't coincidence. Someone who knew about those deaths had wanted *me* to investigate. That explained the recent tip on my podcast chat. I figured Ayden was making the same connection.

We made better time on streets where other cars had gone before us, but the large flakes continued to limit our vision.

I turned to Kip. "Was this Seren good with computers?"

"I think so. My dad knew him. That wasn't really his name. He called himself Seren because of Dacretown. It's shaped like a star."

I caught my breath. "It is?"

"Yeah, the five exits. If you draw lines from one to another, you can get a star." He drew it in the air. "So, Seren chose a name that would link him to the place. I remember the star thing because he kept saying he was the star of the program. Like he was *the one*. You know? The exceptional one, the one they were searching for. The North Star. I kind of think my dad thought so, too, which didn't make me feel too great. Dad spent a lot of time with him, cuz they were both into biology. They even invited him to the Gray Hollow Group meetings."

"Did Maisie like him?"

"He was younger than her, like three years younger, but he tried to persuade her that together they could rule the world. He said the starfish regenerated limbs to protect the center, and he was the center. He thought he could transfer personalities from others to make himself stronger. With enough of them, he could replace the dead guy and be this awesome healer. *He* wanted that left hand, let me tell ya. He did a lot of digging."

I felt cold. "How do you know all this?"

Kip shrugged. "He wrote it down. It's in code, but I figured it out. It's in notes he left behind when they kicked him out of the program."

"That's Merrick's idea," Ayden said. "Personality transfer for personal improvement. Sounds like Seren pinched it." The Rover slid again, and Ayden corrected for it.

Kip snorted. "He wouldn't like hearin' you say that."

I returned to Kip. "Have you ever heard of a Lee Bandisi?"

Kip nodded. "I met him. Smart guy."

My heart raced. "Where?"

"At your dad's house, where you live. They discussed how to extract the neurotrophic stuff from the preservative and refine it. My dad wanted Lang to get involved again. Bandisi was helping them. He was some kind of biologist."

Ayden looked at me. "I think that guy drowned. I was on search-and-rescue then."

"In Hatteras. Did Natra tell you about this case?"

"Yeah. Didn't seem suspicious at the time."

"And then my father was murdered," Kip said, "just a few months later."

I looked at Ayden. "This is too fluky. How can our case be related to all this up here?" Then I had a thought. "It started for us with that Tennessee case. How did JoLynn get called into that?"

"A colleague at the weather station there." Ayden went silent, then said, "He knew she was working with you. I think she told him. And she introduced me to 'im."

"Hmmm. We need to talk to that guy. I sense there's more to our starfish cases than we thought. Someone might be steering us. I'll text Natra about this Seren character, although he might be using another name now. She and Joe can start looking. With a possible victim here and one in Hatteras, and now a guy with a starfish philosophy inspired by a star-shaped property, that's got to be related to Dad."

I texted Natra. *Look for Seren, last name unkn. Has starfish philosophy. Was in this area in...* I looked at Kip. "When was Maisie sent away?"

He looked out the window for a moment. "Well, I was ten or eleven, so ten years ago, roughly."

I mentally calculated. "So, mid-twenties for her, and he was a little younger." I typed in the likely range of years when Seren was in Dacretown. I also texted JoLynn, hoping I could get her to go collect Kamryn, since Kamryn knew her a little, but she didn't respond.

To Ayden, I said, "Okay. What's the deal with Merrick Hunter?"

Kip leaned in to listen.

Ayden glanced at me. "Hence, the wine. You won't like this, boss."

Chapter Fifty-One

It wasn't unexpected, but Ayden's report disturbed me.

"Your ancestor was a con artist and cheat," he said. "Big time. That's why he's been erased from the records of the ASPR. He was a black mark on their reputation. He even acquired Dacretown by cheating at cards."

"Why am I not surprised?"

"You've got quite the family legacy. I sent the documents to Natra, but here's the rundown."

Ayden found a track in the snow where the pavement showed through and kept his eyes on the road. "Merrick was nineteen when he came from Scotland to study with the ASPR. He'd met William James in England, apparently, and wanted to join him in scientifically researching proof of an afterlife. I found this among unpublished papers, which also contained an account of why Merrick didn't acquire membership."

"Any idea what he knew about Dacretown?"

"Getting there, boss. While he was in Boston, he also met—and you won't believe this—Julian Hawthorne."

I gasped. "Hawthorne's son?"

"The same. *That's* how he heard about Dacretown. Julian knew about it, and he was a follower of a mystic named Swedenborg. He told Merrick about personality transfer, like Kip just said, and the human potential for telepathy and psychic projection."

"That's not so bad."

"The bad part came from Merrick. He was obsessed with spiritual enhancement. He thought certain people were exceptional. He wanted to figure out how to distill their essence so he could use it to enhance himself. The Perfect Perceiver Project."

I made a face. "Sounds like spiritual eugenics."

"Right."

"And ideas like that were popular then. Lots of supposedly superior people tried to manipulate human reproduction to erase negative traits and enhance desirable traits. They proposed things like forced sterilization and human experimentation, even extermination."

"Merrick being one of them, and he thought his goal was noble. When he heard about the legend of Dacretown, he thought he could attune to this healer and penetrate...what's that word you always use? The boundary between life and death?"

"Liminal." As I said the word, I remembered that Dad had aimed for the same thing with his search for portals. This was all sounding crazy. I turned to Kip. "When did this thing start affecting our fathers negatively?"

"Not sure about Lang, but Dad seemed to realize it a couple years before he died, around the time they brought in Bandisi. He figured it would hit Lang as well. He found some accounts about how Judson got rich off wealthy people paying to take excursions into Dacretown for its healing properties. But Dad discovered that some of those people had really bad reactions later."

"And Bree subjected her own daughter to it, and Maisie became violent." I leaned into my seat and took a deep breath. Spiritual eugenics via neurotoxins that destabilized the brain.

Ayden looked at me. "There's more, Annie. This is probably why your dad wants you to keep control of Dacretown. This part of the story might've gotten lost in the lore, but it was in the report about Merrick. He tried to get the ASPR to excavate Dacretown. He said the dead guy had been a seer. He wanted the Society's help finding the dead guy's parts, especially the left hand, like Kip said. He claimed it was a decoder."

"A decoder?"

"For automatic writing. What the Society was studying and what your dad's into."

"Oh God!" I looked at Kip. "You're right. That's what I was tested for. He wanted to see if I was receptive to automatic writing. He built his whole app around the idea that written spirit communication is real. Not just real. It's the way to penetrate the portals." My eyes teared up as I turned back to urge the SUV to *move*. "I wish I'd never left this morning. My brain-poisoned father's in Concord. So's my daughter, and she's with a woman who knows him! What if they try to test her?" I wanted to jump out and run, as if I could get there faster on my own power.

Ayden grabbed my arm. "Annie, she'll be okay."

To Kip, I said, "That's what Lehr wants. They have it, don't they? This preserved hand, this bone decoder. Judson even cried out before he died, *don't let her take it.*"

His eyes widened. "He did?"

"You said Marti had it. She was the brilliant mind they used to locate it, right? She handled it, and it destroyed her brain."

Kip looked pale. He rubbed his jeans.

"Did she tell you where it is?"

"She didn't…no…she didn't tell anyone that."

I stared at him. Whenever he'd rubbed his face today, he was telling only part of a story. I wanted to jump in back and throttle him to make him spill the rest.

I texted JoLynn to call me ASAP. My text tone chimed. It was from Kamryn. *Going to play in the snow.*

My heart pounded. I flashed on the man in the cemetery the day we'd gone up Authors Ridge. Was it Dad? Had he been watching us? Maybe he was watching Kamryn right now.

Chapter Fifty-Two

I texted Kamryn. *Stay inside. Be there soon.* She didn't respond, so I called her. She didn't pick up. I told myself she might have left her phone in the house or turned it off for her lessons.

But maybe they'd taken it from her and sent the text to make me think she was fine.

But no. We'd set up good security.

Unless they forced her to do it.

A rough patch jerked my thoughts back to the snow. Ayden came up to a line of cars. A snow-covered Mazda coupe and Honda sedan sat stalled on the side of the road. I sensed Ayden fuming. Or maybe it was me. We didn't need this delay.

I turned back to Kip. "Has Lehr ever tried to hurt you?"

"He just shot at me."

"I mean before. Isn't he concerned that your dad told you things?"

"Someone broke into our house and went through things. Maybe that was him. We didn't have a security camera, but my dad's notes weren't there."

"He didn't break into the Crypt?"

"Didn't have it set up then, but when we bought it to renovate a year later, someone broke the lock and tossed it. Now we have security." He shrugged. "It's funny how people who work with geniuses still think like idiots."

I went still. His offhanded remark signaled something. Wherever this thing was, it wouldn't be obvious—or stupid. Kip knew something.

Ayden interrupted. "Annie, have you considered that your dad's doing... well, some..."

"I get it, Ayden. Worst case, Dad's involved in these murders. Maybe he's even killed someone. Or he's still experimenting. I wouldn't have believed it, but I'm the last one to say that people are who we think they are."

"Lang didn't care about the project," Kip offered. "He left. My dad's work distilling the juice to find a cure got him back involved, but then, you know…he didn't have my dad or Bandisi to help."

"Do you know why he went off the grid, then?" I asked.

Kip shrugged. "He came here after my dad was killed to help us. That's when we formed the Skeleton Crew. He wanted us to watch the place. He thought someone might try to use the building. Told us not to contact him but said he'd be back. He came a couple times."

"And Judson covered for him."

"We all did. Seemed like he was the next target. Judson put out the word that Lang was dead. Suicide."

Ayden looked in the rearview mirror at Kip, then at me. "So, you were right. Pseudocide."

"And that's why Judson resisted my attempts to find him. I must've been as annoying as hell to him."

My phone rang. "It's JoLynn." I picked up. "JoLynn, where are you right now?"

"In a ride-share on my way to the inn. It's slow, but I'm close."

"I need you to do something for me. Redirect to Judson's house." I gave her the address. "My daughter should be outside in the snow. She has a key to where we're staying. Please take her over there. We'll be there soon."

"No problem. Natra said you have a good lead for me."

"We might. And it might involve whoever tipped you about the Tennessee incident."

"Bruce? Right, he's a friend."

"Will he mind answering questions?"

"Not at all. In fact, he helped Joe figure out the weather game, the one that gave him the idea about the challenge."

This was new information. "Does he know who created it?"

"I don't think so."

"Did Bruce tell you why he wanted you to look at the case?"

Silence on the other end suggested she wasn't sure how to say it, so I helped her along. "JoLynn, if he called you because he knew you had resources, like our team, that's important."

Ayden put his hand out for the phone. I gave it over. To JoLynn, he said, "I already told her. It's fine. But if Bruce was trying to direct this to us, we need to know that, so don't tip him that we're coming."

He listened to her response and signed off before handing the phone back to me.

"Ayden's right," I said to her. "We don't want Bruce to prepare."

"Got it, Annie. I'm a little rattled, though. You think he might know Starfish?"

"I won't assume anything. It's just a lead we want to follow up. What did you learn at the ME's office about Ralph Steiner?"

"They stand by their finding of accident or suicide, leaning toward suicide. They said they're still investigating, but I sense they're done."

"Did you see the photos?"

"They didn't have many. The cliff top looks too rough for shoeprint impressions, but it's also a hiking spot, so evidence that could prove a specific person was there with him might be compromised. The ME didn't think the body's position was odd for a fall, but I'd like to go out and see if there might be any Starfish signatures his investigator didn't notice."

"Can't go now in the storm."

"No, I know, but if it's carved in a tree or rock, it'll still be there. The autopsy report didn't show any tattoos or markings on the body, so if it's related to Starfish, it'll show up somewhere. Hey, Annie, I'm at the house. I'll call you back."

Relief flooded through me. Kamryn would soon be safe. I left a text on her phone directing her to go with JoLynn.

"You think Seren killed Ralph?" Kip asked.

I looked back at him. "I don't know. We're still investigating."

He looked out the window on his side. He seemed worried.

"Did you ever meet this guy, Seren?" I asked.

"I was a kid. I saw 'im around my dad. Didn't like 'im. Kind of an ass." Kip looked at me. "My cousin knew 'im better."

"The Bone Head cousin?"

"Yeah. He's older. He thought we should dissolve the group."

"Because he was threatened?"

Kip shrugged. "Didn't say, but I thought something happened. He told me to just stop talkin' about it."

"Did he know where the relic was?"

Kip shook his head. "He said it was just a ghost story. Said we should leave it all to the Hunters, let them take the rap. But, ya know, Maisie's our family too."

"Briana Duncan also knew Seren, then."

"More than she wanted, but Dad knew him best. He was Seren's mentor. Some people think he put Seren and Maisie together to hurt Briana. But I don't think he knew what Seren wanted Maisie to do."

"Why not?"

"They talked like they were committed to the vision. They seemed like the best chance to make it happen. Guess that blinded him. Dad wanted to find the hand to harvest the remaining cells in their most natural state. They were helping."

I briefed Ayden about Maisie and Seren before I turned back to Kip. "When they forced Seren out, did he make any threats?" I shifted a little more in my seat.

"Dad said he was mad. They had meetings about him. They were worried."

"Did Galloway know about Seren?"

"Yeah. When he contacted me after Dad died, he said Dad told him about the program and the sponsors. He wanted access to Dad's records. At first, I helped, so he read about Dad's work. Later, I figured out Dad *hadn't* told him. He tricked me."

"So, these sponsors must've known that Seren was the most promising candidate. How many names on the sponsor list?"

Kip shrugged. "A dozen, maybe. Judson's associates, some politicians, the police chief, some lawyers, people like that."

I breathed out. Ayden glanced at me. We'd wondered if Galloway was blackmailing people. He'd had the supposedly missing file all along. Keeping it for himself was his oil well, much more lucrative than keeping his job.

"Did he ever try to find Seren?"

"Said he would. But I stopped talking to 'im."

"Did Seren know Bandisi was helping your dad on a fix?"

Kip lowered his eyes.

"Kip, did this all start because Seren knew our fathers were trying to neutralize the toxin and terminate the Dacretown project?"

He shifted. "Maybe."

"So, they discussed him."

"They were usin' his calculations. He wasn't there, though."

"But they were erasing him, right? Bandisi, a cellular biologist, was helping them to identify something in Seren's work they could exploit for a reversal. That would derail his ambition."

"He couldn't have known that."

"Enlisting Bandisi was a clear signal they were working on something like that. And Bandisi drowned shortly after that meeting at my Dad's."

Kip paled. He blinked back tears.

Ayden held up a finger. "If he sent Gregory the invitation to meet in Boston, that's consistent with his MO, except for the weather part."

Kip leaned forward. "You think Seren killed my dad? Not Lehr?"

"I'm considering possibilities. Right now, we know that the Hunters and Hawkinses ran this program that hurt people. Our dads were trying to mitigate the damage, but someone wanted to thwart them. Leaving aside for now the people named in the file, we've got Briana, who wants to continue the mentalism work. We've got a journalist who *should* be exposing the program but isn't. We've got an unstable former trainer, Lehr, and also Seren, a disgruntled program reject, all trying to stake their own claims."

"All good suspects," Ayden commented. "We need a break that puts us on the right trail."

"Are there other starfish victims?" Kip asked.

"Yes," I said. "In other areas."

"Were any in the program?"

Ayden looked at me. I hadn't even thought of that.

A burst of music from my phone startled me. It was JoLynn. I picked up.

"I'm sorry, Annie. I didn't find Kamryn. I looked everywhere around this house, but she's not outside."

Chapter Fifty-Three

We were nearly to Concord. Kip had directed us off a main road, which had its challenges, but stalled traffic wasn't one of them. The Range Rover proved its worth. I could hardly breathe as we moved through patches of unplowed snow. We couldn't get stuck! I had to find Kamryn.

JoLynn had knocked on Shona's door and got no response. She'd gone to the guesthouse, but the place was dark. She'd seen people going into Judson's house for the viewing, but I'd told her Kamryn wouldn't be there without me. JoLynn wanted to go inside, anyway, to check. She didn't call back.

As we neared Judson's house, I scanned the parked cars and pointed. "Lehr's SUV. It's right there in front."

Kip sat up, alert.

"Looks empty," Ayden said.

"He's probably inside. That's bold."

Ayden parked on the street. Two cars in the driveway suggested few people in the house.

"Don't go in," Kip warned.

"I have to."

I felt something nudge my side. I looked. Kip was handing me his gun. I shook my head. "I don't have a license here."

"Won't matter if you gotta defend yourself."

Ayden held out his hand. "I'll take it."

I grabbed it. "I have legal resources here. You don't. Also, I'm family.

They're expecting me. There's still an hour before the public viewing, and the lunch is over."

"JoLynn hasn't come out, Annie. Something's up."

"I know. I'll keep my phone on so you can hear...Hey!" I saw a figure dart around the front and to the far side of the house. "That's Elyse."

I got out and ran after her in snow up to my calves. When I rounded the corner, I tripped over a fallen branch and fell hard. I got up, dazed, and looked around. I didn't see the girl, but I saw her tracks. I followed them to the back of the house.

"Mom!"

That was Kamryn. Quiet but urgent. I spotted her in her pink coat hiding behind a snow-covered bush. She held her mitten in a way that indicated to be quiet. I ran to her and grabbed her in a hug, so relieved she was all right. "What are you doing out here?"

Elyse ran up. "It's clear," she said.

I looked at her. "What's going on?"

"Someone's inside with a gun," Kam told me. "He's yelling at everyone."

"Where's Jeannette?" I asked.

Elyse pointed toward Judson's house. "In there. She went to get us some cake. We were in there, too, in another room. We came out through a window."

I knew before I asked, "Is the man someone you know?"

Elyse nodded. "He's the one who talks to my mom. He's always mad."

I heard someone yell inside. I knew that voice. "Where's the window? Can I get in without him seeing me?"

Elyse pointed. "I'll show you."

"And then you and Kamryn go back to your house and lock yourselves in." I looked at Kam. "You understand? Everything locked. Open it only for someone you know."

Elyse showed me the window on the other side of the house, still half-raised. I urged her to get to her house. "You're in charge. Be careful."

She left.

I heard an angry exchange inside between Lehr and Bree, like things were escalating, but the window was higher than I could easily enter. I looked for something to raise me up. Then Ayden came around the corner. I gestured for him to approach and stay quiet. In a low voice, I said, "Need to call police."

"Already did, boss. Left Kip with the Rover runnin', 'case we need to chase someone."

I heard a shot inside, then a scream.

Chapter Fifty-Four

I gestured for Ayden to help me get through the window. "Then you go in through the front. The parlor for the viewing is at the front of the house. It has two doors. We can approach from opposite sides, catch him off guard."

"No weapon."

I dug out my pocket knife and handed it over. "You see all those downed branches? Grab a thick one. It'll work."

"Be careful, boss."

Ayden boosted me up, and I scrambled through. I heard Bree yell, "Get out of here!"

"He ruined me!" That was Lehr. "Where is he?"

I crept into the hallway. A man lay on the floor outside the parlor door, bleeding. I stopped. His eyes and mouth were open. It was Peter Hillman, Judson's attorney. He didn't move. Not far from him, tipped over, was a red two-gallon container, and the floor looked wet. I smelled the woody odor of gasoline.

Lehr had crossed a line. He'd entered potential mass murderer territory. I wondered how many people were in the room. The private lunch and viewing were over, but some might have lingered. JoLynn was in there, and probably Shona and Bree, and maybe Jeannette. It was too early for the public viewing. I anticipated half a dozen inside. He probably had them clustered.

"Everyone, please stay calm." That was JoLynn. She must have walked in on a hostage situation. I hoped Ayden wouldn't rush the place to protect her.

"Shut up! Get over there." Lehr wasn't about to be directed.

I tried to think from Lehr's perspective. He'd taken me to Dacretown; I'd escaped him. He'd chased the Bone Head brothers; they'd bested him. He'd charged at us with apparent intent to harm; we'd lost him. So, he'd come here, thwarted, humiliated, and furious. He believed he was ruined. Nothing to lose. People to punish. That's a deadly combination. *One day he's gonna blow.*

I heard the front door open and cringed at the noise. I hoped it was Ayden. Time to move.

Against the wall, I edged toward the viewing room and readied Kip's Ruger semi-auto nine-mil. I stepped over to an open door.

Bree and Lehr continued to shout at each other, with Lehr dominating. "I saw Lang! He's here! Produce him!"

"He's not here! He didn't come. Don't hurt anyone else. I'll tell you where to find him."

"Now!"

Much as I wanted to know this myself, I couldn't delay. I metered the room to figure out where Lehr was standing. Then I entered, took a stance, and shouted, "Stop. Drop your gun!"

He turned, surprised, then swung his gun toward me. I touched the trigger, but from the other side, Ayden swung a thick branch down on Lehr's arm. He yelped and dropped his weapon. I bent down to grab it, but Lehr kicked my shoulder so hard I lost Kip's gun. Bree yelled, "Stop, stop! Everyone, stop!" Then, "Don't, please!"

I felt a hand grab my arm and pull me. A woman screamed, and someone ran from the room. A burst of heat made me look at the casket to my right. It had erupted in flames. So had the drapes behind it and the floor under the table that held it. Flames licked the table legs. Bree grabbed a fire extinguisher from a wall near the fireplace, but the blaze spread fast across that side of the room.

Ayden struggled with Lehr for control of his gun. Bree ran to the fireplace and grabbed the poker. She swung it at Lehr. He blocked it and twisted it from her hand. Then he slammed it against Ayden's face.

Ayden fell back, releasing Lehr's gun. Lehr aimed at Bree. She held up her hands. "No, no, I'll tell you. I'll show you." I heard a loud bang from behind me. Lehr recoiled. Blood on his forehead said he'd been hit. But he recovered. I looked back.

JoLynn had Kip's Ruger. Lehr raised his gun and shot Bree. She cried out and fell back against the burning casket. It slammed shut. She dropped to the floor, shielding herself with her arms. Lehr then aimed at JoLynn. Ayden dove for him, knocking him into a side table. Lehr's gun went flying. He slugged Ayden hard. Smoke filled the room.

JoLynn grabbed a large vase. She raised it to use as a weapon, but Lehr pushed Ayden into her, and they both went down.

Lehr picked up the poker and came at JoLynn, but I used the branch Ayden had dropped to block him. He spun me and hit me between my shoulder blades, knocking the breath out of me. I went to my knees and gasped, then coughed hard from the smoke.

From her position on the floor, JoLynn fired over my head. Lehr cursed at her. Ayden took the Ruger, got to his feet, and ordered Lehr to freeze.

Then the table bearing the casket collapsed at the head end, and the casket crashed to the floor. Bree's black dress caught on fire. She screamed and batted her hand at the flames. Lehr fled. I rushed to Bree, stripped off my coat, and smothered the flames in her hair and on her dress. She watched me, terrified. I saw that she'd been wounded in the right shoulder.

"I got you," I said. "I'll get you out."

She grabbed the front of my coat and tried to talk, but smoke made her cough. Blood gushed from her wound. She could die. I had to move fast. Smoke was making it hard to breathe or see. My exposed skin felt sunburned. Bree's had already blistered.

I dragged her away from the casket. Someone tugged on my arm, and I heard my name, "Annie." It was Ayden. With JoLynn's help, we got Bree out of the parlor. I looked back just as flames consumed the head end of Judson's casket.

Hawthornean karma.

Chapter Fifty-Five

Outside on the porch, I heard sirens. I took deep, gulping breaths. A parlor window had exploded outward, leaving shards of glass on a bench. Intense heat from inside told me we'd have to flee our precarious perch. Accelerant-fed fires get hot fast. That meant moving Bree, who lay unconscious under my coat on the edge of the porch. I couldn't just dump her in the snow, which already covered several steps. I leaned down and felt for her pulse. Weak but there. She was panting. Shona handed me another coat. Ayden added his jacket before he sat near the bottom step. I rolled one coat under Bree's head. Each move brought pain from my back where Lehr had hit me, and Kip's brew cramped my empty stomach.

Shona looked around. "Elyse?" She made a move to return inside.

I held up my hand. "She's safe. She's at your house, with Kamryn."

Shona looked stunned, as if in shock.

"I'll look after Bree. Take the girls to the guesthouse. They'll be safer there, away from all this." I didn't like leaving Kam in Shona's care, but I had to attend to the situation here. I trusted Elyse. She'd already kept Kamryn out of harm's way. In dress shoes, Shona made her way through the snow.

Lehr's Mercedes was gone. So were the cars that I'd seen in the driveway, as if those intimates of Judson's who'd come for the lunch sought to vanish before cops arrived. Then I realized the Range Rover was gone as well. Kip must have followed Lehr. Not good. Lehr wouldn't hesitate to include Kip in his victim toll, and we had Kip's gun.

I went to Ayden. He waved me away, but I could tell he was hurt. He'd been hit hard at least twice. I winced at the bloody purpling welt across his cheek and gripped his shoulder. "Thank you. Help is coming. Where's JoLynn?"

He looked around and made a move to get up. I stopped him. "I'll find her."

JoLynn rushed out the front door with a quilt she'd grabbed. She removed a towel she'd tied over her face. "I used another extinguisher on the fire, which reduced the spread, but it's still bad in there." She grimaced. "I think your grandfather's…"

"Saw it. Thanks for the quilt." I took my coat off Bree and covered her with the quilt. I gave Ayden his jacket and put mine back on. It stank of smoke. Blood from Bree's right shoulder soaked through the quilt. I assessed the rest of what I could see. The right side of her hair was singed, and she had burns on her face and throat. We had to get medical help ASAP.

A paramedic team pulled up, followed by a police car. Uniformed people soon swarmed the porch. I told a cop about the vehicles to look for and warned that Lehr was armed and dangerous. He'd shot a man inside, wounded two on the porch, and set the fire. To be sure they didn't arrest Kip, I added, "The guy in the Range Rover's with us."

Two paramedics carried a gurney through the snow and placed Bree on it. A cop urged us to move away from the house and started clearing a path. Another ambulance arrived. JoLynn, Ayden, and I went down to the end of the driveway. I mentally urged the paramedics to hurry; I was freezing. A young female in a blue uniform shirt came over. "Need help here?"

"He does." JoLynn pointed at Ayden. "He got slammed in the face."

"There's someone inside as well," I said, "but I think he's dead."

"He is," JoLynn said. "I have medical training. I checked. Shot in the head."

The ambulance with Bree inside took off.

A fire truck, siren blasting, arrived. We moved so it could come up the driveway. The female EMT urged Ayden to get in the ambulance.

"No," he said. "I'm fine."

"Looks like you need stitches, and you should be tested for a concussion."

"Please, Ayden," JoLynn said. "He hit you hard."

I gave him a stern boss look. "Go, Ayden. That's an order." I leaned closer to whisper. "Let Jo take care of you." He looked at me, and I winked. "I'll get Kamryn and come."

"I'll go with him," JoLynn volunteered. "Stay here. They'll probably need someone who knows what's going on." She handed me Kip's Ruger. "Can't take this."

"I'm so sorry," I told her. "I never expected you to run into an ambush." I peered at her. "Did you get hurt?"

"Some bruises, probably. I'm glad you came when you did. He threatened to shoot us all and torch the place."

"Thank you for helping. Especially with Ayden. Please tell me what they say, and don't let him leave unless they clear him. He'll try, I promise you."

"Don't worry."

Ayden finally complied. JoLynn helped him to the ambulance. I waved as they pulled away.

An officer asked me for a statement. I decided to give only the necessary facts so I could get to Kamryn. "I'm Judson Hunter's granddaughter. He recently died. Twenty minutes ago, I arrived for the viewing, and this man was here, armed and threatening people. He'd already shot one. My associates and I tried to break it up, but he'd poured gasoline—I didn't actually witness that, but I was in there when he lit it. He shot my aunt, Brianna Duncan, who's in the first ambulance, and assaulted my associate, who just left in the second one. The perp fled in a maroon Mercedes G-Wagon. His name is Richard Lehr. He was wounded, but I don't know how badly." I recalled three numbers from his license plate.

A fire crew took a thick tan hose through the front door. I moved onto the street. The scene seemed surreal. They were about to douse Judson's body. I told the cop where he could find me, gave the names of other witnesses I knew, said they could find JoLynn Wilde at the hospital, and asked permission to leave to attend to my daughter.

The heat was getting intense on one side of me, and falling snow chilled me on the other. The officer took my number and address and let me go. A police SUV pulled away fast. I hoped they were looking for Lehr.

People had started to gather across the street. I saw Rob Galloway among them, watching the house. He'd come for the viewing. I pulled my hood up. I didn't want to talk with him just now. Another fire engine roared up the street, and people were herded back. In the chaos, I made my way to the guesthouse. I turned around once. Even half a block away, I felt the penetrating heat. Dark smoke billowed skyward as flames crackled inside. I hoped they could save the place.

Snow came thick now. I turned and walked as fast as I could. It was over the top of my short boots, making my feet cold. I listened to the racket of voices shouting orders and thought of Judson's corpse going up in flames. I despised him for the secrets he'd kept about my father, for making me doubt my belief that he was alive. And I was sure Lehr had seen Dad, who'd been in the house. Maybe he'd been there the whole time.

I hoped Bree would survive. I didn't want to bear the weight of this odious legacy. My father should be the heir, but he was "deceased." Then there was Maisie. What shape was she in, and how would I even locate her? The Hawkins family had some interest in this too.

That reminded me of Kip. I looked at my phone to see if he'd left a message but realized I hadn't given him my number. I saw a text from Natra. *Heard from Kam. Call when u can.*

I called and filled her in. "Can't say much now because I'm outside and I'm freezing. I think we're close to figuring out Starfish, but I need to attend to stuff here first. We think he was here at Dacretown. Get this. The property has a star shape. This whole thing is about biological specimens."

"That was Bandisi's expertise," she said.

"Yes, and apparently everyone involved could be a target."

"Is Ayden with you?"

"At the hospital getting stitches, and I'll have to go over there when Bree's awake, but right now I need to see Kamryn."

"Copy that, Annie."

"And I need to locate Dad. He's here in Concord. I wish you were here. You're so good at keeping loose threads coordinated. I'll call you when I can. Look through the Merrick papers. You'll see where it started."

I climbed the guesthouse steps and knocked at the door. The lock clicked and Shona peeked out. Kamryn ran over to hug me. "Mom, are you okay? You're all dirty and stinky."

I hugged her back. "Thanks. Just what I needed."

She looked behind me. "Where's Ayden?"

"He got a little banged up. He's with the paramedics. JoLynn's there, and she'll call us after he's treated. He'll be fine."

The place felt wonderfully warm. I took off my coat and boots, so glad I'd purchased them.

"You smell like smoke," Shona said. "Why don't you go get a hot shower. We've made tea, and I brought over food from the luncheon." She took my coat. "Should I go back and make a statement? I'm the house manager. Or should I go to the hospital?"

"They're busy. When we're ready, I'll call over. They'll need your statement, but we can't drive anywhere. The Range Rover's gone, my rental's in another town, and Judson's other cars won't get through this snow."

"I have a Rav4."

"Good. I'll clean up and we'll form a plan."

Chapter Fifty-Six

I took Kip's gun to my room. The shower felt great, but my relief was short-lived. I worried about Bree and Ayden. I called JoLynn and she assured me that both were getting care. Bree was in surgery, but her wound wasn't life-threatening.

I went downstairs. Kamryn and Elyse were in the library, seemingly none the worse for what had happened. They'd missed the most harrowing stuff, but they'd likely heard Hillman get shot. They were watching a weather channel. Kamryn waved at me. "More snow, Mom!"

"Great." I was not enthused.

In the kitchen, Shona produced a blue porcelain mug and made me a cup of tea. I needed it. "Do the girls know about the fire?"

"They heard the sirens, but I took them out a back street to avoid the house. I'm so grateful to you for getting them away."

"Elyse would've done that. She's resourceful."

"They know someone was killed. Elyse saw the body in the hall. That's why they went out the window."

"Thank God they did." I lifted the mug to take a sip. "Where's Jeannette?"

"She went home. She was in the kitchen getting food for the girls, so she wasn't in danger, but she's still upset."

"Yes, I'm sure. What an ordeal."

Shona hugged herself and nodded. "She said she'll help with the girls if we need her. I wrote down her number for you."

"Good to know." I sat down and took a sip of tea. "So, here's a plan. I think you should go to the hospital so you're there when Bree wakes up.

You know her affairs better than I do, and she's worked closely with you. She'll need someone there. And you should hire some private security for her. The cops will be stretched thin during this storm, and I'd like her to have protection."

"We use a local company. I've contacted them."

"And please stop at Judson's house on your way to see what needs to be done. At the very least, you'll have to arrange to move whatever's left of his remains to a crematory when they're released. It's a crime scene, so you'll have to stay clear, but they'll need a contact. They have my number as well, and I'll take care of the paperwork."

"Hillman's dead."

"Yes, but he has an assistant, and partners. I also know an attorney that Judson's dealt with. You take care of your end. I'll take care of mine."

Shona glanced toward the library. "I need to—"

"My turn to watch them. If I need Jeannette, I'll call her. I'll try to keep tabs on what's happening at the house so you can tell Briana."

Shona leaned toward me. "What about that awful man?"

"Lehr? You know him, right? Elyse said he's spoken to you."

"He's *threatened* me. Tried to bully me. He used to work for Mr. Hunter. I don't know why he—"

I held up my hand. In a low voice, I said, "Let's get this clear, Shona. You know what Lehr's after. So do I, and we both know my father's alive. You're from Morvern, the location of this toxic tomb that's caused all these problems, so I think I know why you're here. Gregory Hawkins met you there. Kip filled me in. I know about the program, too, and I've been in Judson's Dacretown facility. I know about the relic." I pointed at my left hand when I saw her stiffen. "I also know you took photos."

Shona looked surprised. "What photos?"

"Of my father and Kip, and some others. I've seen them."

Shona breathed out. "Did you take them from my house? Where are they?"

So, she didn't know they were here. "Before I answer any questions, I have one of my own. Where's my father?"

She shook her head. "I wish I could tell you."

"You haven't seen him?"

"He's been to see Mr. Hunter, and he's been in the house, but I don't know where he is. Ms. Duncan can get messages to him."

"How?"

"She doesn't tell me."

"But you've followed her. Where does she go?"

Shona hesitated. "He tells her where to meet him. It's not just one place."

"He's an heir. Why's he hiding?"

"He has information from his work with Gregory. He said someone wants it who shouldn't have it."

"Who?"

"That man, Lehr. He thought Lang would be at the viewing. He came in, and Mr. Hillman told him to leave. He blocked him from going into the viewing area. The man left but came back and shot Mr. Hillman. Then he poured gas across the door thresholds and on the coffin and threatened to burn us all alive if we didn't tell him where Lang was."

"None of you knows? Not even Briana?"

"Ms. Duncan tried to get him to leave, but he said if he lit up the house like a torch, Lang would come. The man's off his head. That's when you came."

She'd shifted me away from my question. More secrets. "What does Lehr think my father owes him?"

Shona gripped the handle of her mug.

"I'm too tired for this, Shona. I know you're doing some kind of investigation related to Dacretown. What do you *think* Lehr wants?"

"He wants…." She pointed to her left hand. "From the cave."

"For what?"

"He used to be a trainer. He says he wants Lang to give everything to him, to protect it. He was trying to see Judson but couldn't get to him."

"And you want this relic, too, don't you?"

She lifted her chin. "I want it destroyed."

"But Gregory had one."

"When they were threatened, he burned it. He was with me. I have the ashes."

"And you haven't found that last item? After all the time you've spent in Judson's houses."

"He had it once. He described it to Lang. I found the box that was made for it. But it's empty."

"Did my father take it?"

"When he was here yesterday, after Judson was taken away, he looked for it. I was with him. He doesn't have it."

Chapter Fifty-Seven

Kamryn sat next to me with a cup of hot chocolate. I hugged her so hard she squirmed. "Is the house burning down?" she asked.

"I hope they can save it. They got there quickly, and the fire was mostly in one room downstairs."

"That was scary, that guy."

"I'm just glad you girls are safe. Did you call your dad?"

Kamryn nodded. "He misses me. I told him what I learned today and that I got to play in snow. He wants you to call him."

A call I dreaded. "I will."

I was glad she hadn't inquired about Judson. My memory of his remains in flames was unsettling.

Elyse ate some mushroom quiche as she watched me from across the table. Shona had left to attend to Bree, and I was still trying to absorb what I'd learned. She hadn't found the hand. She'd never overheard Judson talk about it. She'd been close to giving up, but when Dad showed up, she thought she still had a chance. But he'd failed too. She'd asked for the photos back. I'd said no.

I called JoLynn, and she gave Ayden her phone. I put mine on speaker so Kamryn could talk to him. "I got some stitches," he told her.

"Did it hurt?"

"Nah. I'm okay. Looks like I was in a pirate fight and got slashed with a sword."

Kamryn smiled. "Cool! You should get a patch. Did you see all the snow?"

"I did, but I can't go out yet. They want to test me some more."

He sounded tired. I put the phone back on a private setting and told him, "Everything's quiet now. I'll get a report on the house soon. Please rest now. JoLynn will stay in touch with me. Shona's there, and she has a four-wheel drive. She can take you to the inn when you're ready."

"Did Kip come back?"

"Not yet. And I don't have his number."

"Boss? You think that Seren guy's around here somewhere?"

"I don't know. We'll talk later. I'll text any updates." I was sure he understood that I had news but couldn't talk in front of the girls. I also didn't want him to think he had to do something.

I pushed away the plate Shona had prepared for me. "So, any ideas of what you girls want to do while we wait for reports?"

"We started a puzzle we found," Kamryn said. "I already showed Elyse how to tie all the knots I know, and I don't know if I should play any games on the computer here."

Elyse sat up. "I know. We could play a detective game."

I cocked my head. "What game is that?"

"From the photos."

"Yeah, Mom," Kamryn piped up. "Elyse says the photos have clues."

"Clues? To what?"

Elyse grinned. "To what my mom was doing. I was with her sometimes. She wouldn't tell me, so I brought 'em over here to look at 'em. Then you moved in so I couldn't get 'em."

Mystery solved. "*You* brought them here? You left them in the staircase?"

"Yeah. It was easy to get in here and I like the staircase. It's fun to sit in there where no one can find me." She beamed.

I made a move to get up. "Sounds like a good game. I'll get them."

Kamryn cleared the table while I went to retrieve the envelopes. I'd taken back the one I'd given to Ayden, so I grabbed it too. I had to admit, this girl's light fingers were becoming an asset.

Elyse opened both envelopes and laid out the prints. I estimated there were a couple dozen. She looked at them and then swapped a few. "I'm not sure if they go together by when she took them or if they should be grouped in some other way."

"Elyse, your mother knows these photos are missing."

She raised her chin. "So? She doesn't know I took 'em. She'd just get mad. I was gonna bring 'em back. But maybe you know what they mean. My mom was looking for something."

I retrieved a pen and pad of paper. "Let's keep track of what we think." I tore off three sheets and gave one to each girl.

"I already know what I see," Elyse said.

I pointed to the photo of Dad and Kip at the forbidden entry to Dacretown. "This is the one that got me thinking."

Kamryn beamed. "I showed you that."

"Yes, you did. It made me realize that Dad had some association with that property."

"The ghost place?" Elyse asked.

"Yes." I tapped the photo of Dad and Kamryn. "But why would your mother have this one? I took this in North Carolina and gave a copy to my father."

Elyse turned it over. "For this." On the other side was a drawing of a genealogical family tree that joined the Hunter and Hawkins lines.

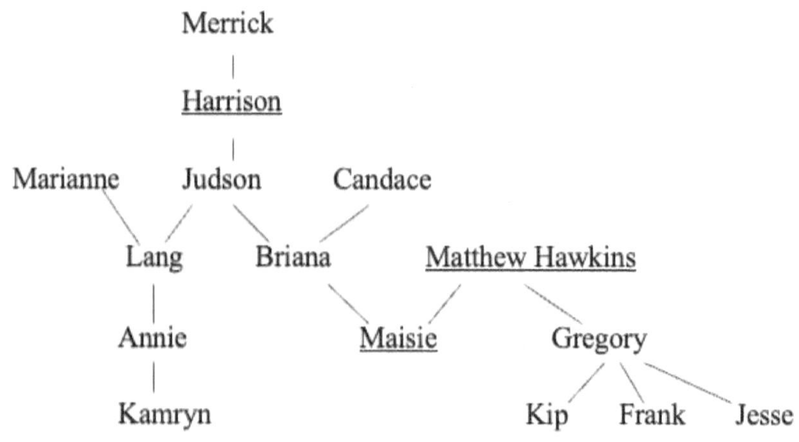

This reminded me that my cousin Maisie was Gregory's half-sister and Kip's aunt.

"My mom took it from Judson. She's a thief."

"What?"

"A professional thief. They hired her to get something."

"Who did?"

Elyse shrugged. "My sister won't tell me. But that's what I'd like to be, so I watched her."

Kamryn leaned in to show me her name on the tree. Merrick Hunter was at the top. His son, Harrison, was underlined. So were Maisie's and Matthew's names.

"Do you know what the underlines mean?" I asked Elyse.

"They're the crazy ones. I heard my mom talking about them." She pointed to Harrison's name. "This one tried to poison this one." She indicated Judson. "So, they locked him up. He was really nuts. He wrote a note. My mom has it."

"Did you read it?"

"Yeah." She gestured toward Kamryn. "We both did. It's short."

Kamryn looked sheepish. I'd already scolded her for snooping. But this was her own family. I'd have done the same thing at her age. I'd do it at *my* age.

"It was kooky," Elyse continued. "Stuff about ghosts and blood and screaming souls. Said his dad ruined them, and no one should survive." She frowned. "There was something else." She opened the envelope and dug inside. "Here it is." She produced a three-by-five card. "This was attached to that photo."

I recognized Dad's handwriting. In red ink, he'd written, "This one has it too." I blinked and kept myself from looking at my daughter. I knew he meant her. The photo was of him and her. What I didn't know is whether he meant she'd inherited the family's psychosis or she had the gift. I recalled his comment on her neurodiverse behavior. He'd said she was like him. But he hadn't underlined his own name on this genealogy. Not crazy? Or just not aware of it?

Elyse watched me. Her eyes narrowed and she glanced at Kamryn.

"What does it mean, Mom?" Kam asked.

I looked at her. "I'm not sure, but your grandfather thought you had the same kind of attunement he had to spooky things."

She smiled. I remained anxious. I didn't like that Dad had made such a chart. I wondered why, and for whom. Judson? Bree? Shona?

I moved the photo and note aside to study later. "Let's look at the others."

Now that I knew Kip better, had been in the Crypt, and had seen Dacretown, I was able to figure out who Shona had followed. I grouped the photos into an order that showed the Bone Heads together. "These guys are brothers. These photos are near a house they use, like a clubhouse. It's near a property line."

"To the spooky place," Elyse commented. "The Dead Line."

"Yes." I pointed to two photos that featured familiar buildings. "These are on the property where that security guard stopped us and told us to leave." I tapped one. "That's Kip Hawkins."

"My mom knows him. He works in town. I've seen him. He's cute."

The photo was taken from behind, but he wore the skeleton head hoodie. A blond female walked next to him, possibly Marti. This was confirmed in the next photo, where she'd turned around. I'd seen a school photo in her file. Another photo caught her going with Kip into the Crypt. Hence, the rumor that she'd joined a secret club. This one showed Kip's profile. Still, nothing in these photos told enough of a story to figure out why Shona had taken them. I wondered if she hoped one of her subjects would lead her to the relic. Kip or Marti or Lang.

I looked out the window. Where had Kip gone? He had the Range Rover and knew about Judson's house, but did he know this one? Yes, Judson had hired his cousin's restoration business. Kip had likely worked on things here.

Another cluster of photos featured the Sleepy Hollow Cemetery.

"Isn't that where we were?" Kamryn asked.

"Yes, where you saw the authors' graves and took a pen." I scrutinized them, then shook my head. "I don't see anything here."

CHAPTER FIFTY-SEVEN

"Maybe the headstones are clues. Like you have to unscramble the names."

I looked at Kamryn. "You're good at that."

She shrugged. "I tried, but I don't know what I'm looking for."

So, this was what had kept these two so occupied. Spy games. I looked at Elyse. "Did you go to the cemetery?"

"We persuaded Jeannette to take us this morning, so we could look. It was so pretty in the snow. But we couldn't find these spots."

"It was cool, Mom," Kam added. "Really quiet."

I knew what that was like, walking in silence, seeing the old gravestones coated in white like a blanket for the dead.

I looked at Elyse. "Did you go here with your mother?"

"She didn't see me. I was careful."

A noise on the front porch interrupted us. It sounded like stomping feet. I motioned to the girls to stay where they were. The doorbell rang.

Chapter Fifty-Eight

To my relief, Kip stood outside, his jacket pulled close. I opened the door and saw the Range Rover parked on the street. It appeared to be in one piece. He held up the bottle of wine Ayden had purchased. *Troublemaker.* I took it and gestured for Kip to come in. He removed his boots on the mat inside before entering the dining room. Elyse's eyes widened, as if she were watching an image from a painting come alive. I introduced them. Elyse continued to stare. I thought she blushed.

Kamryn waved. Kip nodded to her. I was sure he knew who she was. No doubt Dad had shown him pictures of her. Kip's huddled posture showed discomfort, 'though we were third cousins once removed on his father's side, or whatever.

"Tea?" I asked. "You look like you could use something warm."

"Or hot chocolate," Kamryn offered.

Kip shook his head. "Can't stay. Kate's picking me up. Just wanted to drop off your car."

I crossed my arms. "Not so fast. What happened? Did you see the fire?"

He nodded. "I was just there, checkin'. It's contained. One truck's already gone. Won't spread but looks like a lot of damage. Too bad. It's a fine old house."

"And where did *you* go?"

"Followed 'im but got turned around too late, so I lost 'im. Then a cop pulled me over, and I had to call Kate to vouch for me. Not my car. More demerits for me, I guess, but they let me bring it back to you."

"Did you see where Lehr went?" I asked.

"South. Could've gone anywhere." He looked around. "Where's your PI? Thought he'd come out when Lehr did."

"Getting stitches. He got roughed up."

Kip glanced at the girls, and I sensed he wanted to tell me more but wouldn't in front of them. I also wanted to probe a little. The photos gave me an idea. I gestured to the table. "Before you go, can you look at these photos? We need some information."

Elyse slid them toward the edge of the table closest to Kip. When he saw the images of him and Marti, his face tightened. Elyse pushed the one from the Dacretown gate toward him with a questioning expression. He looked at her. "Where did you get these?"

"My mom. She followed you."

He nodded. He knew that. To me, he said, "Don't show these to Emmie."

I understood. These photos proved his close association with Marti. That wouldn't be good for him. He still had a problem—alleged assisted suicide.

Kip looked at the other photos. He shrugged at one, shook his head at another. Then, for a micro-second, he tensed, and the lines around his eyes deepened. Something had caught his attention. I followed his gaze. He pulled away. "Can't help, sorry. I should go. Kate's waiting."

I patted his arm. "Of course. Thanks for trying." But he *had* helped.

At the door, he pulled his boots back on. I gave him my cell number and asked for his. He hesitated, squinting at me as if looking for reassurance. Then he told me.

"I'll keep you updated," I assured him. "Sorry I stranded you in Concord."

He shrugged. "I have places to stay. JJ can get me when the snow lets up."

"Tell Kate that Judson's attorney was shot today. He's gone. I'll need her assistance."

Kip paled. "Shot?"

"Lehr killed him, so whatever Hillman knew might be lost to us, or at least delayed."

"I'll tell 'er." Kip cocked his head. "D'you have my gun?"

"Of course." I retrieved it and gave it to him. "It helped. Lehr was wounded. I don't know how badly."

Kip put it in his coat and looked outside. "He seemed to drive away okay. Maybe you shouldn't stay here. What if he comes?"

"I'll call the police."

He made a *good luck with that* face before he nodded. "Maybe you should keep this." He tapped the bulge in his coat.

"I've got kids here. I'd rather not." I lowered my voice. "Kip, I need Briana's list. Did you make a copy?"

He pointed to his head. "Safest place."

"Would you write it down for me?" When he hesitated, I said, "I have names of victims. If they match, it's likely Marti's part of that. It helps you."

He lifted his phone, paused, then typed something in. My text tone sounded.

"That's eight I'm pretty sure of. But Seren had partners. Like Maisie. Maybe that's what Briana's list is. Maybe the M.F. isn't Marti but someone else."

"Partners?"

"In his notes, he called them the Ring."

I lifted my phone. "Thank you. This could help."

Kip crossed his arms, lingering. He still had something to say. He shifted his weight from one foot to the other.

"What's on your mind?" I asked.

"Just...if you had it...you know...what would you do?"

The question caught me off-guard. He meant *it*, the dead hand. I had to think. "I don't know, Kip. Maybe...I'd hide it, I guess, to make sure...hmmm." Then, I had an idea. "What would your father do?"

Kip blinked at me. "I wish it worked like they said. Healing, and all. But...seems like it's best left alone. Like you said, it's probably dust by now." He shrugged. "Guess I better go."

I closed the door but watched him through a window. I saw no vehicles nearby with lights on, warm and waiting to pick him up. Kate wasn't out there. Something in one of those photos had spooked him. I saw Kip stop, call someone, and walk away. He was leaving tracks.

He'd said it, but I hadn't heard him. This slender young man who looked like a stray wind could carry him off was a shield. For *it*. Kip had the hand.

I mentally organized what I'd heard today.

Marti Fielding had seen it, maybe handled it. But the box made for it was at Judson's house, empty. Judson had used the restoration business where Kip worked, so Kip had been in Judson's houses. I surmised that Kip had noticed the hidden stash and acted on an opportunity. As a son, he'd want to finish what his father had started, show the man who'd displaced him with Seren that *he* could achieve something too. He'd watched Bandisi and his dad work on the other one, and he knew how to make the detox. He could handle the thing without risk. He'd wanted to help Marti. He'd tried it and failed. But he'd kept the hand. Shona had photographed his hiding place without realizing it.

I returned to the dining room. "Hey, girls. I could use a walk. Shall we go over to the cemetery? You said it was so pretty, I'd like to see it myself. We can look at the photos later."

They scrambled to get their coats and boots. I looked at the photo that had caught Kip's attention. I'd been doing this all wrong, thinking about a piece of property and some ancient lore instead of considering the people involved. My specialty was behavior. I had enough information now to follow my instinct.

I ran a finger over the photo to memorize distinct landmarks. Then I gathered them all back in their envelopes and placed them in the library. I finally had a solid lead.

Chapter Fifty-Nine

I called Natra. "There's something about a ring that Seren developed when he was here. His allies. And I'm texting you a series of letters. Each pair is a set of initials, like MF for Marti Fielding. Compare them to the Starfish victims."

"We've got something cooking here too," Natra said. "Joe backtracked two of the victims to someone on the dark web involved with the game. It's kind of shocking that people are volunteering to be assigned. One idiot posted a photo of his trophy. Looks like one of our victims. We've alerted law enforcement."

"These games can lure the worst."

"Also, there's been a call for more minions. Joe designed a honeypot on the I2P market in the form of an applicant. Sort of a Trojan horse with a unidirectional disappearing tunnel so it can't be traced back to him. Opening the applicant's credentials triggers a malicious file that will expose the gamemaster's IP address. Someone's nibbling. If we get access to an app on the suspect's phone, that confirms it. And, Annie, heads up. Concord's a target location."

The girls ran into the room, ready for snow.

"Copy, Natra. Good plan. Gotta go before I lose my lead. I'll check back soon."

While Elyse and Kamryn threw snowballs at each other and sometimes at me, I kept my eyes on Kip's trail. No one else was out in this weather, so it was easy to follow. I didn't want to catch up. I only wanted to see where he took us. Having the girls provided cover for me should he catch sight of us, and our activity covered his tracks should anyone else have the same idea.

It was no surprise that Kip had entered the cemetery. I strolled along, enjoying Kamryn's snow angels and Elyse's perfect pitch as she tossed snowballs. I loved hearing them laugh. I kept slightly ahead of them so they wouldn't mess up Kip's footprints before I saw them.

I arrived at the place where I'd seen the man in a black coat on the day I'd shown Kam the monuments here. I'd surmised that he could be Dad. I now felt sure of it. Shona had probably told him where she'd taken photos.

But Kip hadn't been obvious. He hadn't chosen the Hawkins family plot. His father had been wrong about him. He was smart. But today, he'd been hasty. He'd revealed himself when he saw Shona's photo.

I reached the spot and looked at the ground. The tracks continued off the path and between some headstones. I followed them.

"Where're you going, Mom?" Kamryn asked.

"Just want to see something."

I looked around to make sure Kip was gone. The spot was farther in than I'd anticipated, up a hill and into some trees. Snow came over the tops of my boots, freezing my feet. I stopped. Then I saw the tracks going to the back of a derelict monument.

I didn't recognize the name, but it didn't matter. The tomb was just a marker at an area no one visited. He'd partially moved snow off a flat gray headstone that had a simple chiseled date: 1903. The year Merrick had acquired Dacretown. Flurries were already beginning to obscure it. But there was no chance this pristine stone was old. In his job, Kip did stonework. I expected if I lifted this stone, I'd find it hollowed out enough for a small handmade bone coffin that contained a dead hand.

I stood for a moment in awe. This ancient toxic body part was just inches from me. My heart pumped. I ached for Kip and the burden he carried. He'd wanted this to work, but it had been nothing but trouble. Like a curse.

I memorized the name on the monument and invited the girls to run up here. I threw a snowball. They threw some back. We played there until we obliterated Kip's trail. I looked around. No one was out here but us. Falling snow quickly obscured our own tracks. I'd resisted the snow, but today it was my ally. When I was satisfied, I said, "My feet are all wet. Let's go back."

I'd get Jeanette to watch the girls and come back with a lifting tool. I didn't think Kip would do anything here until after dark. During snowstorms, I recalled, the entrance gates were closed. He'd be alone. He'd know this.

We'd reached the bottom of the hill when a dark gray Lexus SUV entered the grounds. That surprised me in this weather. They moved along slowly, as if looking for a specific site. I scooted the girls along. The Lexus stopped near where our tracks came down the hill, which made me wonder if someone else was watching Kip. I'd seen a Lexus outside the guesthouse a few days earlier but thought it was a Lehr associate.

"Let's go, girls."

I didn't want anyone to take an interest in us. Better to seem just a family taking advantage of a fresh snowscape.

At the house, the girls went into the library to warm up by the gas fireplace. I looked out the window but saw no Lexus. I called Jeannette and asked her to come to the guesthouse in half an hour. She was willing.

I checked with Shona, and she updated me. "Ms. Duncan" was in recovery, and the fire at Judson's had been doused. No one could go back in. Firefighters had moved Judson's remains, and the designated funeral home had come for them, with a plan to cremate him once law enforcement gave the okay. Shona was fielding calls from people who'd come for the viewing and from reporters. A security guard was there, but she hadn't seen Lehr. I assured her the girls were fine and told her to stay there for now. I didn't want her interfering with what I planned to do. "Let me know when Briana's able to talk." I had things to ask that woman.

Before I could call anyone else, someone knocked on the front door.

Chapter Sixty

I told the girls to go upstairs and lock themselves in Kamryn's room. "If it sounds like there's trouble, hide in the stairway. You can lock it from the inside. Keep your phones, in case you need to call someone. Don't open for anyone but people you know and trust. Understand?"

Kamryn nodded. She'd been abducted earlier that year. She knew there were dangers associated with the work I did. I strove to reassure her. "It's probably just the police letting me know about the house. It's just a precaution."

"Maybe we should stay with you," Elyse said.

"No. I want you both upstairs. Now, go."

Another rap made me jump. I watched the girls run up the steps before I went to see who it was. I hoped it was a cop. I didn't think Lehr would just walk up and knock, not after what he'd just done. He was wounded and enraged, not to mention wanted for arson and murder.

But he was also crazy.

I looked through the peephole. Rob Galloway stood on the front porch. I didn't want to talk to him, but I opened the door.

"Good afternoon, Dr. Hunter. May I come in?"

"I'm afraid I have no statements about my family or what happened this afternoon."

"I didn't expect you would. I have some information you'll want to hear."

Recalling Kip's caution about Rob's exposé and his possession of the "missing" file, I invited him inside. He brushed snow off his coat and wiped off his boots before entering. "Not such great weather for dealing with this all, I imagine."

"I have someone coming over," I said. "Let me just text her. Please go into the library."

I texted Kamryn. *It's safe but stay in your room.*

I offered Rob coffee. He declined. "I don't mean to intrude. I know you've had a rough day. In case no one's told you, the fire at Judson's house is contained."

"That's a relief."

"Heard you tussled with Richard Lehr."

"Like I said—"

He held up a hand. "Not asking. I know you have to circle the wagons. But they'll get Lehr soon enough. He won't be happy to know that Owen Kringle's awake."

I stared at him. "The kid in the hospital?"

"That's right. And he's talking. He said a man pushed him. It's likely Lehr. It's already on social media. There's an APB out for Lehr."

"Wow. Good. He's dangerous. But why would he try to kill Owen?"

"From what I've learned, Owen was talking at some party about…well, about Marti, the girl Kip Hawkins was dating."

I didn't correct him. I sensed he was here to lead, not inform me.

"Why's that a motive for murder?"

"Apparently, he said Marti was about to publicly accuse Briana and Judson of running dangerous experiments on kids."

I feigned surprise. "On kids?"

"It goes back a few generations. Your father was involved."

I shrugged. "And now he's dead."

Galloway squinted. "I heard he was seen near Judson's house this morning."

I felt myself flush. "From whom?"

"Someone who was there. Forgive me if I protect my source."

I wondered if Shona, or even Jeannette, was his source. "If he were alive, and in Concord, why wouldn't he contact me?"

"Good question." He leaned forward. "Has he?"

I gave him a direct look. "He has not. I was in Judson's house. He wasn't there."

Rob's left nostril flared, and he curled the fingers of his right hand over his thumb. No scoop to be found here. "Maybe he just doesn't want to pay his debt. Isn't that what Lehr's after?"

I decided to throw him a bone, so he'd think I still trusted him. "I'm Judson's executor, so I'll know more after I've reviewed the paperwork."

Rob's eyebrows raised. "That's a surprise, isn't it?"

"It was, but now that my aunt's injured, it's a good thing I have that authority."

"But wasn't Hillman killed?"

Rob knew more than he should. He had an inside source.

"I can't speak to the events today. You'll need to ask your police pals."

Rob put a hand in his pocket. "Speaking of that, the chief says they're pretty sure Kip was involved in Marti Fielding's death. That's your case, right?"

"Not anymore. It's not a suicide cluster, so they've ended my investigation."

He looked disappointed. "You were at his attorney's office after he was bailed out. Didn't you talk to him?"

He almost caught me. How did he know about that appointment? "He wasn't there. I picked up some paperwork."

Rob looked annoyed, and now I was worried. This reporter knew more about my movements than I realized. If he were blackmailing the people from the file Kip had described, he was invested in the status quo. He'd realize that today's events and my status as executor could disrupt his income. He'd want to choreograph a discreet exit.

The door knocker sounded. "Oh, I'm sorry. That's who I'm expecting."

Rob rose to his feet. "Thank you for talking with me. I'll let you know whatever I hear."

The loose ends no doubt irked him, but I was relieved to terminate the conversation. I let Jeannette in and sent her upstairs to Kamryn's room while I ushered Rob out. Jeannette seemed unfamiliar with him, so she wasn't his snitch.

I called Natra. "We've got a confirmed murder attempt. Owen Kringle said a man pushed him onto the track. Galloway just told me."

"He's there?" she asked.

"Gone now. He thinks it was Lehr."

"Maybe you should move into a hotel."

"Not a bad idea but getting a reservation could be tough with the snow. Have you found out anything more?"

Natra cleared her throat. "Starfish likes his metaphor. The ring is part of the starfish hydraulic system, using reservoirs to transport water to its various arms."

"So, his partners, whoever they are, keep things moving. Maybe, like Joe suggests, they're killing for him as part of a challenge. I realize that narcissists are magnets for sycophants, but could the payoff really be some role in his fantasy?"

"Maybe there's a financial benefit."

"Yeah, maybe. Judson might've paid Seren to go away. I'm sure I'll find a few secrets like that in his financials."

"Also, Annie, four of those sets of initials from Kip match our victims, if you include Marti."

"I figured. It's circumstantial, but—"

"One more thing. Our other Dunbury victim, Ralph, worked as an aide at a private psychiatric facility. Isn't your cousin Maisie locked up somewhere?"

"She is. I wonder if Seren thinks Maisie's getting an inheritance."

"There's a BD on the list. Like Briana Duncan."

"But it's Briana's list."

"Just telling you."

I took a moment. "Send me the names of our Starfish victims so far, all of them. I have an idea."

Chapter Sixty-One

Jeannette offered to take the girls to her apartment, where they'd be safer. It was the perfect solution. I'd need time to get things done, and they'd get to explore a new place.

In the kitchen, I found a flashlight, a large spoon that could serve as a shovel, and a long screwdriver to pry up the stone. I didn't want to remove the thing. I had no safe place to put it. I wanted only to confirm my suspicion and take a photo. Then I'd pressure Kip to help me find my father. *What would you do if you had it?* Exactly this. Then together, we'd decide the relic's fate.

I put on my boots, still wet inside, and left the house. As soon as I felt the cold air and nearly slipped on the snow-covered sidewalk, I started having doubts. What if I exposed myself to something just by lifting the stone? How long did Kip's remedy last? I no longer felt nauseous. I could only hope the immunity hadn't faded.

I got in the Range Rover. To avoid Judson's house, I took a longer route than necessary, passing only one other car on the road. The snow had stopped, but dipping temperatures were icing the roads. Plows were out. I had a small window of opportunity.

I parked near the cemetery, then walked through the western entrance. The snow deadened all sound, except for an occasional passing car. I smelled smoke in the air, possibly from the fire. A set of cross-country ski tracks alerted me to someone else in the cemetery, but I saw no one. In case anyone was watching, I acted like I was taking a winter stroll. My fingers, in lined gloves, were already freezing.

I looked around, trying not to seem obvious. Being alone in a cemetery as darkness encroached wasn't my idea of fun, let alone knowing I'd be heading into woods.

The snow disoriented me as I took the winding lanes. My earlier tracks were erased, but I recalled some directional markers. I stopped to listen. I thought I heard movement. I turned around. It was hard to see. I turned back and took the route I thought seemed right. Left, then left again. I turned on the flashlight, though it wasn't dark yet. The plan had seemed so simple. Now I felt foolish.

Suppose I wasn't the only one who'd followed Kip this afternoon. But no. I'd seen no other tracks near his. We'd been here right after him.

Unless the person had been watching from a hiding spot, or with binoculars.

In that case, I was already too late. It had been nearly an hour since we'd been here.

I strode along at a faster clip. My feet were numb. Across my path, I spotted another set of tracks. They were fresh, large enough to be an adult male. I peered around.

Then I saw a figure. I moved toward a tree to hide and watch. He wore a long, dark coat, like the man I'd seen here when I'd shown Kamryn around. I'd thought he was Dad, but now I wasn't sure. The figure moved out of my sight.

I thought I should just go back, forget about this venture. But then Kip might retrieve the relic. Maybe Shona's photograph would prompt him to move it. I couldn't let my leverage slip away. Kip was vulnerable. He might do something he shouldn't. Or he might get hurt.

I heard a car engine start up nearby. I was close enough to the Melvin Memorial to run to it and hide. The car came slowly in my direction. It was not a tourist, not at this hour. I squatted down behind a wall. When the car sounded close, I scooted over to a position that would better shield me, then peeked out.

The vehicle moved past the monument. I gasped. A dark grey Lexus SUV. Someone sat in the passenger side, a female. I breathed out. She glanced in my direction, but I ducked out of sight.

I couldn't be sure, but I thought it was the same vehicle I'd seen an hour earlier. It stopped momentarily before turning to the right to take one of the narrow lanes in the direction where I'd found Kip's trail. I went to where they'd turned to watch their red taillights. The vehicle continued to crawl along as if they were looking for something.

It was possible that someone had planned a trip that happened to coincide with the storm and were determined to see what they'd come to see. There were many notable people buried here. Maybe these tourists had limited time to accomplish their goal. But they'd already been here today.

They stopped. The driver's door opened. A man emerged. He wore a long, black coat. So, he'd been walking around before fetching his Lexus. He looked up the hill toward the spot where I'd aimed to be. Then he turned and said something I couldn't hear to his companion. She responded. He got back in. The rear lights came on. They were backing up.

I returned to my hiding place, hoping they wouldn't spot my tracks. I had to get out. The main entrance wasn't far. I listened and thought I had time to get to Bedford Street before they saw me.

I jumped up and sped toward the entrance, slipping on a patch of ice. I stayed on my feet but knew I had to be careful. I crossed the street and took a route toward town. Looking back, I saw car lights at the gate I'd just used. I didn't wait to see what that couple would do.

Soon, the cemetery would close. It would be dark. I could still go in, but I was too cold. I'd been thwarted. I needed a new plan. I could only hope the snow would deter an after-dark excursion. The gates would close, as they usually did during storms like this. From what I could tell, if that man was looking for Kip's hiding spot, he hadn't figured it out. Was he part of Seren's "ring"?

I got in the Range Rover. I had another pressing errand. Next stop, Emerson Hospital.

Chapter Sixty-Two

I found JoLynn in a waiting room. Ayden was going through tests for a concussion. "He's impatient to be out of here," she said. "They're almost done. He'll be cleared."

"Make him rest," I told her. "It's been a difficult day for us all."

"I want nothing more than to have a nice dinner and watch the snow from inside a warm room. He wants to get back out there, but I won't let him. I've checked with Natra. The honeypot's set."

"Just keep up your guard. We need a code in case Seren or his associates try to lure one of us with a text. If I need something, I'll include…" I sorted through possibilities. "I know. Mortmain. No one else will think of that. It will be our code word."

"Sounds good, Annie."

"I'm checking on my aunt. I'll send Judson's manager to take you to the inn."

In Bree's room, I asked Shona to drive Ayden and JoLynn to their suite. "Jeannette has Kamryn and Elyse at her apartment. You can pick them up there, but you might have smoke damage in your house, and I don't want them at the guesthouse."

"I can take them to a cottage I prepared for someone who canceled," Shona said.

"Great. Let me know where. I'll pick up Kamryn when I can." I also warned her about texts that might lure her out. She left, and I entered my aunt's room.

Bree looked miserable. The left side of her face and neck were bandaged. I was sure she was on enough drugs to be pain-free, but she seemed sufficiently alert to answer my questions. I hoped to exploit her drug-weakened defenses.

"You probably know why I'm here," I said.

She looked at me.

"I need to ask some things, Aunt Bree. I've learned about what the Hunters were doing with this perception project. I thought you should know that Judson signed over the Dacretown deed to me before he died."

She blinked. Her lips looked cracked, but she managed to talk. "He didn't tell me."

"Then why did you forge a false one?"

Bree's eyebrows came together. She shook her head.

I tried again. "Hillman said he had a deed, too, so it had to be fake."

Her response was so faint I could barely hear. "Not from me."

She seemed genuinely confused. Since Hillman was dead, I couldn't ask him about the circumstances. "Did they tell you he was killed?"

Bree nodded.

"Do you know what was in the note Judson left for me? You said it was an apology, but I don't believe that."

She closed her eyes.

"Aunt Bree, if there was something in the note—"

One eyebrow went up. "A warning."

"About?"

"He didn't...trust..." She coughed and moaned. "I ruined it. Disappointed him. Could never please him." She looked defeated.

I thought of Judson's plea. *Don't let her take it.* "Because of Maisie?"

Her eyes shot wide open.

I persisted. "I know about Maisie. She was in this program. She turned violent. You put her in an institution. I need to talk to her. Where is she?"

Bree shook her head.

I told her the address of the place where Ralph Steiner had worked. "Is that it? We're trying to stop someone Maisie knows who's killing people. I need information."

Bree shook her head. "He can't…"

"He? You mean Seren?"

To my surprise, Bree reached for my hand. I gave it to her. She squeezed. "He can't… He…helped her…she escaped."

A chill gripped me. "What?"

"She…lured…Gregory…" Bree swallowed. Tears formed in her eyes. "We made a monster…need to help her…my fault…"

I hadn't expected this. *Maisie* had lured Gregory to Boston. Her own half-brother.

"It could be…reversed…" Bree said. "We can help her."

"Is she with Seren now?"

"We found her, then she escaped again."

"Does she contact you? Can you reach her?"

Bree let out a long breath. "She'd come for the…*thing*. He wants it. She'd come for that."

Now I knew why Bree had wanted the relic. "So, you were going to use it to get Maisie to come, and then you'd quietly lock her up again? Was that your plan? Let these murders go unsolved? You made a list. It was with those papers you asked me to bring you."

"No, not me…"

"Bree, it's your handwriting. You sealed your own fate. You're deep in this, and now you're going to help me." I pulled out my phone and looked for the text from Natra. "Do these names sound familiar? Carmen Ashford, Michael Levy, Craig Warren, Derek Houde, Ralph Steiner. Know them?"

Tears wet her face. She nodded and made a move to get out of bed, but I said, "You stay here. It stops with us. Isn't that what Judson said? Who has the full list of past candidates in your program? We have to warn them. I think this Seren's trying to eliminate his competition."

Bree's lips thinned. "Not competition… compassion."

"Compassion?" The room felt hot. My adrenaline spiked.

"The sickness. Maisie wants to release them."

Released. The word at the top of the list. I lost it. "You can't really believe that. It's a game. They're having fun!"

Bree shook her head and looked away. She *did* believe it. "He helps, but it's *her* list. I only copied it. I wanted to show—"

I fought to contain my rage over this family loyalty. "To show who? Dad?"

Bree frowned.

"I know he's alive. He's in town. People saw him. Judson knew it too. You've all been covering for him."

Bree looked at me. "Lang warns them, the ones he can. He helps you."

"Helps me?"

"Tips."

I recalled the anonymous tipster on my podcast chat. "Lee Bandisi. That was from Dad?"

Bree nodded. She arched her back as if in pain.

"Now you tell me, how can I find him?"

"He'll find you. He tried today, but the fire..." She raised her right hand as if that was all she could do. "Be careful. He was at Judson's house."

"Dad? I know—"

"Seren. He's here."

Chapter Sixty-Three

I texted Shona to stay away from the guesthouse. I didn't want my daughter anywhere near it, not if these deranged terminators were close by. The couple in the car in the cemetery could have been them. I recalled seeing them there the first day here. They'd been apart, so I'd thought the male was alone, but they'd both been in the cemetery, and they'd been watching me. So, they'd seen Kamryn that day and both girls today. I texted Kam to urge her to do whatever Shona asked. Then I got on the road to drive back. The snow had stopped, at least, but the streets remained tricky to navigate.

When I arrived at the guesthouse, I saw a light on that I'd left off. I looked around for the Lexus, but the cars parked on the street were covered in snow. Still, there were other ways into this house than from the front.

Downstairs was a set of knives. Not great weapons if the intruder had a gun.

I parked away from the house. Keeping a wide berth, I walked around it. The wind had kicked up, causing drifts that hindered my progress. A set of tracks went to the back door. I followed them out to another street but saw no Lexus parked there. The street had been plowed, so I couldn't tell if whoever left the tracks had gotten into a car. I followed them back to the house.

On the back porch, I tested the door. The knob didn't turn. The intruder had a key or had found a key back here I didn't know about. But there was no evidence in snow on the porch of a search. So, the person had a key. I tried mine, but it didn't work on this door. I returned to the front. This door was also locked. I looked through the window but saw no one inside.

I texted Shona: *Did you come to the guesthouse?*

She returned a text: *No.*

Who has a backdoor key?

Me & Ms. Duncan. Something wrong?

I'll let you know.

This place had been updated and painted recently. Anyone on a work crew could have made a key, including Kip. Or Lehr or Seren could've paid someone to get one. Elyse had easily filched the staircase key.

I unlocked the door and slowly opened it. A car went by, so I waited until I could listen. I stepped onto the mat inside and closed the door. Again, I waited for a telltale noise that someone was there. A light was on in the library. My heart beat so hard I thought whoever was in there would hear it.

Maisie. I hadn't seen her since childhood. I wondered if she even remembered the "idiot" she'd repeatedly duped. No compassion in that one. She'd probably offered that justification for murder to Bree as a ruse. Still, I couldn't see her as a Bonnie-and-Clyde type. Something about Seren's vision must appeal to her arrogance.

I wished Ayden were with me. Action was his forte.

I removed my boots and took a tentative step toward the library. Surely, whoever was in there had heard the front door open. I felt a sense of ambush, as if the light was bait to draw me into the room and my would-be attackers were hiding. Ignoring the slush I left on the wood floor, I moved to the library entrance and pressed against the wall along the left side. Again, there was no sound. I metered the room, then leaned in. The place looked undisturbed. I stepped to the doorway's other side and looked around. No one was in there. I entered. I'd left nothing out that might be of worth to someone. The photos were behind books. I pulled the books out. The envelopes were still there.

I noticed the door to the hidden staircase. It wasn't quite flush with the paneling. Someone was in there. My heart raced. I backed slowly out of the room, turning on lights as I moved. I could call the police or set off the alarm. But in this snow, how fast would they come?

I crept up the steps. Halfway up, I stopped to listen. A wind gust rattled an antique glass window, making me jump. I took a deep breath and went to the top of the stairs.

But I didn't make it to my room. I stood still, staring at the open door to the staircase. Someone had definitely been here. I went over to it. At the halfway point, the cubicle light was on. Maybe Kip had returned to look for the photos. He likely knew about this staircase.

"Kip?" I sounded scared, so I said it again with more authority. There was no answer.

I pushed the door all the way open. I didn't want someone to rush out and close me in. If Maisie and Seren were here, one could do it from the top, one from the bottom. At least, I had my phone.

Illumination from the cubical drew me. I took tentative steps down. When I was close, I pressed myself against the wall. Then I looked inside. The bare bulb showed the small space. No one could be hiding in here. I entered. Everything seemed as I left it. Then I noticed hardcover books on the shelf that hadn't been there before. I counted five. One was the copy of Hawthorne's *Mosses from an Old Manse,* the collection Dad had beside his bed when we lived here. Stories about greed, betrayal, and obsession at the expense of humanity.

My heart raced. *He'll find you.* I took the book from the shelf and opened it. A sealed envelope lay under the cover flap. I held my breath as I dug at the seal, pulling out a single page. On it was a list of names. Five were victims we knew about. I put my hand to my mouth as tears welled up. Dad had come. He had a key, of course. He'd placed a message where he knew I'd find it, where we'd left each other notes. I looked at the back of the list. He'd written nothing to indicate where to find him. I looked through the other books, but they seemed to be props.

I took a photo of the list and texted it to Natra, with a message: *List of targets.* She'd know what to do. I sent the same text to JoLynn and Ayden, urging them to work with Natra. I added *mortmain* so JoLynn would know it was from me.

I had to return to the cemetery. Just walk over and get the cursed thing. I put my phone down, bundled up, stuffed rubber gloves in my pocket, and grabbed the spoon and a plastic trash bag. Picking up my phone, I opened the door.

A man in a black knit skull cap and a long black coat stood there with a gun. He cocked his head and asked, "Ready for a ride, Dr. Hunter?"

This had to be Starfish.

Chapter Sixty-Four

I got into the back seat of the Lexus. The woman in front pointed a pistol at me. Her dark eyes looked dead, but I recognized Maisie. She was thinner than I'd expected, and she'd dyed her ash blond hair black. In a flat voice that suggested over-medication, she greeted me. "Hello, Annie."

My memories of her malice flooded back. "Why are you doing this, Maisie? It's sick. The police know you're here. They'll find you."

Seren got into the driver's seat. "She's fulfilling her destiny." His voice had an unnaturally low pitch. "You know what we want, and you know where it is."

"I can't find it in the snow."

"We also know where your child and your friends are. Can you find it now?" He looked back at me, pulling his thick lips into a sneer. His pupils were so large I realized he was high on something.

I reminded myself we had a plan. If he took our digital bait, we'd locate him. We could also warn his still-living targets. I had to give him the relic. I just hoped I could find the spot again. "Let's go, then."

"That's more like it." He started the SUV. I heard another car behind us and looked back. I recognized the lights. It was Lehr.

"We patched him up," Seren said. "Good as new."

So, Lehr had partnered with Seren. He was a goon but not for Bree. I was in real trouble. Seren had made me leave my phone at the house. I was on my own.

As Seren drove, he kept up a narcissistic patter. "It's so flattering how you've studied me, Dr. Hunter. Too bad we didn't meet before, although

I've watched *you* for a while. I'm a remarkable specimen, the most unique person you'll ever meet. Lang can tell you. He knows that Maisie and I are the Adam and Eve of a new era in brain science." He reached over to ruffle her hair. She didn't move.

"Killing off the competition doesn't make you look so good," I commented.

"Oh, I haven't killed anyone. If you have a grand mission, it's remarkably easy to find lackies to do things for you. They *compete* to be chosen. It's amazing what social media can attract. You should see what's been offered. Once Maisie inherits the works, we can spread even faster."

"Maisie," I said. "Your mother was hurt today. She's in the hospital. You should go see—"

She turned, her eyes furious. "The bitch! Lehr was s'posed to finish it. He's a loser. We'll do it ourselves."

Her venom shocked me. She intended to kill her mother. "She's not the Dacretown heir, if that's what you're after. I am."

Maisie smirked at me. "Not if you're dead. We already filed the deed."

So Seren and Maisie had forged the false deed. Somehow, they'd gotten to Hillman with bribes or threats. Judson must've seen one of them. That's why he'd abruptly changed his arrangements and urged Bree to get me here. *Don't let her take it.* He'd meant Maisie, not Bree, and he'd known Bree was weak. I figured Lehr was gunning for Dad to clear the way for Maisie, but he wanted the relic—the means to a cure. That's what he thought Dad "owed" him.

Seren turned onto Bedford Street. The gates were closed. We were too late. He drove past the first entrance, following the wall to the second one. In some places, only low chains separated the street from the cemetery. The snow, if packed, could provide a bridge over them. But Seren kept driving. Seemingly, he hadn't counted on the snowstorm. Typically, the gates are open, even at night. Now we couldn't go in. I quietly checked my door handle. Didn't work. He had the child safety lock engaged. I couldn't jump out, anyway, or he'd go for Kamryn.

We were nearly to the end when Seren turned toward the cemetery. Then I remembered: the service road. He'd found it. The gates meant nothing to him. Lehr stayed on the road, parked with lights off, while Seren drove along the lane inside, made another turn, and stopped. He kept the car running. "Right around here, I think." He got out and opened my door. "Let's go."

I looked up the hill. It seemed about right. I saw a distinct monument I recalled. It wouldn't take long to get up there. I felt sweat form. Once I found the relic, I thought he'd shoot me. Seren went to the back. I felt for the child lock on the open door and flipped it up. He got a half-size shovel out of the back and motioned to me to proceed. Maisie stayed in the car.

As I made my way up, I saw dimples in the snow off to the side. Tracks. The Starfish Killer didn't seem to notice. Maybe they were his own tracks as he'd looked for where I'd been. Normally, cops patrol this place after hours, but with the gates closed they wouldn't come till it was plowed. I couldn't hope for rescue. My mouth went dry.

When we came around to the back of the monument where I'd seen the flat headstone, I kicked snow away to find it. Seren handed me the shovel. I used it to tap until I heard the metal tip hit stone. I cleared off the slab and saw the date. 1903. I worked the shovel along the edges.

Seren pushed me away. He dug his gloved fingers under the stone and lifted. It moved. He held his hand out for the shovel. I gave it to him, wishing I had the courage to hit him with it and run. But Lehr was out on the street, and they knew about Kamryn and the others. Better to comply.

Seren dug around the edges as well as he could. I saw the stone budge. He got the shovel under it and lifted again. It came away, and he flipped it to the side. He turned on a flashlight. We both looked at the dark spot the headstone had covered.

It was empty. I felt doomed.

Chapter Sixty-Five

"You got the wrong spot," Seren growled. Even in the shadows, I could see his tense expression.

"This is the place. Someone got here first."

"Back to the car."

On the way down, I heard him talking to Maisie on the phone. He was furious, thought I'd duped him. Seren forced me back into the car. His dark eyes, under the cap, drilled into me. He got in the driver's seat and said to Maisie, "Let's text them. Get them out. Use her."

I realized they were about to lure Ayden and JoLynn to "rescue" me. Thank God I'd thought of a code.

"They know how you operate," I said. "They won't fall for it."

Maisie gave me a smug look. "Have you forgotten? Idiots always respond."

Seren hadn't checked the child lock, but it hardly mattered. Without a phone, I couldn't warn anyone. Lehr's presence made it too risky to jump out.

We arrived at the service road and rolled onto the street. As Seren turned right, a tall blond man stepped into the headlight beams, several yards away. He held up a small oblong box.

I gasped. "Dad!"

Seren stopped. Maisie said something under her breath, then told Seren, "I'll get it. Unlock the door." I heard the doors click open. Before Maisie could move, I jumped out. Maisie yelled, "Get her!"

Seren exited, grabbed my coat, and yanked me back. I struggled to break free, but he overpowered me.

Dad lowered the box. "A trade, Seren. This for her."

Seren put the hard muzzle of a gun under my chin. "I don't need either one of you."

Dad held up his phone. "I'm on with cops. They know where I am. If you shoot, they'll hear it. They're coming. Take this and go."

"Show it to me!"

Seren had me in such a tight grip, I couldn't breathe. Dad opened the box and displayed an item in the left headlight. It looked like a mummified hand. Maisie gasped.

Behind me, I heard a command. "Let her go!" Kip!

Seren turned and forced me between him and Kip's gun.

Up the street behind Dad, headlights flashed on, and an engine revved. The G-wagon screeched to life and raced straight at us.

I shouted, "Dad!"

As Seren turned to look, Kip grabbed my arm and jerked me free. Dad jumped to the side. Maisie screamed. I scrambled out of the way just before Lehr slammed straight into the Lexus. The crunch of metal and shattering glass deafened me as the Mercedes pushed the crumpled Lexus backwards. I crouched to protect myself.

Dad ran over. "Run! Go!"

He helped me up. In his grip, I passed Seren on his hands and knees on the road amid broken glass. The box lay open on the street, the hand projected five feet from it. I reached for it, but Dad kicked it and steered me away.

"Get her to the shop," he told Kip.

"Dad!"

"Go!" he ordered. "Get away from here."

We hadn't gone ten steps when an explosion dropped me to the street. Flames shot into the air. Kip covered me, then helped me up and urged me to run. I tried to look back, but Kip kept pulling me. I heard a siren. Cops! Dad wasn't bluffing.

I saw a dark shape on the ground near the cars.

"Can't stop," Kip said.

"But—"

"Come on!"

We cut through several yards and went down a street. I gasped and thought my lungs would burst before Kip directed me to the back door of a brick building. He opened it and ushered me in. We were both out of breath.

"Dad's back there!" I panted. "Can't just leave him."

Kip held up a finger to keep me quiet. "He'll come."

"But the cops—"

"He grew up here. They know 'im."

Kip led the way up some concrete stairs to the second floor, flipped on a light, and opened a door into a studio apartment.

Chapter Sixty-Six

I went to a chair and sat down to catch my breath.

"Are you okay?" Kip asked. He pointed to my left knee.

I saw a hole in my jeans. My knee, scraped, was bleeding. Kip went to a sink and got a cloth to wash it off.

"The thing's in the road," I said. "I'm sure he saw it. He'll take it. We should—"

"No, it's not."

"Did you grab it?"

He looked at me. "What were you doing with him?"

"He's been following me. He forced me to show him where you hid the hand."

Kip raised an eyebrow. "So, you followed me."

I nodded. "I thought you'd lead me to Dad."

He sat down. "Guess I did."

"Is he okay? He was close to the explosion. I saw someone on the road."

"He's coming." He got out his phone and showed me a text to prove it.

"Where's the hand?" I asked. "Did you pick it up?"

"That's a decoy. I saw you in the cemetery when I went back to get it and realized you'd figured it out. I also saw the couple driving around, so when they left, I went up and got it. We were bringing the decoy to replace it because Lang knew Seren was here. He put a tracker in the box. He thought Seren would grab it and take it to where he's staying before he realized it was fake. But the Lexus was there again and then we saw you get out, so Lang thought the box would make Seren think he had the hand."

"You thought he'd just stop in the street?"

"We didn't have a plan. Just buying time till cops got there. But Lehr acted first. He probably saw Lang and just floored it. Told you he was crazy."

I hugged myself. "That was close. And so bizarre. He slammed right into them, no brakes, no attempt to avoid them. Just *bam!*" My heart raced at the memory. "He had to be suicidal after what he'd done. There was no going back." As awful as Lehr was, I shuddered at his shocking act. "He said he was my guardian angel. Guess so, but…"

"My brothers are coming. We'll get you back to the house."

I looked squarely at Kip. "I'm not going anywhere until I see Dad. Do you have any of that nasty anti-toxin here?"

He looked surprised. "You want more?"

"I want to hug my father."

Kip nodded. "Got it. You're fine. It's still working."

"Is the real hand here?"

"Yes."

"Can I see it?"

"It's…not…"

"I've seen dead things in all kinds of stages, from liquid to bones. I want to see it."

Kip shrugged. "If Lang says okay."

I looked around. "He's staying here?"

"On and off. He doesn't stay anywhere for long. Judson told him Seren was here, so he moved around. Our shop's downstairs."

I squinted at him. "You found the hand at Judson's. You stole it."

He cleared his throat. "Borrowed."

"For Marti, right?"

He frowned. "Didn't work."

"If Dad had it, why did you ask me what I'd do?"

"He didn't have it. Didn't know I had it till I figured out you knew. He went to the house to tell you what we wanted to do, but you weren't there."

I heard the door close downstairs. I stood up. I barely had breath as I listened to footsteps ascend the stairs. I went to the door. Dad came in, and

I threw myself at him.

He hugged me, but then stood away. "You shouldn't touch me, Annie."

"It's okay. I drank Kip's brew. I tried so hard to find you. I missed you." I hugged him again. He made me feel safe.

"I know. I'm sorry. I missed you, too, and Kamryn. I couldn't tell anyone."

He led me back to sit down and handed me a red cellphone. "Yours?"

I shook my head. Dad put it on the table next to me. "I think it's yours."

Then I realized. It had to be Seren's or Maisie's. Natra said the perp's phone would help to prove the digital tracks. We'd need it. I slipped it into my pocket. "Yup. Thank you."

Dad looked years older than he should. He still had an air of authority, but I could see he was ill. He took a breath. "Maisie's dead. She went through the windshield. Broke her neck. Lehr had gas containers, which exploded. He probably meant to go back and burn down the house. He's dead too."

"And Seren?" Kip asked.

"Fled. He grabbed the hand, but he left the box. We can't track him."

"So, he's still out there," I said.

"He's hurt," Dad told us. "I saw blood on the street where he fell. Tonight, he'll be more focused on getting away than getting even." He looked at Kip. "Let's get this over with."

Kip gestured to me. "She wants to see it. I told her everything."

Dad nodded. "Is the stove ready?"

"Should be."

"What?" I asked. "You're burning it? Don't you need it to figure out the cure?"

"I need to end the mess our family started."

Kip led the way down to a room on the first floor, where I felt heat from a coal-burning stove. "This is where my dad burned the other one," he said. "Shona was here."

Dad put on a heavy leather glove. He slid a small wooden box out from under the stove. The intense heat prevented me from getting too close, but I had to see.

The back door opened and closed. I looked over. JJ entered with a kid who resembled him. The Bone Heads had arrived. We had the whole outlaw gang here, the Dacretown caretakers. I was now one of them. JJ nodded at me.

Dad opened the box. I leaned in and saw a shrunken grayish bony object lying inert in some black dirt. It smelled musty. The healer's hand, the automatic writer. All that trouble over this? I expected someone to take a picture, but no one did. Dad closed the box, opened the stove door, and placed the entire bone coffin onto the red coals. He closed the door tight. We watched through the glass as flames consumed the thing. I almost expected to hear a preternatural scream.

"JJ will take you to your place," Kip said to me. "This will take a while. We'll give the ashes to Shona."

I looked at Dad. "Will I see you again?"

"I'll be here a few days, but I'm going with Shona to Morvern. If there's a cure, it's in the soil. It's not as bad for me as for the others, but it still affects me." He let me hug him again and he kissed the top of my head.

To Kip, I said, "Seren may have slipped your tracker, but we have some ideas about finding him. We might need your help."

He gestured toward his brothers. "Whatever we can do."

Chapter Sixty-Seven

I ended up with Shona and the girls at the cottage. The guesthouse wasn't safe. I wanted to tell Kamryn about her grandfather, but I couldn't let her see him, so I said nothing.

The following day, the storm had ended. Kamryn got to play in the snow, but I asked Ayden and JoLynn to take her home. I filled them in on the night's events and told them to go interview JoLynn's friend at the Chattanooga weather station. "We still need to know his part."

I had to clean up loose ends in Concord. First, I broke the news to Bree about Maisie. She seemed more relieved than grieved. From her hospital bed, Bree gave cops enough information about Galloway's long-running blackmail scheme for them to search his house for the purloined file and arrest him. Kip added what he knew.

When we retrieved Seren's papers from Dacretown—the pages Bree had wanted me to bring to her—they contained enough evidence about her part in the experiments that she'd face serious consequences. She'd believed in Merrick's ideas, maybe to win Judson's respect. She'd trained Maisie rigorously. She'd helped Seren gain prominence in the program. She'd known that Maisie might be killing off her competition and had covered for her. She'd also bribed city officials to remove hindrances to her development. I decided not to tell her Maisie's plan for her.

I finally saw what Judson was hiding about his will. He'd made Lang his heir. He took full responsibility for the program and designated funds for damages. He'd figured there was no use pretending that Lang was dead, but he hadn't wanted Bree to know he was cutting her out. He knew she'd aided

Maisie even after it was clear Maisie was homicidal. When I discussed it with Dad, he said, "He wanted to remove any means for Bree to continue the work. The Institute will collapse now, as it should, and I'll be able to work on a cure."

I arranged to move Judson's will to Kate Gardiner's firm, and she promised to help me figure it all out.

"I want to sign the Dacretown deed over to Kip, if he'll accept it," I told her. "He's been the caretaker, he and his brothers. His father and grandfather had a stake in it. Judson's estate will pay for remediation, as well as the taxes for a couple of years. And I plan to hire Kip to restore Judson's house."

"That's generous," Kate said.

"They deserve it. They lost their dad because of my family."

Shona helped me arrange for Maisie's final disposition. Police found where she and Seren had been staying, 'though he was long gone. Maisie's journals proved how truly disturbed she'd been. She'd targeted Ralph Steiner because he'd once thwarted her escape, but Seren had pushed him to his death. Maisie had also bullied Marti Fielding. She'd lured the girl out of hiding with a fake text from Kip, approaching her at Gilly Pond and forcing her in. Kip might have come later—too late—but he hadn't hurt the girl he'd tried to help. He was off the hook, especially when Blackburn resigned. Dad gave Kip his pick from Judson's vehicles. He chose the Range Rover.

I spent as much time with Dad as possible before he left. He wanted to know everything about Kamryn. He promised to keep in touch. One day we drove by the Old Manse, where Hawthorne had penned those grim tales. "It's as if he knew the Hunters were coming," he commented, "with all our terrible flaws."

That same week, Joe's honeypot worked. Seren, desperate for partners, had dropped his guard and bought the false narrative of an exceptional follower, which helped us snag his URL. Maisie's phone provided more digital proof. Joe had the resources to tip the right authorities, who then traced more of Seren's incriminating activities. I told them about the forged deed, so they lured him to Concord to make his claim on Dacretown. Like Maisie had said, "Idiots always respond."

I spent an afternoon touring Dacretown with Kip. He eagerly described his plans, including toxic mitigation. Clearly, he loved the place and envisioned a complete overhaul that would restore its beauty.

"No more Skeleton Crew," he said. "No more Dead Line. No more curse."

Chapter Sixty-Eight

Back on the Outer Banks, I was glad to be warm again. Kamryn was with her father and back to her classes. She kept up with Elyse online and now she wanted to go to Scotland.

I looked forward to my team's case debrief. Although it was usually just my primary team, I made an exception. JoLynn would join us since she'd led the Starfish case, and Joe Lochren had given us the right stuff to close it.

Natra chose the wine. "It was a tossup between something from Hawthorne Winery and this." She showed me the label. *Dead Man's Hand* cabernet sauvignon. I groaned but said, "That's a bottle I'll keep."

Ayden's cheek was healing nicely. He admitted he'd enjoyed being pampered, but he was ready for another case.

When everyone was settled in place with wine and dinner, I began.

"As all of you know, this investigation was personal to me. I've spent five years looking for my dad, unaware that his absence was partly for my protection. When he heard Natra's call for tips, he sent us the Bandisi info. He also urged Kip to help. As a result, Seren—the star of Dacretown— will be prosecuted as a mastermind of multiple murders. I think one of his Challenge flunkies—the guy who posted the photo of his victim—has agreed to testify in exchange for a reduced sentence. Maisie, the driving force of the violence, is dead. So's Richard Lehr, who would've otherwise been arrested on multiple charges. Galloway's been exposed for extortion, and my aunt, Briana Duncan, also faces legal consequences. Judson would have, too, but he's deceased. He wanted me to return the relic to Scotland, and it's going, but not quite the way he expected. On a sad note, my father's ill from Judson's program, but he's working on a cure. It's been great having him back in my life."

"Get anything in the will?" Ayden asked.

Natra punched him. "That's her business."

"It's all of our business," I said, "because whatever benefits me benefits the agency. I'm not a named heir, but I'll oversee the estate sale, which comes with compensation." I held up my glass. "There will be bonuses. I appreciate each of you. JoLynn discovered and worked the cases, Natra spotted the patterns and kept it organized, Joe figured out the game and designed the trap, and Ayden found the connections that led to Maisie and Seren. As a team, you are spectacular."

"And I have a contribution to my profession," Joe said. "A hitman challenge using weather as a cover. It's unique. Just glad we figured it out."

Natra looked at JoLynn. "Your friend Bruce started it."

"Yes," she said. "He dabbles on the dark web. When we really pressed him, he admitted he was paid to contact me because I was working with you, Annie. The guy who paid him told him about the weather challenge and said your father, his mentor, had killed Bandisi to show how it was done. From what we could tell, it was Seren trying to set up Lang as the mastermind."

"But Dad had an alibi for Bandisi's death," I said. "And your interview with Bruce erased the apparent coincidence."

"What about the curse?" Ayden asked. "Seems like that played out with practically everyone who stepped on that property."

I took a sip of *Dead Man's Hand*. "I'd say the tragedies were more about human failings like greed and ambition."

Natra held up her glass. "So, here's to Hawthorne, your mentor in all things dark and twisted."

I touched my glass to hers. "I couldn't have done this without him."

A Note from the Author

Although the story is fiction, many of its aspects are based on genuine lore, methods, and discoveries. My original inspiration sprang from the myths surrounding Dudleytown, CT. I located my fictional Dacretown near Concord to exploit the amazing Sleepy Hollow Cemetery and the sense of Hawthornean gloom I experienced there.

Acknowledgements

I want to thank my alpha reader, Susan Lysek; my digital forensics consultant, Joe Pochron; my beta readers, Sally Keglovits, Ruth Knafo Setton, Ruth Osborne, and Dana DeVito; and the DeSales MFA directors, Juilene Osborne-McKnight and Steve Myers, who placed our summer residency in Concord, MA. Nothing replaces immersion for inspiration. I also appreciate tips from the Sleepy Hollow Cemetery supervisor Tish Hopkins, which assisted the plot. Special thanks to my enthusiastic cemetery-loving LBB editor, Verena Main Rose, and my long-time agent and friend, John Silbersack. I was in Concord when Verena bought this series, so it's fitting to come full circle with this tale.

About the Author

With her Nut Cracker Investigations series, Katherine Ramsland brings her expertise in forensic psychology into her fiction. She consults for coroners, teaches homicide investigators, and has appeared as an expert on more than 250 crime documentaries. She was an executive producer on *Murder House Flip* and A&E's *Confession of a Serial Killer: BTK*. The author of more than 1,800 articles and 73 books, including *The Serial Killer's Apprentice* and *How to Catch a Killer,* she also pens a regular blog for *Psychology Today*.

AUTHOR WEBSITE:

http://www.katherineramsland.net

SOCIAL MEDIA HANDLES:

Facebook: https://www.facebook.com/katherine.ramsland
Twitter: **https://twitter.com/KatRamsland**
Blog: http://www.psychologytoday.com/blog/shadow-boxing
Instagram: https://www.instagram.com/katherineramsland/

Also by Katherine Ramsland

In the Damage Path, Level Best Books

I Scream Man, Level Best Books

The Serial Killer's Apprentice, Crime Ink (Penzler)

How to Catch a Killer, Sterling

Track the Ripper, Riverdale Avenue Books

The Ripper Letter, Riverdale Avenue Books

The Blood Hunters, Kensington

The Heat Seekers, Kensington

Heartless: Iowa's Bloody Murders, Notorious USA

Murder Alley: Nebraska Fiends and Felons, Notorious USA

Cold-blooded: Kansas Murders, Notorious USA

Confession of a Serial Killer: The Untold Story of Dennis Rader, the BTK Killer, University Press of New England

Haunted Crime Scenes, with Mark Nesbitt, Second Chance Books

Blood and Ghosts: Paranormal Forensic Investigators, with Mark Nesbitt, Second Chance Books

The Mind of a Murderer: Privileged Access to the Demons that Drive Extreme Violence, Praeger

The Forensic Psychology of Criminal Minds, Berkley

The Devil's Dozen: How Cutting Edge Forensics Took down Twelve Notorious Serial Killers, Berkley

The Human Predator: A Historical Chronicle of Serial Murder and Forensic Investigation, Berkley

The Criminal Mind: A Writer's Guide to Forensic Psychology, Writer's Digest

The Forensic Science of CSI, Berkley

Ghost: Investigating the Other Side, St. Martin's Press